MW01681431

THE EDUCATION OF A MACK

THE TRILOGY

BOOK 1 (**THE MAKING'S OF A MAN**)

Copyright 2020 Wordsnlyrics.com

All rights reserved. This book was printed in the United States of America. No part of this book may be reproduced in any form, or by any means, without prior consent from the Writer/Publisher. The only exception being brief quotes used in review.

For permission on printing any part of this book write, Raashad@juno.com For autographed copies or bulk purchases, write email address above or call 916-507-3352.

ISBN-978-0-692-10374-6

This book is a work of fiction. Any references or similarities to actual events, real people, living or deceased or to real locales are intended to give the Novel a sense of reality. Any similarity in any other names, characters, places, and incidents are entirely coincidental.

With undeniable authenticity this book was not written for children. Considering it lives inside street life with a truest sense of reality and language, you must be over 18 to purchase or read this book.

Although a work of fiction, it is based on real life experiences and is as real as the characters portrayed. The words of this book shall breathe life into the truth that is street life. This book series ultimate goal is a vision into the perils of real-life relationships and the streets, along with the redemption of the black man.

Also available from

Wordsnlyrics.com

THE EDUCATION OF A MACK BOOK 2

A TASTE OF BLOOD

THE EDUCATION OF A MACK BOOK 3

A FAMILY AFFAIR

CHAPTER 1

Martell

THE MAKING OF A MAN

The Los Angeles coastline could be considered the essence of awe when you think of California's natural beauty. The large, life like boulders and rolling hills seemed to display Southern Cali's most redeeming qualities. During the spring, it felt as if the greenery wrapped around you and made you a part of the lush surroundings. For these reasons, the Orange County and Malibu areas could be observed as paradise in the minds of many outsiders. This kept those blessed with deep pockets, sprinting their way to its sunny shores.

The word Hollywood fell from the lips of people as if the word was magic. Throughout the globe it was and is treated as if an Island located in the middle of life itself. However, it's underbelly of sex and drugs loomed as dirty as anywhere in the world.

The beautiful views and beaches were known to strike awe into the romantic emotions of its visitors. A casual drive was known to transform a common, sex stingy, female into the most insatiable, passionate, animal on God's blessed planet.

The ocean appeared to grab the giant rocks as if the two were born at the same moment and inseparable. The hypnotizing waters crept about like soldiers in the night, hungry for battle.

The famous, green, Highway one, wound across the coastline in a wondrous splendor and dropped the driver directly in the heart of the San Francisco Bay area.

However, crossing the bridge into Oakland would serve as the wakeup call from that euphoria, and sober you up quickly.

While Los Angeles shadowed several lifestyles, the East Bay was known as the land of hustle by any means necessary, in retrospect.

Largely because, anything a person craved, no matter how perverse was surely to be available for a price. The aggressive trends offered every vice humanly possible. Its under-life was one of the most active in the United States. It was also quite secretive and dynamic in its own way.

For those familiar with street life, the Bay offered a large array of pimps, players, cons, drugs and ladies of the night on display.

A drive up toward the peninsula would reveal the lush, green counties of Marin and Half Moon Bay.

The appealing surroundings appeared to open up like miraculous legs giving birth. The awesome shore seemed to reach forever.

California's weather was a true gift, recognized globally for its seasonal ease. It was fortified by one simple fact. The heat never overstayed its welcome, while the cold wrapped around you, like a needy child during the winter months. As quickly as you prepped for the winter, it was sneaking out the back door and running away. It was like a lovesick boy longing for his first girlfriend.

The surrounding cities crossed each other like an amazing puzzle with water being the glue.

At day's end almost, everyone traveled through the Oakland's streets with pleasure being their goal after a long, days' work, or hustle. Most rushing to gather a piece of an American dream, that remained just that, a dream to most Americans.

However, things changed drastically at night and so did the mentality of the locals.

Those not cemented in the hard-core game of life became prey. They became what were commonly known as suckers, marks and johns. In most cases they had no idea what they were in for, until it was too late. I knew it to be God's test to mankind. He would allow the Devil to test our resolve. The problem was, as man evolved, his ability to fight temptation did just the opposite.

The gifts offered were as simple as they were priceless. They continued to make California, the place to be for tourist and transplants from all over the world. But the east bay had mean streets and they were not to be trifled with. If you were unaware of the potential for danger, without notice you would become a victim. Stabbings, gunfire and the will to survive were the things most prevalent in Oakland, Richmond and the surrounding areas.

A baby's cry might be the banana on a string to pull you into one of the project apartments. Next you would get peeled for your cash and left for dead.

The large numbers within the population played cat and mouse until it was their turn to be had by the system of East Bay hustlers.

As for me, I'd been on earth for ten long, years, but mama always referred to me as an old soul. She also swore that I'd been blessed with some kind of uncanny ability to gauge life, like she'd never seen before in a person so young.

I rarely felt like a kid of ten years; therefore, I guess there was some truth to her words. I was often afraid to remind her of why she felt that way. Truth suggests, she'd been anything but reliable and had never stayed in one place long enough for me to call it home. I was treated like a grown man by everyone in my life and I rarely had a chance to be a child. I sometimes thought God had sent me there to test mama's ability to love and show affection. It seemed as if my mama and the word ***love*** seemed to miss each other's outstretched hands at the crossroads.

Because of our moving in the midnight hour so often, my thoughts were like that of an old owl at night. We'd already moved in and out of approximately six to ten neighboring towns in the area, from lavish surroundings to downright dirty!

I was glad we'd landed in the cultural oasis of Oakland. It was the center of all aforementioned areas, with life on the streets as rough as anywhere in the world, and deadlier than most. This was bad juju if you were a single mother raising a so-called black, man-child. However, a magnificent move if your goal was to raise a street smart, hustler with no compassion in his heart.

Oakland had a mystique that would draw a person in with daytime splendor. It would pierce your heart until you became a part of its love or its wrath. Oakland's his-story suggested white folks held prominent positions, but black folks ran the city.

The mix gave way to days when you could plainly see its rich culture and hope for a promising future. While at night, money, sex and drugs ran the city. Self-hate, mixed with a love for money, created an environment that resembled crabs in a barrel. When one crab attempted to climb out the barrel, another crab pulled you back down. In essence, never allowing any single crab success, thus, no one gained real success for long.

Another plus to living in Oakland city limits was the exploding population of little, black girls. They were always void of the guidance from, a father for many reasons. The lack of daddy's in their households made them easy prey for little boys like me.

Fifteen minutes across the bridge from Oakland, was the forever busy, San Francisco. The "City" was known for its eye capturing buildings, multi-lane highways and pornographic nightlife. The freaks came out at night and this hill enriched terrain was a Mecca for every type of creature manufactured on this small planet. It was also hailed for its willingness to accept alternative lifestyles at any cost.

San Francisco was a melting pot of nationalities and sexual desires. A trip on the main strip would make you believe in,

"**the wilder the better**."

Homosexuality was generally paraded and displayed as a natural thing. It was treated as normal as apples falling from a tree. It was also home to *the* famed Alcatraz prison. Alcatraz was an island built on command to jail the throwaways of American society in the early days.

Layers of concrete ran recklessly through the streets and highways of San Francisco. This made San Francisco a far cry from the awesome greenery, alive and thriving just twenty minutes across the nearby Richmond Bridge. The bridge was a steel corridor leading to the quaint, attractive town of San Rafael.

Standing alone in the clearing, stood a daunting landmark. It was a visual strike to the soul. The driver had to pass it, prior to reaching the unique little town. Once again, the realization of mental torture lived deep in the heart of societies supposed failures. Thanks to the maximum-security prison resting along the beautiful ocean line: San Quentin.

This penitentiary rested in the clearing, as large as life. It was produced as another stronghold for men, killing the heart and soul of its inmates. On a good day, the rolling of the fog would bless you with a breathtaking look at San Francisco in all its glory.

On the other side of the bay, Richmond had been known to amaze law enforcement throughout the Country. They'd proven it had some of the darkest and most deadly streets in the country. The homicide rate had maintained elevated and staggering numbers for over forty years. Thanks to the lack of resources, not to mention an unrelenting will to survive, against all odds. Richmond locals were known for their resilience. Traveling into those parts, you'd find a lack of white faces, because Richmond was black. However, just like everywhere on the planet, the Mexican population was currently climbing like an invisible staircase to the stars.

This was a large contrast to the beautiful city, just North of San Francisco. It was known as Marin. The terrain felt as if it was laced with money, and the ocean ran through it like a continued taste of paradise. Rolling through this lovely area would convince the driver, there were more cops than citizens running about, thus crime was at an all-time low. Deeper in the line of fire was ground zero, North Richmond. In North it was difficult to find an area not laden with project housing for the financially challenged, and an array of sporadic gunfire.

This made North Richmond a bloody battle zone, with one way in and one way out. Hustling was more than a way of life for its inhabitants, it ***was*** life!

Even for those who hustled the welfare system. This system provided a check and food-stamps on the first and fifteenth of the month. Thanks to those county peanuts, it made life possible to survive without starving, but never blessed us with enough to keep us from being hungry.

At this juncture in my young life, I recognized North Richmond and East Oakland as home and the money grove for black folks. Mama did her best to make sure that grown was my middle name, as my little sister Tina, and I suffered the consequences of mama's ugly habits.

We suffered because, instead of buying food, mama hustled our food stamps in the local, black market. I felt as if that particular market was named after black folks, because everything had to be accomplished from the bottom up, and that hadn't changed since the first slaves came here on the slave ships. Black people in America always struggled.

The food-stamp hustle was a game spreading throughout the ghettos, supplying party money for the mamas in the hood, while pushing boys like me into the street game.

The money was spent in non-deserving hands, because the stamps often detoured and transferred into the hands of the men who lived like kings compared to us.

A perfect example of a money man living better than us was Uncle Jamie. I enjoyed the days that he'd snatch me up and venture me back into the projects as his ride along. He wasn't my blood uncle, but mama told me to call him uncle. Just like a million other black kids were ordered to call the men that bounced in and out of their lives, "Uncle". As well as the secret, sick-minded, older bastards that hovered around father-less children. They often waited for a chance to sexually strike the naive girls or boys.

Luckily for me, Uncle Jamie wasn't that type of old dude. I could never imagine him trying to do an underage kid for sexual desires.

He was instead, one of those Hugh Hefner throwbacks, living by the playboy playbook. His short afro stayed flawlessly groomed as if he lived in the barber's chair. Only to compliment his razor-sharp goatee, which rode closely cropped to his chin. His threads were always boss clean and in style with a colorful flair and not to mention expensive. He was a bit on the heavy side but moved with an air of confidence for a big man.

Thanks to me being that old soul, I was already blessed with an eye for bullshit. I was smart enough to know he was more of a mark than a playboy, but I would've never led on to my keen observations.

My thoughts were, anytime you had to pay a woman for her time, you became a john, or a trick in my eyes. It didn't really matter whether it was dinner, a movie, or just plain old paying for some unattached sex!

There was a churning deep in my gut, and it continued to feed my soul when it came to the ways of women. I continually observed black men treating their women the wrong way and losing them.

Besides the Mack's and the preachers, they all fed into the black women's powers of suggestion. The trick was to give them anything they desired as long as it equaled sex in the end.

This happened especially when a woman's strength towered over a man's ability to take his natural God given place as leader. For some reason, deep inside me, I couldn't fathom that being the way to win in a relationship with an American taught, black woman. Yet I observed men sucker for them daily. All except for the hustlers, wino's and pimps.

Uncle Jamie was the only man that was capable of talking mama into letting me leave the house.

I was sure he was paying mama on the side, because my mama was cold blooded when it came to the game of life. Uncle Jamie was wise enough to know her mean streak. It was only tamed with money.

I could clearly see his game was simple, but worthy.

According to his own fantasy, he thought his was the slickest process in the world. On the first and fifteenth he would sneak away from his loving wife and pretend to attend work meetings.

Then he would visit us and grab me, as if I was his best nephew, and we would roll. Another stop would be to his connections house to buy food-stamps.

Charlie Trey was the neighborhood fence, and his house was packed with assorted items from one end to the other.

He purchased food stamps from women in the hood like mama.

There was no doubt in my mind that he dreamed he could purchase my mama in the raw as well.

Charlie would sell anything that brought money to the table. He weighed about three hundred pounds and struggled to get around.

His breathing was always labored, and his struggle for air was ever present, as he wheezed with every step. I can recall times when mama would refer to him as a,

"Jet black gorilla!"

She would also call him, **"Fat black bastard**!"

These names would bellow through the house once the guilt settled in, from the selling of our stamps. At first glance, one would've thought of him as an easy target for larceny. To think that would be a big mistake. He was known to have an extremely well-trained and quiet, Doberman pinscher waiting to attack.

He also kept a Saturday night special strapped to his side at all times.

I would get excited whenever Uncle Jamie and I entered his crib, because it was like going into a Newberry's department store.

I never had the money to buy anything, but I did a lot of dreaming. After about fifteen minutes of jive talk, they would get down to business and make the stamp exchange.

Once the stamps were in hand, Uncle Jamie would aim his big, pretty, green, Lincoln toward the Lucky's store to get some groceries.

Uncle Jamie did something mama never chose to do by allowing me into the store with him. Of course, there was a reason for this particular kindness, and it wasn't my happiness. Jamie knew the women were far more likely to give him action if I was observed walking by his side. Most black women shared a soft spot for black men willing to be seen with their kids.

Like clockwork whenever an attractive, black woman was in eyeshot, he would pretend I was his son. As long as they figured there was just one child, he got action.

It was my job to put on the shy face, and act is if I was a great kid. Even at a fresh ten years of age I knew how to sell the con. It always worked like magic and Uncle Jamie had a grand smile to go with the con. Together, with my loving, childish look, we couldn't lose. Quite often he came up with at least two telephone numbers, and future possibilities.

After getting groceries he would spend a few moments trying to decide which female he would bless with his manly ways. Once decided, the Lincoln was rolling again, and we were on our way to play.

There were at least five different women amongst those in his lust traps. Each stop had a different feel to it. My favorite stops were the ones with little children at home.

It would be my job would be to keep the kids busy, while he and the chosen woman went behind doors. They would need twenty to thirty minutes in order to get their freak on. The more difficult days were the days when I would just sit and keep myself company while the victim's kids were off at school.

My job would largely depend on the age of the children living at home. I often wondered how it was possible that mama would keep me home from school on the days he came by. I later found out; it **was** the money. The one thing that made these special visits possible was the much-needed groceries. This was the first chance I got to see what was supposed to be big Pimpin' 101, according to Uncle Jamie's dossier. I knew even then it fell short. There was no doubt I could learn from this old playboy, but I planned on being harder than him.

For some reason I felt his lessons were inconsistent with what the winos had informed me a true Mack was. I felt as if he could be taught some things, himself.

My personal thoughts were more in line with what I'd learned from the winos drinking by the liquor store. Their teachings were simple and made more sense. First, I was taught if you wanted to impress a woman, you needed a dynamite ride. If you were ugly, a bad ride would get you some cookie!

Second, you had to have bad threads, which usually included, having gators, or snakes on your feet.

Third, if you had something a woman wanted bad enough, you could get some cookie, no matter what the situation! But, from what the winos were teaching me, those things also equaled to what was called a tender dick. None of which was part of the pimp parade. It meant suckering for some ass.

However, their actions puzzled me, as they staggered with toothless grins and lethal habits.

It was obvious each had fallen in love with the same cookie they protested, and their current condition was the end result.

They were living like vampires, alive at night and stagnant in the day. Unlike them however, Uncle Jamie had achieved his goal at least. He walked out of those bedrooms with a renewed brightness in his smile, and I found myself envying that.

One day stuck out in my mind as if I created the day just for that particular memory. I couldn't believe the smile that lived happily on Uncle Jamie's face from ear to ear! It was as if he couldn't stop smiling no matter how much he tried.

We were at Miss Flo's house, and as usual I was happy to be visiting. I always loved visiting her because she was finer than most of his conquests. She had long, black hair, attached to a mellow, yellow, skin tone and without a scar, or blemish on her attractive face. The tone of her skin made her appear as if she was black with a mix of Native American. Her breasts stood firm, and erect. I knew they would refuse to bounce no matter how high she'd jump.

My hand moved downward. It was like fighting a small snake that refused to die. My hands suffered a continuous struggle to keep it under control. I figured she would run if she knew the head was ready to spit at will. The day had been one of those special days that I was able to watch T.V. for a change. I started the morning watching a popular television show, "***I Dream of Genie***."

The actress on the show was named, Barbara Eden. She was blonde and voluptuous, with very little clothing on her body. She was my personal muse and left me, and my private part in a wrestling frenzy whenever I was fortunate enough to watch the show.

I was usually great at my job because I sat extra quiet and waited without

a stir for my sexually motivated Uncle to finish.
I fought with the thought of sneaking to the door in order to listen to the moans and groans, that had to be present. It didn't take but a few more moments for me to lose the good fight and tip toe to the door for a listen. For the first time I could feel the hairs rise on the back of my neck. My palms begin to sweat, as I listened to about the most exciting thing I'd ever heard in my short years. Her melodic voice resounded sweetly through the thin door.
She purred,
"***Oh Daddy!***" Over and over again. The words sounded off and slipped beneath the door, as if they were sticky. I felt my manhood rise to another level as he demanded her,
"Suck this dick, bitch! Suck this big ole, soul brother dick! You, big booty, pretty, black assed fox!"
I found my pants taking shape in my private bump area again. I continued to rub it. I clutched and jerked my member around, like if it was forged from a piece of super steel and unbreakable.
I aggressively massaged until Uncle Jamie grunted like a mule and blew out a mass of air. He sounded like a hot air balloon going flat.
I quickly limped back to the couch. I pretended as if I'd been there the whole time. But I didn't know what to do with the stick that was testing my pants like a hard pencil. Things became worse, as Miss Flo floated and sashayed into the room. She was wearing a short, tight fitting, silk robe.
I noticed a wet spot riding the back of the robe, near her ass. It soiled in direct correlation with the exercise she'd just finished.
There was no shame in me, as I stared directly between her legs in order

to be blessed with a view. I had to have a view of the space dripping between her legs, so I moved closer.

Bingo, there it was, thanks to the robe falling open. It was just enough to reveal the hard nipples of her firm breasts. Her areolas were pointing at me, as if they knew me personally. Her body sent me a message that suggested I not even try to contain my rock hard, private and let my passion do its thing. Without notice she bent over to retrieve a sock from the floor allowing me to see the panty free space riding between her legs. There was no doubt she'd done all this on purpose. She shared a sly grin when it was time to bid her goodbye. However, she was still able to muster a surprise for me as she pulled me in close for a hug.

I looked at Uncle Jamie in order to gauge whether he'd get pissed at me squeezing on his squeeze. He gave me a small nod and I knew it was a pass. My erection was there to stay, and it was too late to avoid poking her during our parting, but it was as if nothing else mattered to me at that moment.

I was in another world as my gaze was stuck peering between her legs. Much to the excitement of my beating heart, she purposely grabbed my jimmy and slid a dollar of Uncle Jamie's money into my pocket.

I felt as if I were the real pimp in the room, and had a difficult time keeping my smile hidden.

I'd gotten paid without giving up a thing, which made me feel like the man.

I was sure Uncle Jamie's stubborn ways put him on notice to the little attention I was receiving, but he decided against blowing my cool and shaming a kid.

On the way home, he did something a bit out of his character, and reached into his pocket and gave me a dollar. I realized it was somewhat of a consolation prize. Uncle Jamie had a great time getting laid, and I had to be satisfied with the dick grab received from a grown woman. My moment would've been counted in the court systems as molestation, but in the mean streets, it was considered a blessing.

Once home, Uncle Jamie chose not to go inside and suggested I tell mama, he'd talk to her soon.

I stepped in and the tone of my moment changed to the usual, as mama slammed Tina's hand in mine.

"I'm glad you're home, buster! Git yo' little ass in here and take care of yo' baby sister, because I got shit to do!" She said curtly.

I'd lived way too many of these nights, therefore, I knew what to expect. I had no choice but to make mamas soon to be absence unimportant to my little sister.

As Mama disappeared into the room, it became one of those nights, that I would sit as quiet as church-mouse with my hand placed carefully over Tina's little mouth.

I had to keep her voice from screaming through the hallways of our tiny apartment. It was hard to believe she was only five years old and privy to the racket that commonly occurred every weekend of our young lives. The beatings and arguing had become far too commonplace. Oh, how I wanted to run for help, but I knew mama would beat me, straight away for snitching.

I knew I could muster help from at least two places in our hood, but mama wouldn't appear to be a victim to most, due to her big mouth.

I often closed my mind and concentrated on things I loved, like music and our tiny apartment. It rested quietly in the center of East Oakland,

directly on the main strip where the action lived.
We didn't live far from the infamous and gritty East 14th Avenue.
I was in love with ghetto life and the ever presence of black folks from block, to concrete block.
In the room with my mama was Doc, a waste of space in my mind.
I was built like a rail; therefore, I knew I couldn't cause the pretty boy much damage. But if it was possible, I would have put a life-long footprint on his ass for hitting my mama!
I found myself dreaming of ways to kill him on a daily basis. My emotion was fueled by the hate in my heart for him.
Maybe I could've put poison in his hair until it bled into his brain!
Or maybe I could've put a pork chop in his ass while he slept and let the Doberman Pincer next door, slowly eat it out.
Doc was a street hustler with a rep for being a made con man, blessed with a flair for the women.
He was a smooth talking, low life, with the ability to talk most fools out their shirts, while they were still wearing them. His dark complexion reminded me of the famed balladeer, Nat King Cole.
I think he hated being a black man, because I would watch mama put white conk in his hair. After a matter of minutes, he would scream like a girl. However, once the process was complete, his hair would be as straight as a white boy's hair.
I often wondered how it was possible that no one had knocked out any of his perfect, white teeth.
I had championed the cause of hiding mama's physical abuse from Tina. Mama had no idea that her acceptance of his behavior, was molding me into a special kind of monster. She staggered, due to the strong backhand

that landed solidly against her face. Tina's anger flushed her little, honey tainted face, until it was tomato red. Much to my surprise and without notice she ran up to Doc and yelled while punching him.

"You mean old man, don't hit my mommy no mo! You fucker! 'FO, I tell my daddy on you!"

I felt murder in my heart but put it away in that special hiding place until the day I'd be big enough for revenge.

I was trying to figure my next move because, Tina caught me by surprise. My dearest little sister upon listening to mama's less than pleasant vocabulary shouted her first cuss word. Mama figured it cute, but I didn't agree. She smiled at my adorable little sister as she dropped the, "F" bomb without hesitation.

Mama had always talked to me as if I were an adult. Unfortunately, the truth she often shared with me was far too harsh for my baby sister's ears.

The shameful tune was a common sentence bellowed in the ghetto.

"Your daddy ain't shit! He's never been shit, and never will be shit!" The women would say.

She would continue, "Dexter is, and will always be a junkie and a drunk! So, you'd better realize I'm all yo' smart ass got! You little bastard!"

Her words would enter my body like venom and cut me like a knife leaving an invisible trail of blood. It was those emotions that would have me talking to the winos and ex pimps at every opportunity.

Quite often I could see men in the alleys burning spoons with matches, and sticking needles in their arms. After slamming the dope, each would release the big rubber band wrapped around their arms. Soon they'd fall limp with their necks bobbing and rolling around as if their necks were rubber. Somehow, I felt as if my daddy was in one of those alleys and had forgotten he had two kids.

Tina's outlook was far more optimistic than mine. In her heart she knew he'd show one day. I didn't have the heart to let her think any different.

After the powerful slap and the scuffle, the room got quiet for a moment. Tina and I scurried about hoping mama and Doc were finished.

It wasn't long before another boom seemed to blast through the small hallway, and it sounded louder than the first.

Doc's voice trembled through the halls.

"Bitch, I otta kill you for fuckin' up my hair! I know you did that shit on purpose, Simone!"

Doc shouted, as mama appeared sharing a devilish grin.

Doc sprinted out of the room and into the bathroom while patting his hair. A dip in his hurried steps allowed me to see a patch missing out of his conk.

I chuckled, because I knew mama did it on purpose. That lady would take a beating from a man on any day and chalk it up to life. However, if you tried to beat her out of money, it would almost be impossible to hide from her.

Mama noticed us watching from the hall and approached us, while wiping blood from her mouth.

She mumbled,

"Motherfucka! You know better than playin' with my money! Next time I'll kill your punk ass! You little dick, bitch!"

The vision of me covering Tina's eyes in attempt to lessen the sting of the situation, caught mama's attention. After observing the concern in Tina's face, she licked her lips in a failed attempt to hide the blood.

Tina's eyes began to water, which prompted mama to grab my little sister from her perch with enough force to shake her big afro puffs. Tina's mellow, yellow, face became flush once again, and almost red with the snatch.

Tina looked at me with a familiar fear in her eyes and my heart wanted to reach out to comfort her. If I didn't know any better, I would have given my mama a resounding slap on the back of her neck.

I figured, it was my turn for torment as mama bent over and began to repeatedly jab her finger to my face while holding Tina. Her anger was displayed in her voice as she blasted at me.

"Look here little Mack! Don't ever let no faggot, or no bitch take you for your money! Do you hear me, little nigga?"

I stayed put, because I didn't want the backhand mama was so famous for to cross my face. I was forced to say whatever she wanted to hear in hopes that my words would save my lip from looking like hers.

I found the strength to rise to my feet and belted out a low response, "Yeah mama, I hear you!"

I could see calm reappearing as her breathing began to normalize, and she began to brush the dust from her clothes. We could clearly hear Doc talking to himself as he primped in the bathroom mirror.

Tina was also slowly returning to her normal state of mind as she lifted her tiny head, and softly spoke, "Martell I'm hungry!"

Mama sucked some of the remaining blood in her mouth and calmly attempted to put Tina's mind at ease. She suggested, "Everything's okay baby! I'll have your brother make you some cereal, okay?"

Although I knew it to be a mistake, I looked at mama and informed her, "Mama we don't have any milk!"

The response would be exactly as I expected when she looked at me as if it was my fault. She frowned, as if I was supposed to buy groceries, but somehow failed to do so.

She snapped. "Well, there's some bread in there and some sugar! Make her a sandwich, little nigga, shit! Stop acting as if you don't know what da hell you doin'!"

I knew it was coming and I'd have to find a way to feed Tina as well as myself. I went into the kitchen cabinet and grabbed the oranges I had borrowed from Mr. Thompson's tree, the day before.

I kept them hidden in the kitchen, in order to avoid Doc's hungry eyes. Mama was wrong as usual, there was no sugar; however, there was a piece of bread along, with a few items I could use.

I sat Tina on the counter next to me and began to cut the oranges. I'd perfected a way to strategically place them around the plate, in order to fool her and make them appear to be more than what was there.

I cut the bread in small squares, just the way my little sister liked it. When our makeshift dinner neared its end, she was satisfied. I couldn't say the same thing for me. After eating the one orange on my plate, my little ass was still starving and ready to go rob a meat truck.

I walked by the bathroom to secretly check on my mama and what I saw, moved my stomach down south toward my feet. The feeling rivaled the time I'd eaten too many rotten grapes and spent the whole day on the toilet.

My mama was burning a spoon with a match, like I'd seen in the alley and my little brain had trouble believing it.

I watched what I thought was heroin sizzle and smoke in the spoon. My mind suggested to me, this was a dream, because my mama was smarter than this.

I figured the devil was visiting as I observed Doc standing, counting money with his sleeves rolled up. I noticed strange marks on his arms that winded like a snake. My soul was on fire, as I realized my mama was the same thing she labeled my daddy, a junkie!

My feet froze in place again, even though my mind told them to run. I stared at my mama with an intense contempt as she was becoming part of the demonic scene in my eyes. The feeling was surreal as the sweating bathroom reminded me of a prison scene, and she no longer looked like my mama. Mama was slapping her tiny leg. She appeared to be beating herself. There was a small yellow, rubber tube tightly wrapped around it. Doc slowly began to drop money on the sink, as I observed drips of saliva slithering out of his mouth.

"I'm a boss number one, con man, with money to burn, baby! That's what I am!"

He bragged.

I looked to the floor at the blood spatters freshly resting on the once clean linoleum. He seemed to have a difficult time keeping his mouth under control. I watched his head bob, like he was a puppet. He was slightly drooling and struggling, with wiping his mouth.

He stammered the words.

"Come on Bitch! Hurry up, so I can clean my tools and put 'em away! Next time we fix, you betta not plug your works, 'cuz you know I don't like sharing my shit!"

He slurred.

That day burned like a small flame, dark in my heart. It became a defining moment for me and would change my life. I instantly felt the

impact of what was in front of me and knew I was changed forever.
The ugliness I felt, made me aware that the change was not necessarily for the best. My stomach was like a pot of water with fire lit beneath it. It was bubbling, but not quite ready to boil.

Without accepting the reality of my presence, mama stabbed the needle in her golden leg.

I soon realized the bathroom scene wasn't a blur just for me, but for mama as well. It had to be, because she wouldn't allow her brain to register me staring on with trepidation. Once she pulled the plunger and observed her blood appear in the dropper, she pushed the substance back into her body and sighed with intense pleasure.

It was at that moment she turned her head to the side, only to see me stuck in my tracks. She looked at me with the coldest eyes I'd ever seen in my short life. My own mama looked at me with a death stare as if she hated me. It occurred to me that she would shoot me dead if a gun was within her reach. Her reaction was no surprise to me, because I'd never fooled myself as to how much hate lived in her heart. As for me, I felt my heart break at that moment.

Mama was never very affectionate to me. Short of an occasional light hug, Tina got all the love. It never really bothered me much. However, now that I was getting older, my heart suggested I was losing her love a little more day by day. Mama looked at me, as if I was the single solitary owner of the cold in the night and she hated the cold.

I didn't understand her building resentment toward me, and it would've been easy for me to share that resentment. But I knew it would have been a waste of time.

The look in her eyes confirmed, she didn't care that I wanted to be treated like a little boy. I found myself wanting to lash out and tell her, "Look, I'm only ten years old and all I want to be is a kid! Can I mama? Can I be a kid? Can I play tag outside, like everybody else? Must I stay in the house babysitting all the time? Can I have a bike or maybe some toys to play with?"

I knew these were dreams, because had I said these words to my mama, I would end up coughing up blood. There was no doubt, she would have blasted my chest to pieces.

I had no idea what was going to happen next, but I knew my lean, chocolate, frame had better find a way out of mama's eyesight, fast! I found myself stuck in a mental quicksand. There was a reflection of hate marinating through her eyes, as she coldly peered through my soul.

I could hear Doc's voice rumble with bass as he grinned.

"I think yo' boy wants a taste of this fast, Simone!"

He mused.

I realized then, mama wasn't just cold to me, as she gave Doc the same death stare. Doc was just too high to realize the trouble he was in until mama yelled like the devil.

"Shut up, you ignorant fool and let me deal with my son! Don't nobody tell yo' faggot assed son, how to buy purple panties and switch his little ass! Like the lil' bitch he is, do they?"

Doc's pain made him laugh at mama's coldness in reference to his son being homosexual. He pulled a four-finger lid of weed from his pocket and replied,

"Them's called jockeys! And don't trip off my boy, he just goin' through a phase right now, you dig? He ain't nobody's faggot, Simone!" Doc lied.

Without notice, mama grabbed me by my collar with one hand and yanked me completely into the bathroom. By the look on her face, I knew trouble would be my middle name. I'd seen her share that look with men in the past. It was as cold as a freezing winter's night on the Aspen ski slopes. It was that look that sent hordes of men to the gallows in medieval times.

The smell of the dope began to ooze through my nose and make me sick. The spoon she held in her other hand was burnt, as well as bent and rounded at the end.

I had trouble holding my orange down as it ripped away at my stomach, and mama stood strangling me at my collar. Her anger was at a level I'd never seen pointed at me before, as she kept jabbing the needle near my face.

She moaned with that scary tone again, while holding me in her clutch. "You see this shit, you little fucker? Do you want some of this shit? I think this bitch assed Doc is right! Maybe you do!"

Just as quickly as she grabbed me, she let me go and reached down at her foot. I thought she was going to hit me with her shoe, but something in me wouldn't allow me to cringe.

Her shoe had been the object of my pain many times before, but to my surprise this day was different. She removed one of her socks and shoe in order for me to see. There were black marks all over her foot that I'd never noticed before.

I couldn't decide whether I was so selfish that I never paid attention to my own mother's feet, or if these were new scars.

After clearing my eyes to see the horror, I realized they were identical to the snake marks on Docs arms.

Mama continued,
"You see mama's foot, boy? It wasn't like that just three months ago! I know the scars ain't cute, but the way this shit makes you feel is dynamite! This here is what they call crystals.
Yo' mama's a bad bitch! I shoot the good shit! It ain't near as hard as that shit Ray Charles and Billy Holiday us! But it's some boss shit just as well; Janis Joplin, Charlie Parker and all the great singers, shoot up with the boy! The big, bad, boy is heroin and be glad I ain't on that shit! This is just a little go fast! But you know what that makes me, Martell Mackie? It makes me a fuckin' potential superstar! I'm a hell of a singer! But when I'm on this here, I can blow up a whole room, like I have giant lungs! All the greats used something to take 'em to another level, now it's my time!"
Mama slurred in a temporary daze.
Doc began to laugh and interrupted,
"That's no bullshit boy! And this here shot into the veins, sends you straight to heaven, fast like! Shit, when you on this here, you ain't even black no mo! You da same as everybody else! You the same as rich folks and superstars like Elvis!"
Mama relaxed her grip and began smiling as she unwrinkled my shirt and joined in on Doc's perspective.
"Yeah, you become the same as whites, Jews, Italians and everybody else. Your skin color walks away like a runaway child and you're left just blowin'! You dig what I'm sayin' kid?"
Mama asked.
All three of us were caught off guard as Tina entered the hallway and looked into the bathroom. My anger was immediate as it traveled from

the bottom of my feet to the top of my head.
Tina looked on in obvious bewilderment. I felt as if I was changing shades of black, as I watched her little face contort due the horrifying sight that lay before her.
There was no way she would understand the blood on the floor, or the blood on mama. Tina's brain had to find some reasoning for what was happening. All she could come up with, was a simple question.
She sadly asked,
"Mommy, why you playin' doctor at night?"
Her observation of mama's injuries made a bad situation worse.
She continued.
"You want me to get you a Band-Aid, cause you bleedin' mommy?" She asked.
I knew I had to act quickly, before Tina got hit by the Simone side of mama. I placed her in my arms and turned away from Simone, and surrendered,
"Yeah Tina, mama playing doctor! So, come with bro-bro and we can play jacks."
Upon exiting the bathroom, a strange feeling crept into my being, as my words felt foreign to me.
I couldn't hold back my thoughts, as I looked back and spoke out of turn.
"God made me black, mama! I don't know anything else, and lookin' at you two, I don't think I want too!"
The lost look on Tina's face gave me a new-found courage. Her shock and bewilderment stood as fuel for my controlled rage. That was the moment I decided, mama was weak, and I would never be afraid of her again. After a blurry moment she snapped at me one more time and

argued,
"So, I guess you wanna say it loud? You black and you proud, like James Brown, huh? Then you'd betta stay away from this shit, little black assed boy! Because, what I forgot to tell you, is this shit'll kill you! And I will too, if I ever catch you in my stash, you understand me?"
Her words had little meaning to me, due to the automatic depletion of respect, forging through my person for her. I answered mama like a smart ass, for the first time in my life and retorted.
"I got it mother! If your stash doesn't kill my black ass, you'll will, right?"
Mama, recognizing my disrespect wanted to get me, but her body was moving erratically, and she had little control of it. I closed the door and Doc called me a jive turkey, upon my exiting the room.
That was the day Doc became my sworn enemy. I would continue to have love for my mama, but never respect her.
I'd come to realize; a person can be loved without the benefit of respect. After a while, I could hear mama begin to sing through the door of the bathroom. Her voice remained melodic in nature, but the haziness of the dope, made it sound quick paced, strained and a bit out of sync. She attempted a rendition of (Billy Holiday's)
"Good Morning Heartache."
The night was long and hot, especially for a little boy having nightmares, and I was having a memorable one for sure. In my tossing and turning, I violently opened my eyes and grabbed at my sweat drenched t-shirt. The visions were vivid and life like.
In the dream, the white horse, heroin, was choking me in my sleep. The all dangerous white ooze was crudely bubbling out my nose, and mouth,

like white fizz from a year-old garbage can. I was covered with a death cloud and it was taking my last breath, when suddenly there was a tug at my shirt.

I was thankful, because I was always told, if you die in your sleep, you die in real life. This made me happy for the shaking of my body.

Within a split second, she had me out of bed and standing on my feet, at four in the morning. My thankful energy didn't last long as mama pulled me into the kitchen, while punching me in the arm. Her screams seemed to emit from the top of her lungs.

She yelled.

"You little, nasty, bastard! All I ask you to do is take care of my fuckin' house!"

Once we reached the kitchen, I noticed a cup sitting on the counter. She grabbed the cup and banged it upside my head, while yelling.

"You see this dirt in the glass? I want your triflin' ass to wash all these damned dishes over, Martell!"

I looked at the cup that had just became her weapon of choice, and noticed it had a small speck on it.

Soon after, she had all the dishes from the cupboard in the sink, with a few broken from the force of her anger.

After washing all the dishes, I found myself grabbing the broken ones with my bare hands, in attempt to hurry back to bed. I pretended the cuts didn't exist and I licked the blood off my hand.

The hallway found me totally exhausted, when I noticed mama sitting in a chair, crying. Normally I would've gone and let her cry on my shoulder, until my t-shirt was drenched with her tears. But the way mama had been treating me of late, I found myself heading straight for bed.

Once in the bed again, I prayed the nightmare wouldn't return, while I cursed mama, until I was sleep.

I was thankful to the morning light that made its way into the bedroom, and even more thankful, that the dope filled nightmare didn't return to my sleep. What I didn't count on, was the lack of energy that plagued me, as I got ready for school. My eyes seemed to stay shut. It felt like they had been stapled with heavy duty staples and drooped as if I were a dope-fiend myself.

The simple truth was this fatigue had become commonplace in my young life. Mama spent most of her nights at the clubs, trying to break through as a singer. It was becoming my job to stay home, while keeping the house and maintaining an innocent Tina.

It was becoming apparent to me, that I would be the one to guide my little sister in the early years of her life.

I was becoming ever so self-efficient, spending more than thirty minutes a day ironing creases in my 501 jeans. Having only two pairs, made it a struggle to wash them. Therefore, I made a system and I'd wash them by hand, on rotating nights. The next task in my morning missions, was to find something for Tina to eat. As always, this was struggle, due to the lack of food in our household. I figured I was skinny, because I never had a chance to eat the way I should've, due to a lack of resources. Lucky for Tina, I kept a stash of oatmeal in the back of the shelf. I wanted her to eat what appeared to be breakfast daily.

I thanked God for the invisible cloak he'd placed over my little sister. I also thanked him for making her too young to really feel my day to day pain, or confusion.

Every morning, I would head for school, after putting Tina back to sleep.

Most mornings, I prayed that mama was in her room. My next concern would be who was sleeping in her room.

Slipping mama's door open was like digging to the bottom of a crackerjack box, looking for the prize. You'd never know what you would get, considering she didn't discriminate sexually.

I've opened mama's door many mornings, only to see some of the nicest booties and breast the world had to offer. I could remember, she had done the nasty with threesomes with no regard. I didn't think it really mattered to her, who landed in her bed, as long as she didn't have to eat of the flesh.

I'd overheard conversations, and mama would speak ill about eating pussy and the possibilities of bloody surprises. Mama was using lust, to drown out some of her inner pain and emotional torture.

A day seared in my memory, one of (mama's) Simone's visitors dropping in on me. Her name was Candy and she exited mama's room and entered the kitchen, I was cooking Tina's breakfast.

I was pleasured by her wearing one of Simone's, sheer nightgowns. The curve of her body caught me right in my little zipper, because she was built like the perfect black princess. The fact, she didn't have on any panties, didn't lesson my erection. Her girls stood at attention, in the shape of firm pears, topped with well- rounded silver dollars.

They became more pronounced, when she became startled by a shirtless, boy standing by the stove, me. Her stomach was flat like a pancake, with a diamond stud pierced in the center, of what was blessed to be flawless, milk chocolate skin.

Her dark bush was revealed just enough for me to know, she wasn't big on shaving, however the gap between her legs needed the hair for cover.

Because there was so much space, without the hair, I'm sure she would have caught a cold down there.

My reputation wasn't that of a shy boy, when it came to women, even at my young age. I stood my ground firm. I pretended to be waiting for some steamy sex. I wanted it to be her job to satisfy me. She stopped in her footsteps and began to clutch her goodies.

She then placed one arm across the top half of her body while covering the hairy V that lived between her legs, with her other hand.

The snake between my legs popped up. It was strong, trying to shoot me in my chin. I refused to move, or waver, one single inch. Without thinking, or having any control of my faculties, I surrendered and praised,

"Damn baby!"

Once she realized I wasn't moving, nor was I afraid, she relaxed and placed her hands to her sides. This was much to my surprise and pleasure as well. I offered her my hand and introduced myself, "How you doing? I'm Martell, pimp daddy, Mackie!"

She softly graced my hand with her grasp, while giggling, and returned, "They call me Coffee! Pleased to meet you, Martell! Is there anything to drink in there?"

I knew there wasn't anything in the box, but water; however, I wasn't saying anything that would stop my action. I was quick witted and thinking on my feet, when I said,

"I do not know what you like, so I guess you'd better look for yourself."

My next lie was quick and worthy.

"Sometimes we keep sodas in the bottom drawer!"

We both understood what was going on, as she slid her superbly, curved body past me, with a slight brush. Her perfumed aroma almost made me almost bust a load in my pants. She walked past me and stood in front of the fridge. Her nipples become more erect, due to the chill from the ice box. My zipper was being tested, beyond reason and I didn't care. She placed her hands on her thighs and bent over to reveal a small, but well-rounded ass.

I was close to blowing up, as she twisted side to side, teasing me with the best body I'd seen, up to this point in my young life.

Upon a closer look, I could see a mound of curly hair, that ran from the tip of her pussy, to the crest of her ass. Her hair made me feel so aroused, I immediately lost control and busted a hot shot all over the front of my creased jeans. Coffee closed the refrigerator and turned back toward mama's room. I tried to hide my wet pants, so not to be embarrassed. Somehow, she could dig into my truth and giggled again. She must have known, I wanted to slap her to cure the way I was feeling, when suddenly she reached down and gently rubbed my wet spot.

"You spilled something on your pants baby, or did Miss Coffee cause you an accidental cream?"

She asked, while licking her lips. I felt my body shake with sex tingles, as she moved her hand to pour herself a glass of water.

Her twisted smile served as the litmus for me to make a promise to myself. I would never allow this to happen again. I would learn dick control, even if it killed me. From that moment, I would master the ability to control my sexual organ and orgasms.

At my young age, I had no girl in my program, to assist me in the training of pre-ejaculation control. The one-armed bandit had to serve as a replacement.

Soon, I was able to control the length of my arousal and control my blast. I was able to stiffen my member upon command, and ejaculation would never be premature, or without a great deal of mind control. Little did I know, I was taking the first step to mastering the art of the being, an unselfish lover. I had no idea the things that were taking place, would impact me for the rest of my life.

Even more of an impact was my strong-willed mother. She was not to be trifled with and controlled every situation within her eyesight, or beyond. Mamma's name was Simone and just loved when she would sing to me. My mamma had the voice of angel, or so I thought.

CHAPTER 2
MAMA SOUL
SIMONE

Mama lay in the bed, just like she did every day, that my young mind could recall. She seemed to be stuck in a time-less blur, of drunkenness and constant hangovers.

I opened the door and let the wind push my tired body, toward school, in a robotic fashion. Most days, I walked in a cloud wondering, if Tina would make it safely, through each day. All she had was Simone, to lead her way.

My mind would be consumed with thoughts, that mama would have difficulty waking up for Tina.

Every morning was the same. Simone would push her small body upward in the bed, while struggling to open her eyes. She was able to strain one eye open and reach for her daily breakfast. The breakfast consisted of a pack of kool cigarettes and the left-over bottle of Boone's Farm, wine. Once the last sip slid down her throat and mellowed her body, she would sit up and survey the mess in her bedroom.

Next, in her process, was the wiping of her eyes and the struggle to remember if anyone, or who may had slept in her bed.

This was about the time every morning when regret would begin to slip into the crux of mama's true personality. She would lay in bed, thinking to herself, ***how different things were just a short time ago.***

If my daddy could only see the fucked-up person, I have become, he would want nothing to do with my high, yellow, ass! And I wouldn't blame him because I barely recognized myself anymore. Daddy expected so much out of me and my life.

The underachieving woman I have become, could never be attributed to my daddy's influence, in my life. He guided me the right way and supported me.

There was no real excuse for me, being a dope-fiend, bitch, with no hope!

I still remembered the pride in his face, the day I graduated. He shook the hand of every white man, that entered his realm. That day was his day and he made it his personal mission, to kick sand in their faces and prove his colleagues wrong. He needed to make them see how wrong they were, about their beliefs, that black people were inferior.

Daddy was raised during that time in His-story, when black men rarely got the same respect, as white men, achieving the same goals. Actually, he never stopped thinking that way and therefore, it made this a special day.

My daddy's one and only baby girl, was receiving a degree from the University of California, at Berkeley.

I was going to teach like him, with the only variation from his pedigree, being my teaching of music. My daddy taught accelerated English, on a much higher scale, than I could ever achieve.

This was the day he stood tall and erect. His energy mirrored him graduating all over again. I however, had a long way to go, before I could touch daddy's credentials. He'd received his Doctorate and was a professor at one of most prestigious Universities in the United States.

He was also a true, Southern gentleman, with a heart of gold and the mannerisms to match. Sometimes, these wonderful attributes didn't matter at Stanford University. Those racist, old, white men wouldn't give my daddy, any love. The emotional trials of his job kicked his ass every day. Although, he would never admit to it, or even show it.

Most of his peers, figured, uppity Negroes such as daddy, should be working in the facilities department. He should be digging ditches and changing light bulbs.

Daddy worked there most of my life and I always thought the mood of racism would change. However, years of looking into my daddy's eyes, made me lose hope that it ever would. It did help however, that daddy was a Louisiana Creole, and spoke French fluently. His tall, slender body and pretty, black mane didn't seem to hold one single nap.

This meant my daddy had everything close to God going for him, while having all things against him, at the same time. His good looks made him a target for the different white women, curious about having a black lover. He ignored them and they began to despise him, for turning down their advances.

Society couldn't comprehend, nor accept a black man being true to his wife. According to powers that be, black men didn't care about nothing but money, a fine ride and dripping sex.

Slavery rendered the black man's nature, one of animalistic breeders.

They silently suggested, daddy would have to dumb down his extraordinary IQ, to avoid trouble, due to white women.

Daddy couldn't stand the prejudice and self-serving power structure, and God knows he had his reasons.

He only spoke of it one time, but I'll never forget it.

Daddy admitted, he had a white granddaddy. His Granddaddy was a slave-owner and he would force daddy's, black grandmother to have sex with him. That is, if they wanted to eat. She chose family, over virtue and submitted her body, while taking her mind on a journey.

Daddy wanted the man and his white family, to acknowledge him. The old, white man would always deny him, despite his pleas. Daddy was quite insistent, until the old man ran daddy away from his land, with his shotgun blazing. The old man eventually became bitter. He was unhappy, occasionally spouting, to his family,

The old bitch gave the, black bastard, the Fontenot name, without my permission.

I can remember daddy speaking that French dialect, to mama. He would sneak up behind her and kiss her neck whenever she stood in the kitchen, cooking.

There were times when his ability would hinder his progress and tutelage because he enjoyed flaunting this dialect. The Dean wouldn't allow daddy to teach it, even though he spoke it, better than the person teaching it at the time.

Although, I could keenly see the apparent hurt in my daddy's face, he would never admit to it bothering him. Not even to his pride and joy, me!

I can still recall my daily question.

"How was your day, daddy?"

He would put on his, I'm a grown man face and his voice would become strong and gruff.

"Little girl, God made this world for mankind! And he made the black man, the strongest. The good book speaks about the righteous being treated the worse. Therefore, when it comes to your dear old dad, that's what comes to hurt me, only succeeds in making me stronger!

Just remember this, I'm strong and that beautiful smile of yours, blesses me with a lifetime of courage!"

He would say these words so often, that I began to mimic him whenever he'd say them.

My daddy was never aware of me recognizing his pain, due to his career pace slowing. I acted, as if I didn't see the dire situation for the black man. However, I clearly saw the world showing the black man its booty, for as long as I could remember.

From shore to shore, people were afraid of ***the*** educated black man, more than any other group, alive.

After taking a good look at my daddy's list of accomplishments. As well as, the great men like him, I understood why the fear was present. If these men ever set their minds on reprisal and revenge, it would be a devastation placed on their enemies, like never felt before.

As for Mama, she was a well-traveled woman, with an IQ to match her husband's. In my opinion, my mama and daddy made the finest couple ever placed on this Earth. Anyone fortunate enough to be in their presence, could see it, and feel it, down deep to their bones.

Mama was short and stoutly built, with the big girl curves often found in the deep South.

Her smile tended to light up any room, that she would enter with grace and reverence.

She was the epitome of a Preacher's daughter, raised to love God and do good deeds. Not the kind of Preacher's kid known to rip up the town, like I'd seen before. But the kind, that spent all her time in church, playing the piano and singing in the choir.

Mama was daddy's opposite, in almost every way, however they shared what was most important to each of them. A yearn for teaching and the mark of intelligence.

While daddy was militant, and willing to knock the hell out of anyone that was disrespectful, mama would be the peacemaker. She would use her love for Jesus, as the answer to all problems, no matter how big or small.

As a little I girl, I played in mama's bras, wishing to be her size one day. She bounced a heavy pair of 44 double D's around. She moved them with ease. However, I thought mama's breast were the biggest things I'd ever seen on a woman.

As I reflect on her personality, I wish I'd taken after her, instead of daddy. She had a strong personality and refused to let anyone, or anything get to her.

She was always extremely casual and so cool, when trouble reared its ugly head; it was amazing to see her iron clad calm.

But there was something deep in mama's past that kept her from touching, or hugging. It was a chore for her to kiss me on the forehead, or any skin to skin contact, was even more difficult for her to manage, with everyone, but daddy.

From the day I was born, I can recall daddy, holding me much more than mama would.

As I grew into womanhood, Daddy was the one to continuously pull my card about men and their evil ways. He even taught me about the birds and the bees when I was twelve.

Once I turned thirteen, I could gauge the actions of the opposite sex, to know if he was going to be satisfied just getting a kiss good night, or if he had other sexual aspirations.

Mama was perfectly content sitting on the sidelines, as daddy taught me the ups and downs of womanhood.

It was daddy that ran through the house, with tissue in hand to wipe my nose when it bled, as well as other things.

I clearly remember the day; I went into the bathroom and slammed the door in a rush. The aching feeling in my stomach exploded, with a life's fluid from the bottom of my dress, which freaked me out.

Daddy didn't even flinch when I came out crying and my hands were full of blood. He explained my period to me, to the very letter of what could affect it. He also suggested, what not to do during heavy flow.

I noticed conversations like that, would take a toll on mama and make her extremely uncomfortable. But oddly enough, she was comfortable teaching in front of hordes of people. That's where she found her calling.

Mama received her Law degree from a prestigious, law school, located in the Oak Park area of Sacramento California. It was McGeorge School of Law.

She was attending school there when she met daddy. He'd won several debates against her school and was there to eat up the debate team, once again. Mama wasn't a member of the team, but never missed a debate.

It's no wonder, she was head of her class.

She suggested, daddy was very sure of himself, as he beat the local boy's down. His tongue was a sharp sword.

"That dude thought he was the Moses of information, when he came to our school!"

She would say about my daddy.

They often played and argued about which one was smitten first.

It really didn't matter, because they were truly in love and it showed in every aspect of their life. From the day, they met each other, it was over for anyone else, to have a chance, at either of their hearts.

McGeorge School of Law was an hour and twenty minutes away from our house, but mama enjoyed the travel time. Considering, the Sacramento area didn't offer a lot of jobs; Mama didn't have to worry about traffic. This made the commute somewhat pleasurable.

Daddy's commute on the other hand was hell, which prompted him to use public transportation, on most days.

I was surprised that mama had taken a job as a teacher and decided against practicing law. One day she explained it all to me.

She began to shake her head, in sorrow as she shared,

"Honey, I was a Lawyer for two months, and in those two months, I'd seen so many miscarriages of justice, it hurt me to my heart. I'd seen the court system, work with two different systems of crap!

One for blacks and a different one for whites, and equality always absent. These things damaged my love for the law and opened my eyes. So, I took my chances on being a teacher of the law, and I've always prayed that I would make a difference. I knew I was winning when, each one of my students passed the Bar exam. I knew I was doing the right thing!" Mama would admit.

I don't think my mama and daddy went more than an hour in each other's presence, without kissing each other. I always figured I would have that, but life would prove me wrong. When it came to men, there wasn't one beacon of light in my life.

I'd had the worst luck with men and relationships. Mama said, I'd never have a man, thanks to me always looking for daddy, in the men I dated. Her assumptions were absolutely on the money, as I often found myself leaving half of my intelligence on the shelf.

I had to do it, in order engage the men, I was attracted too. I just loved them bad actors and they loved my innocent look. The problem seemed to be, most of those cats, were so dumb that I became bored. Far before, the relationship would have a chance to flourish.

Who would have ever thought, the first time I laid down and opened my legs to a man, I knew I was in trouble? I would have to tell my parents, I was pregnant. The pain in daddy's face, cut through me like a sharp switchblade. I watched him cry for the first time, in my life. I felt like killing myself, when this, six foot plus, hulk of a man, become child-like in front of my very eyes.

He appeared more hurt to think I had sex, without being married, rather than me being with child. Maybe that part was easier, due to him looking forward to having a grandson. I was the one and only child in his life. Considering they were both professionals, it was amazing that my parents, had the time to have a child at all.

I knew how to work my daddy for anything because I was his bunny. Mama was different; I had never experienced, her being pissed off to that level. She was beyond angry, when she admonished me, due to my condition.

"You mean to tell me, you been out there screwing these low life's, child?"

She rendered, with scorn.

"Those negroes don't care about you, or the future you just threw away! They can't take care of you or help you through college! As a matter of fact, do you have any idea, how difficult it is to finish school and take care of a baby?

I can't believe you could hurt us like that! You thank-less, spoiled excuse, for a grown up!" Mama yelled.

She calmed down enough to regain her composure and even her tone, as she continued.

"You've broken your daddy's heart, today! But even more importantly, you've put your life, in a state of struggle! And it's all on you, Simone! You've been blessed with far more than your father and I, ever had! You've never had to work hard, not one single day! Now, you've just placed all our dreams for you in jeopardy. I'm so hurt about you having a bastard child; I don't even know what to say! Do you have any idea, how many parents struggle, because there's no money to raise their kids? It's hard to imagine my child, would do it willingly!

Simone, you've just become an average bitch, in the streets!" Mama scorned in obvious disgust.

I struggled to get a word in, as she treated me uglier than she'd ever done before.

My embarrassment and humiliation turned my stomach, as I pleaded, "Mama please! I can't handle you treating me like this, please! I know, I made a mistake! It wasn't on purpose! I didn't plan on it! It just happened!"

I cowered.

Mama looked at me with a hate, like I never thought her capable of, and strongly blasted me.

"You don't happen to fall on a man's dick, stupid! You lie down, open your legs, and give them the passage! You give them passage to the only damned gift, you'll ever get, that's supposed to be unique! Your body is a gift, as long as you live! So, don't hand me that weak assed, I didn't mean too shit, Simone! In ten minutes of selfishness, you've made my life's work, seem worthless and I'm, fucking upset, like you'll never know!"

She spurned.

My heart dropped to my knees and I knew better than to say anything else. This was the first day, I'd ever heard my mama be this mean, or use profanity. I knew I had played myself way out of her favor, and at this point, I'd hoped daddy hadn't felt the same.

It didn't take long, before I got my answer, as my daddy entered the room. The look on his face was dismal. For the first time ever, my daddy spoke to me, without looking at me. True sadness was written all over his face.

I realized at that moment, how much influence the love of a woman, or a girl could have on a man.

This tall, proud, handsome warrior had been broken down by a disappointing daughter. With his head hanging down, daddy surrendered, "I don't know what your plan is, and I can't begin to tell you what to do with your, God given, body. But I will tell you, we Fontenot's, don't kill our babies! However, when all is said and done, that's your choice to make. You can stay here with your baby, but I won't be in the delivery room. Afterwards, you will need to get a job and have your own money, because you don't deserve mine! Right now, I need some space, so stay clear of me for a while."

Daddy requested, in a withdrawn and surrendered voice.

He quietly left the room, still hanging his usually proud head down.

Mama walked outside and began to pace up and down the hill, located alongside our house.

It felt like, a bad dream, but my eyes were open. To make matters worse, I couldn't bring home the man responsible for my condition. I was sure, that upon meeting him, my daddy, would've hated him and hated my choice, in him.

I thought of myself as a rebel, because I always did the opposite of what I was taught, when it came to men. I later found out; I wasn't a rebel at all. I was just plain gullible and stupid, as a young girl.

Dexter was the man in my life, and he was everything daddy hated. He was a pretty boy, and he knew it. His smooth, caramel skin was as flawless, as his manicured fingernails. If you didn't know any better, you would think he was a sissy. Especially if you watched his mannerisms and the way he moved. His walk, was more like a glide and his hair, was always braided, into a long ponytail.

I think, he figured himself prettier, than me, on most days. But I surely loved looking at him. I might have been able to get away with all these things, upon introducing him to daddy, but there was a bigger problem. He had no ambition, and no job. He made money in his only professions, selling weed, and playing women. Somehow, I had become one of the women. He played me from the day we met, and I was helpless to stop him.

I felt, he had a spell on me. There's something about your first love, as a girl, that would remain special for your whole life, for good or worse. He was my first, therefore I couldn't gauge just how good a lover he was, but he had a lock on my heart, and he opened it at will.

Some women say you lose more than your virginity, with your first lover. Well I'm here to say, you lose your mind, after your first love, and it doesn't really matter if the sex is good, or bad. In the beginning, I was nowhere in love with this man. Once the sex was over, he spent so much time in the mirror, I was wondering if he was a girl.

However, after the passing of some time, he began to win the battle of hearts. After he got into my panties, he spent plenty of time getting into my head. I would later find out, he worked all his women in the same manner, and I was one of many.

He would make us all feel like, we were royalty. We showed that loyalty, by buying him clothes, shoes, and silk shirts. Unfortunately, he was far too preoccupied with himself, to realize his full potential, and just how silk his tongue was. But it was that same tongue, which prevented him from really achieving anything notable in life. He would always be a low-level hustler. I believed, he could have achieved anything he wanted, had he any ambition.

The first time was enough to keep me wanting more of his passion, and that was all it took. After two months of relentlessly chasing me and popping up everywhere I spent time, he finally pulled me into his web.

I was pulling out of the school parking lot, in the cute, red, 1965 mustang convertible, that daddy brought me.

I hit the corner and there he stood, like he was the man, and I was lucky to be a part of his world.

Flash had to be his mantra. His afro sheen, laden braid, was lying perfectly across his back. His blue alligator shoes evenly matched the overlapped collar, of his blue silk shirt. His smile was a pretty white example of perfection, except the two gold teeth that would blind you into surgery. To make matters worse, this ghetto Romeo had a box of chocolate cherries in his hand, which just happened to be my weakness. I didn't have it in me, to turn him down again.

I found myself attracted to him for a long time, and I was also impressed with all the trouble, he'd gone through, to impress little, old, me.
I was impressed, because none of the dudes in church, did anything like this. Not to mention, in all my years in Church, were they nearly as persistent.
He flagged me down, as I drove by. He teased, the chocolate in my face, with his dazzling smile and summoned,
"Hey there Princess! I was hoping, I could be your servant today! I'm fit, willing, ready and able to do anything, at your command!"
I couldn't do anything, but smile and ask,
"Are those chocolate cherries you just happen to have in your hand, my brother?"
He responded instantly, with the sly look of a fox.
"Why yes, they are! Boy, they're already meltin' all chocolate-ee and smooth, just like they're ready to melt in ya mouth, ya dig!" My curiosity was digging deep, and I had to know, therefore I asked.
"Who told you about my chocolate, cherry, weakness?"
His confidence flared at the question, as he gloated.
"Well, seems as if church boys want to meet project chicks, and would sell their souls for anything to get a phone number, ya dig! Supply and demand, of what we all need! I gave up info on a couple project chicks and bam, I got your Bio!"
He bragged.
I observed him trying to keep his language above street as he spoke. He was beginning to struggle with it, which made me throw him a lifeline.
My mind remained cautious, and I wasn't sure when I spoke.
"Okay, you've worked yourself up on little time, thanks to all your

antics. So, what's the deal, and what is it gonna cost me?"

I asked, with curiosity.

I couldn't believe what I was doing, but I was a bit eager and trying to hide it.

"Well, Princess, I need you to meet me at three forty Plymouth, East Oakland; tomorrow when you get out of school. If you can do that, I will be your royal servant, as long as you can dig it!"

He smiled.

My curiosity was getting the best of me. I had been totally smitten, on this thug wanna be, for a long time.

The next day moved along quickly. I couldn't wait for school to end. As the day endured, the clock appeared to slow down. I began to stumble over schoolwork, while sitting in my last class. I should have been focused on earning my second degree. But, for some strange reason, I found myself continuously struggling to keep my hand away from my lap. There seemed to be an invisible magnet present and it kept moving my hand to my lap and I didn't know why.

Finally, class ended and I almost tripped, trying to get to my car. I started cussing at myself. "**You a stupid bitch? Why'd you put those three-inch heels, anyway**?"

Here I was with heels, lipstick and make up on, in school. I was fooling myself into thinking, that Mr. Pretty, thin, yellow Negro was a big deal. I knew he wasn't anything, but the trouble my daddy warned me about. For some reason, I couldn't pull away from his advances. My mind and body were having an internal battle and both, were losing.

I reluctantly aimed my mustang toward East Oakland, while feeling warm all over. I wanted to stop and drop my top, but it would have taken too much time. I'd heard mama and her friends talking about women having hot flashes, but hell, not at my young age.

I rolled the window down and took deep breaths, to avoid hyperventilating. The wind did me a lot of good and cooled me off, as I took the Ninety Eighth Avenue turn off.

I was making a right turn, when the vivid streetlights, began to appear blurry to me. It seemed extremely dark and fear of my surroundings, crept into my person, like quicksand.

Thanks to daddy being such a militant, I never had any fear of the hood, or my people. This night felt different. I was beginning to understand my mistake and was feeling vulnerable.

I was also having second and third thoughts about this foolishness I was driving into. I wondered, what in the hell I was doing? I hadn't told anyone where I was going and even though I knew this cat, he could mean me nothing but ugly.

I was close to turning around when there, in my truth, was Plymouth Ave.

Reality was exploiting my fear, in all its glory. Why hadn't I turned around and headed home, like a smart girl? Why hadn't I stopped at one of the phone booths, and called my mama, to get her opinion?

I parked the car, in front of the big, old, house. The porch light gave me a splinter of hope. I began to pump myself up, like a football player, before a game. I needed the false confidence required to man up, and head to the door.

I also verbally began to scold myself.

"What's your problem girl? Mr. Fontenot didn't raise no punks! Be the bad bitch, you're supposed to be! Besides, he's skinny anyway;

you could probably whoop his ass!"

I said to myself.

Even though my body wanted to go into the house, my mind was still hesitant. As I reached the door and pulled downward on my tight, blue, mini skirt, the door swung open.

The house was dark, with nothing but candlelight, as my guide. I could hear, Marvin Gaye in the background, crooning his hit, love song,

"***Sexual Healing.***"

In the shadows, I could hear Dexter putting on his sexiest voice, as he mellowed,

"Come on in, lovely! I'm in here."

He spoke softly, but his voice seemed to echo through the house. I followed it with curiosity, and foolishness as my guide.

Once I rounded the small hallway, there stood an open door. It was leading to the room, with the music softly, rolling out of it.

There was a lamp on the table, with a red light, dimly lighting the room. The bed was small, with very little space to get away, had I decided to sit on it. A bright white sheet was the only linen, lying across the bed. There was also a dark sheet, tacked across the window.

Dexter was sitting on the bed, shirtless, wearing a red silk robe and pair of sexy, silk boxers. I must admit, I had never imagined Dexter in this light, or imagined him as this sexy.

Searing a hole in the depths of mind, was a barrage of questions. They were questions, I wanted to ask Dexter. The main question, was why was he so bold, to think I was willing to have sex with him? Did this fool know I was a virgin?

As I began to speak, he stood and softly placed two of his fingers over my mouth and nodded for me not to say a word. Had it not been for the great smelling cologne, that emanated from his hand, I would have bit him.

However, something inside of me, made me obey his wishes.

He placed his body so close to mine from behind, I felt as if he was in my skin. As his slow breath, breezed on the nape of my neck, it raised the hairs, that usually lay without bother. I was so stunned at what was taking place, within my body; I could not hear what he was saying for a moment.

The complete picture was surreal, and I was moving kind of slow motion, as if in a movie. Soon he began to tenderly kiss me on the back, while moving upward to my neck. This sensation sent tingling chills up my spine. I could hear myself whispering for him to stop, but I didn't know if the words were leaving my mouth or stuck in time.

Maybe I didn't really want him to stop at all. I noticed my hands were stuck, by my sides. They were held down by large rubber straps, or it felt that way.

Without even a thought of really stopping anything, I could hear the thump, as he dropped to his knees. At the same time, he was softly kissing my warm, lonely ass, through my clothes. I say lonely, because prior to this very moment, my ass had never experienced this type of attention.

My body began to perspire, for the first time ever. However, I was far too occupied to worry about it. Every inch of me, had become a wet bar, with a water spill, and Dexter was sucking up the water, like a sponge. His tongue was moving, like it was on a personal mission, to become my best friend. At this point, my body and his tongue were stranded on a deserted island, as best friends forever.

I could feel him really enjoying himself.

Dexter licked my backside at every corner of my flesh, and I couldn't stop my leg from jumping, in small spasms of pleasure.

He slid his tongue into the very center of my back and licked straight down my spine. His tongue moved like a credit card swiping on a machine.

I tried to play it off, by easing my hands to my legs and holding on. My actions were to no avail. I found myself losing control. The feelings that were consuming me, were intense. I knew at any moment; it would be impossible to not to share my internal juices. Deep moans of pleasure were begrudgingly leaking into the air, while I was trying to maintain some amount of self-control and dignity.

He was in total control and I was still fighting the small war inside my head. My mind kept telling me to pull back. Without notice and much to my surprise, his head manipulated deep between my legs and his mouth rested securely on the crest of my wet panties.

There was no more fight in me, as my juices began to run like a leaky faucet. His grip on my ass was firm but forgiving. He swayed me side to side. I could feel his tongue playing with my panties and touching secret hot spots, inside my thighs. The work he was putting in suggested his mouth was completely at home, between my legs. I was starting to think my pussy contained a hidden breathing tube.

He treated my vagina area like it was a ripe orange, waiting to be eaten. Dexter was a master chef, prepping the orange and not allowing a single drop of juice to run free. He licked every, hot drip.

Considering, I had never been this close to a man, the hair around my vagina lay wet, straight, and plentiful. I was a student with no time for pleasure activities such as swimming; therefore, I never shaved anything pubic. Thanks to that reasoning, the hair around all my private areas had the fresh making of African size bushes. My hair was the pure sign of our endeavor and my personal snitch. I found myself wanting every inch of his tongue lodged deep in my mound.

Because the hair was so sticky and wet, it moved just clear enough to avoid him getting stuck. At that point, had he attempted to pull his head up. Had he pulled it up however, there was no doubt, I would've have broken his neck.

Amazingly enough he worked his swirling tongue well enough to move my laced, red, panties to the side. He did this, while sliding his agile, pink flesh into my steamy box.

Mama always told me, a woman should always take pride in her underwear, because if it feels good against your skin and moves well with your body, it's priceless. In this case there would never be shame in visiting the doctor's office and removing your clothes. She always suggested this would help me to marry a doctor, but her vision was wasted. I fell in love with lace and pretty panties instead.

The way he was licking me now, was so intense, I thought my head was going to explode. The last thing that I would allow to slow down my pleasure, was my lace, panties. I was on the verge of embarrassing myself and ripping my underwear off, if he didn't do something fast. With timing being the key, his manhood took over, without a moment to spare. He softly asked me to hold on to his shoulders, with a promise of tenderness. Without a second thought, I held on as he wrapped his arms around my legs and lifted me into the air.

Once I was suspended in the air with a GI Joe grip, he turned my hot body toward the bed. I don't know to this day how he was strong enough to lay me on the bed, while his tongue stayed planted in deep in my wetness.

He went to work with zeal. He was a skillful technician and quietly removed my panties and his boxers, without breaking the mood. I found my hands glancing across his shoulders, chest, and arms.

I can remember thinking,

"**Damn this boy got guns! I never knew he was this built like this**!"

I ran my hands across his chiseled body and found myself loving on his ripped, six packs. My body was no longer mine and I began to shutter uncontrollably. I surrendered it to my emotional capturer. Surrendering was no longer a choice, due to the strange wonderful feeling that was taking me over. I had goosebumps all over my body and I was on the verge of exploding, in a brand-new ecstasy. Suddenly this fool pulled his tongue out of my dripping slit.

I found myself breathless, wanting to scream and choke the life out of him. My hands were searching for his neck, however, at the same time he found a new sensual, licking spot. I had no idea, just how sensitive my breast could be, until they were being treated like apple suckers.

The intensity wasn't the same, but it kept me in place and dripping on the sheets. He mustered a Barry White, bass tone and whispered in my ear.

"Touch it, so it's not a surprise when I give to you! I figured a good girl like you don't do this a lot, so I don't wanna hurt you, Mama!"

His voice moaned with a sincere confidence.

"You don't know how I do my thang, Mr. Nasty!"

I painfully replied without thinking.

My hands moved away from his wide shoulders and grabbed what I felt was the biggest dick I'd ever touched in my life. I thought his girth was as big as a jar and his length was as big as a summer squash.

I felt fear slip between our bodies because it was at that moment, I knew it was going to hurt. I hadn't started my day prepared for this. After a few moments, the truth crept into my mind. I was reminded I had no way to know how big he was, because this was the absolute first time, I'd ever touched a penis in my life.

Within minutes there was a pressing at the tip of my vagina. The head of his tool felt awkward to be rubbing between my parted hairs. I didn't have to wonder, because there was so much juice and moisture present from his licking and my excitement, that it was obvious he was in the right place. My automatic reaction was to grab his shaft in a death grip, like a handle and break it. No matter how big he really was, there was no way I was ready to put that thing in me! It didn't matter how good I was feeling. The sound he made was somewhere between a moan and a very loud surrendering, as he begged me to release the pressure on his pleasure tool. Control was momentarily mine and whatever was to happen next would be my choice and his racing heartbeat left me no doubt.

I was listening to him plead like James Brown, which prompted to lesson my grip. Although I didn't feel I was ready, I gave him a quiet okay. He then promised he'd be careful. Once he gradually, but forcefully pushed into my region, there was a pain that words could never describe. The jolt that ran through my body, felt as if a butcher was taking a knife and ripping me from rectum, to my vagina. The pain all of a sudden hurt like hell. My nails had found a new home, as they dug into his shoulders and

I could feel his blood running.

"OH MY GOD YOU'RE KILLING ME! PULL IT OUT!"

I surrendered.

I was looking for my tongue in order to bite a hole somewhere. I held in a silent scream. The language I began to speak was anything but English, and foreign to anyone who would ever try and interpret my ramblings. The one thing for sure, there were plenty of four-letter words in the sentences.

In my pain, I could see this simple bastard drooling at the mouth. He appeared to be blessed with a fresh new life, thanks to my oozing virgin. I wanted to scream like a white girl in a scary movie. At that moment, I felt like I was having a baby. This hurt like nothing I'd ever experienced in life.

Something began to change after the pain was easing, just a bit. I held him away from me for a moment, but he never stopped his slow strokes, while continually whispering in my ear. He sounded off, repeatedly like a recording.

"It's okay baby, I'ma go easy. I promise! I promise I'ma go easy!"

Dexter's breathing was hard and heavy, with an overt passion. The noise he was making was nothing I'd ever heard before. I was halfway trying to pull him out of my pussy at that time, to no avail. It was like attempting to move a pack of starving wolves off a meat truck!

I was feeling foolish at this point because it was me that secretly chose this rendezvous and not Dexter. He just didn't know it and I wasn't going to tell him. However, the pain thrashing about in my vagina region had me thinking twice about my decision. Luckily for me the pain wasn't as intense, as the start of our endeavor, and now it was slowly being replaced with something else. I had no control of the legs that seemed to separate from my mind and seductively wrap around Dexter.

The muscles in my body started moving on their own and something in my sexual awareness began to speak for all of me, without using any words. My movements took on an erotic motion I'd only seen in the movies. I was pushing back in his rhythm space.

I could hear him struggle in my space, but I didn't have the heart to admit that I'd never been touched in that area by any man, except my doctor.

Here I was locked in place with a foreign strength, and my body began to shiver, as if I was freezing.

I was feeling quite strange and became a different person. I gripped, and ripped at Dexter's back and shoulders.

I was subconsciously unwilling to release my legs. He, on the other hand was enjoying my virgin box so much, that he struggled to speak at all.

I found myself drawing blood with my grip. After the initial begging was over and he was all in, all he could muster were strange noises and grunts. There was something exact with our movement. We moved sexually on one accord and he became weightless with a quickened pace. I was fighting myself the whole time and found it difficult to find the fun in what I was doing. I could hear myself thinking,

"***Damn bitch, your Daddy's gonna hate you! What in the fuck are you doing, giving your virginity away to this lazy, bastard? You must be stupid, stupid, stupid!***"

I had to admit this shit felt like nothing I'd ever felt before, but I couldn't say good described it. There was something about that very moment that made me understand God's vision when he placed Eve next to Adam.

But I wasn't sure if sex was the answer. My whole body went into some weird convulsions. They consisted of painful, pleasurable shakes and I found myself erotically purring like a female cat.

Suddenly there was nothing but an intense, odd explosion between my legs. It was wet and extreme, as my passion took complete control of me. I captured every inch of Dexter and cut his breath off, until we both just about passed out.

I thought I was burning up with fever, all through my body. I was gasping for breath and this new experience had me perplexed at the time. I didn't know whether to scream for joy or die in embarrassment. One thing was certain; this was the best and the worst feeling I'd ever had in my life.

I wanted to run and hide, because I knew I had just allowed a fool to think I'd been suckered for my goods.

I was stuck for a moment as the odd juices streamed down my legs. I found it difficult to look in his face, as he let out a major yawn.

This time, the wetness felt different and I knew it wasn't just the flow from what was there earlier. After a moment I recognized this flow, it was blood, and I knew it.

Dexter just laid there like a bump on a log and bragged about how good my pussy was, over and over again. I thought he was going to put his thumb in his mouth and coo like a baby, as I searched for my clothes.

I grabbed my panties and ran to the bathroom. The warm, red, muted light was a full blessing to me, because I was too ashamed to have a good look at myself. I had never taken a shower in a strange house before. However, after seeing my blood on my legs, I knew I couldn't enter mama's house like that. I had to get rid of the blood in order to put my panties back on and sit in my car without making a mess.

After finishing, I peeped out of the bathroom and crept through the hall, only to hear the heavy snoring bellowing from Dexter's mouth.

Once I was safely in my car and driving home, I began to second guess what had just taken place, in a strange house. I had surrendered my virginity to a man that wasn't my husband. Not to mention, neither of us had ever declared love for each other.

There was a nagging voice echoing in my head, but it seemed to be coming from my stomach. It was telling me, I had just fucked up and got pregnant, thanks to our endeavor happening with no thought of protection.

The thought of being pregnant made me feel ill. How could I be so dumb, screwing a man with no ambition and no real desire for anything, but pussy? And I lay without any thought of a rubber? What if his nasty ass had the clap, or another S.T.D.? No, I assured myself, I couldn't be with child after one exchange.

For the first time in my life, I tried as hard as I possibly could to sneak into the house. I knew, I wouldn't be good at it, because I never had a reason to creep into the house before.

Mama wasn't having it and she stopped me on my way up the stairs.

"Hi honey! How was school?"

She asked, as I held my shoes in my hand. I mustered up my best attempt at a fake smile and replied.

"Hi mommy, school was good! I'm just tired, because I was served up a long, boring lecture."

Mama's face contorted, as I put it on a bit thick. I also found a yawn hidden deep in my body and let it release on cue. She looked at me strangely and twisted her head sideways. I couldn't help but think my mama knew something was up. Maybe she knew I was being the type of whore that my daddy begged me not to be. She cleared her throat and inquired,

"You alright honey? Lord knows you seem a bit strange tonight!"

Without waiting for my reply, she continued,

"I'm doing a lecture tomorrow on abstinence and safe sex; would you like to read my notes? I know you're a smart girl, but maybe you'll be inspired!"

Mama suggested.

I knew she was looking straight through me and I had to bolt, or I was going to turn red in front of my mama.

My face would have been a dead giveaway.

I mustered up a fake laugh and giggled,

"No Mama! I don't like boys enough for that! But good luck with your lecture, anyway, and goodnight!"

There was fear looming in my soul and a burn in my stomach, as mama replied.

"Goodnight baby girl! We'll see you at breakfast!"

She smiled, while returning to her favorite chair. It was a blessing that daddy played chess on those nights and wasn't there to observe my behavior. I was never any good at lying. My daddy would have known something was up. Although, we talked about everything, I wouldn't have the heart to tell him, I was no longer holding my royal goodies. My walk of abstinence was a thing of the past. Although, I hated what I'd lost, I was developing real feelings for Dexter, from the day we first met. Not to mention that little nasty thing everybody called sex, was now a bond we shared.

It gave me a bond with Dexter I couldn't explain. I didn't crave it all the time like some girls, but I did enjoy it a little more each time we did it. That damned Dexter had magic lips, and a busy tongue to go with them, which kept me interested. He always said, he'd lie, if I told anyone he ate my apple. Because, according to all the men in his family, black men didn't eat the apple. At least that was the lie they led people to believe.

I couldn't believe nine months from that eventful night, my life would be changed, forever. It would never find its course again.

My mother and father barely spoke to me after my belly began to show. They had a difficult time explaining my big belly to their friends. The Stanford crew looked at daddy like a man that couldn't handle his household. It was my fault; because I let my hormones take over my better judgment.

It was the first day of my sixth month being pregnant, and I had received bad news at my Doctor's appointment.

They were putting me on medication to ease what was discovered to be false labor. The pains had me up late nights, moaning until the early hours of the morning. Luckily, our house was big enough to keep the noises from daddy, but mama knew something was wrong.

She was too disappointed in me to dig into my affairs. It had become obvious; she didn't want any more bad news. After the ultrasound and the meds, all I could think about was the beautiful little boy, on his way to bless my life.

The day that helped to shape my future. I placed my key in the door, only to realize it was unlocked. This was unusual because my folks should've been at work.

I crept in, so that I would be undetected, however, what I heard and observed broke my heart, and left me a changed person forever.

My daddy was sitting on the floor, sobbing, and admitting to my mama that he was a failure, because he'd lost his daughter to the streets. He was crying for the first time I'd ever seen and blaming himself for my acting like a whore. He found it hard to accept my departure from his teaching, despite all of his hard work and love.

As I ear hustled their conversation, a stream of tears began to run down my face uncontrollably. I was stuck, trying to wipe the tears as fast as they appeared, but nothing would mend my broken heart.

A broken heart that was now plunging deep in my stomach and about to burst.

I grabbed my eyes firmly, without ripping my corneas and tried to control the flow. Next, I reached into my soul, twenty feet deep and gathered my fake smile. I placed it on my face like a mask. I cheerfully walked into the room and prepared to lie to my parents with a straight face, while looking them in the eye. I gleefully stammered,

"Hello people, I got great news! I finally got my own place and just need a small loan from my dear old parents, and I'm officially a grown up!"

My lie was controlled and believable. Daddy tried to wipe his face, without me noticing his tears. We both manufactured smiles to cover our broken hearts. I looked down, pretending not to see my daddy's pain, as mama began to massage his back.

To keep the farce alive, I asked,

"What's wrong Daddy'o? Is your back bothering you today?" Before daddy could speak, mama took over the conversation and interrupted,

"Your dad pulled his back today, while working in the yard, but he'll be

alright!"
She cleared her throat and continued,
"I'm glad you got a place Simone and of course we'll give you some money!"
With all of us pretending, the moment was odd for a household of just three people.
Breathing became difficult for me, due to the air being so thick. The heavy emotions looming about, forced me to run into my room before the mood got any stranger. My tears were close to giving way, as I lauded,
"You know you're my man, daddy! I hope you feel better and get some rest! I'm going to go and lay down, because thanks to this ball in my belly, I'm really tired!"
I turned my gaze to Mama and lied again,
"I'll come down later mama, so don't worry about me and dinner! I just knocked out a juicy, Casper's hot dog, so I'm not hungry."
Once in my bedroom, I realized that life was to change forever.
Until that very moment, I pretended like being pregnant was just something that happened, and my parents would come around eventually. They would come to embrace my baby and I knew it. But they were so right about my situation. I had no idea of how much I had altered my future, choosing to have my baby, while still living like a baby.
It was a good thing I kept my credit stellar, because it was time to find an apartment quickly. Considering the bullshit, I had just fed my parents, there was no turning back now.
I banked on my daddy's old school ways. I knew he would never ask me

to abort my baby, no way!

He was truly pissed, but I knew he couldn't hold out for long. I was having his first and possibly, only grandson.

However, life was different now, due to me observing my daddy broken down on the floor, in tears. I didn't fool myself; I knew it was due to my negligence of his heart.

I was playing handball against all the pride he'd placed in me and hitting his emotions against the wall one slap at a time. But the biggest slap in my face, was the fact I'd never seen him like that before. I was burning inside like a cast iron stove because he'd always shared his life and love with me.

The only spirit in this world with the power to take a black man down, next to God, was a woman.

Much to my dismay, I had become the evil woman to take my daddy down, and now I had to find the cure to picking him up. I was also aware of it resting on the soul of my son. My son would have to be the baby boy, my father never had.

I tried to sleep that night, but there was a dark cloud looming over the house. It was my cloud and it felt gloomy. It was mine and all mine.

I lay in sweats for most of the night and my pajamas were soaked with perspiration and tears. By four o'clock, I needed to change my wet clothes.

After changing, I slipped down to the fridge to get something to quench my thirst, because I felt as if my lungs had survived a major case of road rash.

After cheating the house rules, by grabbing the orange juice carton and drinking directly out of it, I could see mama sitting in her chair. She was

sipping on a cup of coffee, which suggested she'd been up for a while.
"You know better than drinking out that carton, child! I guess you've forgotten everything you've been taught, huh?"
Mama admonished.
Her tone suggested drinking the juice out of the carton was the just the starting point. I just wiped my lips and let out a deep sigh and responded.
"I'm so sorry mama! I never meant to break your, or daddy's heart! I was just stupid!"
Mama stood up and snapped,
"Stupid my ass! That's for the ignorant! And you aren't ignorant! But I'll tell you what you **are**, Simone! You **<u>are</u>** inconsiderate, and self-centered! You **<u>are</u>** a selfish, spoiled, little bitch, and you have taken me and your daddy for granted, for years now!"
Her words couldn't have been more damaging if they were rifle bullets blasting straight to my chest, as she continued.
"Simone? In the thirty years, that I've known and loved that man, I've never seen anything break that wonderful heart of his down to tears. Not even being called Nigger at every turn of his career, by the gaggle of white men, standing in his way!
Not even being shunned by his own family, because they figured he'd gotten too high and mighty. The called him the biggest Uncle Tom they'd ever seen!
When in truth, he changed his militant ways, because he had a little girl to bring up. This man didn't even break, after I confessed to having an affair in the early years of our marriage!
I used the excuse; we'd been separated for too long and I was lonely. That man shook that shit off and pretended it never happened. He stood

like a king, and reminded me, I was a Queen, and needed to act like one. When all was said and done, he put all this work in for a daughter that's paid him back, by having a bastard child! I guess you've got your mothers bad genes, huh? You've found a way to bring back his past, as if it's never changed. I will always love you because you're my child! But I will never understand your reasoning, Simone!

I've got to be honest by telling you, I can't say when all this is going to be okay. I do know, it's a good thing you're moving out. You've hurt my man and I am not happy. We will do whatever we can to help you, but we need time to accept the damage you've done to this family!"

Mama sternly lashed.

I found myself stuck, cowering over, like I had just received a sucker punch to my gut. In all my life, I had never heard my mother use that language. There was nothing I could say, as my tears seemed to be drowning me. I struggled to catch my breath and without saying a word, I ran upstairs without looking back. It felt like my mamma had surgically removed my heart and placed it in my hand.

That night I cried like my best friend had been shot and killed, and I had just finished identifying the body.

CHAPTER 3

Martell

MAN-CHILD

Life was rolling along quickly for me, and the years seemed to pass like days. My teen years resembled the years prior. I was still being treated like an older man, by everyone in my life. A man at least ten years older, than my actual age.

I was happy to have my 1975, Buick Electra 225, as my first ride. It was also known as a duce and a quarter, according to the street lingo. Approximately three Months prior to the day, I had purchased it from an old white dude in San Jose. I was scanning the local newspaper for a new ride. I was growing far too cool, to be riding around in the Dotson B-210; I had taken from my young, grey girl.

I'd already learned in my young life that certain white girls would give me damned near anything, just to be with a handsome, black stud. Mostly thanks to the racist white daddies that kept them curious. While black women, on the other hand wouldn't share anything, but their bodies upon first knowing you. A marveling thought, because in retrospect, it should have been the last thing they shared. I'd chalked it up to white girls not having to fight as hard for the things in their lives as black women had, since slavery.

I made sure she saw the two-year-old Electra parked in all its glory and I put on a pouting party for not having it. I was certain to make face appear as if I'd eaten sour lemons all day. Upon seeing my unhappiness, she handed me some bread. It was enough to put down, on what was to be my new ride.

In the long run, she assisted in paying for my car, in order to stay next to me. I had no interest in grey girls at the time, but I loved their parent's bread.

I had a problem with the way white men looked upon me with hate. I had seen footage that showed their white women standing behind them in their hate, lynching us. So, I had no doubt their girls just chose black boys to rebel. It was the money that prompted me to let her accompany me to San Francisco a few times. I would also take her to the most popular white folks hang out in town, Farrell's Ice Cream.

In order to keep her satisfied, I would make the trip once a week. Every now and then, she would pressure me to service her sexual needs.

There was something deep inside of me that made me aware that sharing my tool with her, could be a disaster. She would have been at my mercy after the first dose.

Had I decided to give her my best, it would be over before it got started. I was afraid; I would've never been able to get rid of her. Therefore, I had to play my cards right and be careful. Her pops spilled money into her hands on a regular basis. He had no idea; he had a young, black, hog, on his payroll, and he was paying me like a son.

At first, she was pushing money at me and insisting I take it. Before I knew it, I was putting in orders, and she was paying her weight in dollars. She was paying just to have a chance to rub on my dick and break her parent's rules, while messing with a darkie.

It was also a perk for her to show her rich, white, girlfriends that she could keep up with a real deal, black boy.

In truth she couldn't, but I hid that truth well. I took their curiosity to a level, beyond their control. The rougher I treated her in the presence of her group of curious puppets, the more she would buy. I often thought to myself.

"**This girl is just plain stupid**!"

The problem was, I had a strong moral compass, which made me feel bad, whenever I thought of my ugliness.

I was too young to realize just how much natural game; I had picked up, just watching cats like Uncle Jamie, play the player game.

I also refused to accept that she just really dug me, and I was worthy of her emotion. It was nineteen seventy-seven and I was trying to understand every inch of the game.

I'd personally decided my life had to be more impactful than your everyday cum freak. I'd decided that I wasn't playing, and my life would be different. I had to become more than just a simple-minded player. I also wondered if I could pull it off.

That answer would show itself in the years to come. For now, I thought to myself,

"**If this broad only knew, I wasn't but fifteen, she would be fresh for suicide**."

But then again it might not make any difference at all, because I lived and hustled like a grown assed man. Whenever I wasn't honing my verbal skills, I was hustling three-card Monty on the piers at Fisherman's Wharf.

The piers in San Francisco would pop off with money on a daily basis, thanks to the constant influx of tourist, and the employees that worked along the docks. This would keep money in my pockets and gas in the

Buick. I knew any normal kid rolling the duce, along with the payment attached to it, would have been worried to death.

But I was a big picture kid, and saw beyond the factory puke green, paint job and basic wheels.

I wasn't clearing enough bread playing con games to satisfy my needs. And riding the Bay area's AC transit bus system was cool when I was a young roller, but not now I was a full-blown hustler. I mean there were always honeys on the bus, but it was no good for a real hustler, and I was getting tired of pretending to dig Julie, my grey girl. It was testing my resolve, because I had love for self, but was never good enough to meet her parents.

On any given day, the brothers we came across, would have given their right nut for a fine piece like my Julie. However, I was young and revolutionary; therefore, my militant ways made me look at her as if I were selling into the easy.

I'd read times in His-story as lies were conjured of black men whistling at white woman. When this happened complete towns were destroyed, and black men were hanged and burned alive in mass numbers.

I often thought,

"Look at all these knew sucka assed black pretenders, running around with these white women. Acting as if they were trophies from the past, while wearing the dashikis of our ancestors.

I'd even read the writings of the brotha, Malcolm X, as a young man being fooled by tricks and the lies. In his youth, he admitted, he thought white women were his right. He did white women, until he realized, he was being made part of the white man's plan by falling for his traps. Simply put, when you assimilate into a legacy of death, and deceit, your teachings become lost in translation. Thanks to my youthful stupidity, I decided to drop her altogether and, fire her from my team, but not before draining every dime into the duce.

I realized in order to do that, I had to bust her virgin, and serve her real dick whenever she wanted it. I served her well, and often, until the duce was clear. I was just happy to have an elite ride. It was a large score for such a young cat, and I was oblivious to how large. My ride was newer than all Simone's dudes.

I enjoyed her pussy and she enjoyed me, so I considered a job well done. Wanting my own bread as well, I kept my gloves and cane dusted, and brought me a new top hat. I began to work the piers even more and performed at assorted talent shows, along the Peninsula and the Bay area. I'd mastered the art of pop locking, and one would have thought I was wired together; by the way I worked the robot, dance moves. Forget basketball, if you couldn't boogaloo, you weren't from Oakland. I clearly remember us moon walking, vibrating, and popping like dominoes before Michael Jackson ever made the dance famous.

However, we would never be seen by industry folks, unlike Mike. Because he was larger than life and we were just that, life.

I made sure she didn't pay the last hundred on the duce. I'd given the last slice of bread to the old hippy dude and paid my car off. I was able to take it out of the dude's name.

With no daddy to lead the way, it was becoming important for me to decide, who I was going to be.

Without trying, I found myself forming my inner spirit base, quickly. There were rules that I would live by, thanks to observing Simone's life choices. I chose to be a person to who would complete all large tasks, one at a time. There was one true financial thought cemented in my brain. It was, as long as money was owed on anything you purchased, it would never really be yours.

I didn't have a driver's license when I went to pick up the title. Thankfully enough, my tongue had the makings of a sharp weapon and was getting sharper by the day.

Tina and I drove my car directly to the Miracle paint professionals and ordered the silver and black color that represented the Oakland Raiders, football team.

Next, was the bus trip to the rim shop and ordering the spokes and vogue tires we called mustard and mayonnaise.

In order to keep my head straight and without worrying, I found it easier to keep Tina by my side. I made sure that anyone that enjoyed my presence had to accept my little sister, because she was tied to my hip at every turn.

I also made sure Tina was my banker. She held and hid all my money. Thanks to her innocent look, she also kept my 380. Magnum in her kiddy bag at all times, without any questions.

I was aware that I should never ask such a thing of a child, but we didn't lead normal lives, thus we didn't live by normal rules.

We played the role by day, but things changed at night. The streets lit a fire in my soul and there was no putting that fire out once it burned.

I had no problem with throwing kibbles and bits to the little girl next door, Veronica. She appeared to be quite content keeping an eye on Tina whenever asked. She was a little, cute, bow legged, caramel colored, honey. With the icing on the cake being she worshiped me, and I loved her for that. Although she was pretty, I could never see myself crossing the sexual lines.

I found myself treating her like a little girl, even though she was my age. She moved me like a little sister, thanks to her sweetness. She seemed to genuinely care about Tina and content to be the sister type, in our lives. Although she was cute, her braces and buckteeth were like a stop sign for me. The terrible acne on her face, served as the full blown red-light to stop any sexual advances. Still, she had cute hidden in there somewhere. It was just behind everything else, and I was blessed to see it.

Veronica's home situation made me realize something I never really realized before. Her home life revealed to me a painful truth. And that truth was, the only thing worse than not having a daddy at home, was having a bad one.

A bad father in the home was a misery, that would shape a monster.

Her mom was cool, but always at work, maintaining two jobs. Her daddy was a problem because he stayed drunk off his butt. She painfully told me of nights, her dad would piss in the sink, thinking it was the toilet. He was also known to walk throughout the house naked and out of control.

My mama's coming and goings at this point had become sporadic at best. She would burst through the door most mornings between four and seven in the morning. Most of those mornings, I was usually one step ahead of her, as she opened the door and checked in on Tina. I don't even think she knew who Veronica was, but she was always too high to complain about her lying next to Tina. I wasn't surprised that she never asked.

My life skills had grown to the point, that I continually stayed a step ahead of mama on the first, and fifteenth. This allowed me to get her portion of the money and pay rent on time.

I often found myself having to place my bread with hers, in order to pay the monthly bills. My heart made me feel as if I was committed to helping mama. And I found myself just doing it because it was the right thing to do.

I often fought with my internal feelings for my mama, due to her continued drug use and bad choice of sleeping mates. It was a chore to love a woman on crystals, and or cocaine most of the time. To make matters worse she treated me like crap every day.

Mama tended to fall for whatever new dope was popular in the streets. She was the true example of an addictive personality. But there was some kind of covert loyalty planted deep in my soul, and it was strong enough to keep me on her side. Although, I was often angry at her, this strange thing inside of me often won over anything else and prodded me to excuse her actions.

As I grew older, those same feelings pushed me to keep food on the table and kept me from peeping into her room after her late-night sessions. I'd finally gotten to the point of accepting the awkward feelings that lay buried deep in my heart. Whatever I felt wasn't the love I once held with care for my mama, but loyalty remained.

It hurt to feel that way about my own mother, but she was a cold and bitter woman with the ability to turn her back on anything warm. There were some days when mama would sober up enough to make Doc stay away from her. Usually it was just long enough to mentally torture him. During these periods she would open her eyes, and marvel at my abilities with consistent contempt. She often rambled,

"How'd you learn to cook and dress so fuckin' nice, man?

Where are you getting' all that money and them nice ass clothes from, little Negro? I noticed you're keeping Tina in Jordache and Vanderbilt jeans, and shit! I even heard you rollin' a fine assed, fuckin' ride, you keep hidden from me!

Where's this mystery car, Martell? You don't even have a damned driver's license! Where'd you learn to drive, and do the shit you doing? 'Cause I ain't taught yo' no good ass, shit!"

She'd spew in anger.

The look on her face left me knowing, my own mama wanted my complete and total failure. I would look at her and laugh most days, just to keep from crying. I never had to think of a clever reply because the truth was always more potent. My response would be automatic.

"It's okay mama. You're just misunderstood, that's all. But I understand you!"

These words I would utter, to keep a lid on my world. I would count to five and mama would snap back and yell.

"Don't you patronize me, you li'l black Motherfucka!"

She'd spill.

"You forget, I'm a college educated bitch! I know what your arrogant ass is sayin'! But that's alright, it's a new day and I'm gonna send your smart ass to juvenile! You had better, keep doing what I say, and winning in school! Remember, I've forgotten, more than your young ass, will ever learn!"

Mama seethed.

She really had no beef, thanks to me being an above average student, without even trying hard. My love for school, left me no choice.

Mama would say these things with the sting of the scorpion, that represented her astrological sign. She couldn't bring me down this day. I was destined to be happy, despite her mighty blows. I had scored some tickets for the concert at the Oakland Coliseum, the night before, and was heading to see the **Parliament Funk-a-Delics**.

It was going to be George Clinton and his boys, backed by, "**Bootsy's Rubber Band.**"

I laid out one of my nicest Nic-Nic shirts and my black Cottler baggie, slacks, with the zoot suit chain. I also topped my fit with a white, Godfather brim, and a long white zoot suit coat. The Chicano's, along with the brotha's themselves, would have been proud of me, as I pulled out my shiny, new, lace up, Stacy Adams shoes.

By eight o'clock, I had given Veronica some money to watch Tina. I rounded highway 101, toward Milpitas. I had to pick up Benita, Pink Lips. I called her Pink Lips, because she had some of the most perfectly rounded, pink lips ever sculpted by the father above. She was a mellow, golden, girl at the fresh age of nineteen, with a figure that defied purpose. Men stared at her body without shame, because her ass was so rounded and firm, it just made no damn sense.

If one was to make a dress for her, a life-sized coke bottle could have been used to gauge her shape.

I'd observed countless men being slapped by their women, just to sneak a peek at my Jr. Goddess. The men that seen us together, could've lived vicariously through my smile, whenever Benita was with me.

I smiled, because no matter where we were heading, she would go directly for my zipper. It didn't take a brain surgeon to drive behind me and see her bobbing head to know I was receiving a fantastic blow job. There was no better way to deal with traffic, than getting your brains blown, and she was a veteran sucker with honors. I had taught her well.

I reached for the tape deck to put the brakes on Bootsy's song,

“**Munchies for Your Love.**”

I didn’t want to ruin seeing Bootsy in person, so I slapped in,

The Spinners, “**Love don’t Love no One.**”

She hummed the song, and I felt an awesome pleasure of her lips doing what they did best, buzzing my lower head.

I was deeply moved by the way, Philipp’e Soul Wynn, hit those soulful notes. Not to mention, her humming during the melody gave me reason to thank, **The Spinners** for a wonderful sexual trip.

The place was packed with funk-a-teers of every type. The Bay never consisted of fair weathered spirits. When the folks of the Bay area decided to back anything, it was usually for life. The locals always lived and died by the code.

On that night, George Clinton got the die-hards from The Bay and surrounding areas, rockin’! This included the funk followers from the toughest parts of the Bay. Areas like, Hunters Point, the Geneva Towers, and the Fillmore district as well. Vallejo, Daly City and East Palo Alto, was in the house too.

During these times, if a brotha was fortunate enough to have a fine woman on his arm, he was respected.

As usual, the brotha’s were almost giving me high fives, for having a top notch swell on my arm, and she enjoyed every bit of the attention.

I’d picked out a tight, red, dress, for Benita, and it stretched over her body, like it was made from thin rubber. It was a Chinese cut, geisha dress, with long splits on each side. It cupped her onion, shaped ass perfectly, with a form fit.

The many men that looked on, had no idea how square, Benita was, or how unimpressed she was, by most material things. Those were the

things that made her attitude precious to me.
This was her first concert in Oaktown, and she was looking forward to it. It was a preview for her, as she prepared for the next month's show. Her favorite artists would also be in the same place in the month to come. She was far more excited about us going to see pretty, Prince (Rogers Nelson) than attending the concert in front of us.
Prince was a new artist in the mix, and he just happened to be as fine as any girl on the set. I was digging his sound because he'd delivered a chart topper, entitled, "**Soft and Wet.**"
I loved that song, and I was known to enjoy both of those pleasures, the soft and the wet.
Benita had one of those, old fashioned, strong; black pioneer mama's at home, and I felt she was as sweet as cherry pie. Her ways represented the old landmark, and she followed what appeared to be the standards given to us by God. I think she took to me, because she had a good man in her life, and I was able to put forth the same efforts.
Even though he was in the service and always gone, he was good to his family. Not to mention my manners were polished to the top of my game.
Benita had a cousin named Mo, and he treated me like a local, folk hero. I'm certain he felt this way; thanks to me taking up for him in battle a couple of times.
He had one of those weird dimpled faces and people made fun of him. I always had a tough time dealing with people picking on and bullying others. I'd only been suspended in school twice, and both times was for taking up for other people.
I believed in fighting for yours at any cost. As a matter of fact, I'd

enjoyed the aspects of fighting, but it always had to be fair. When Mo was informed that Benita and I would be at the concert, he rushed out and purchased tickets. He was planning on taking his ugly girlfriend.

I personally liked the cat and had no problem with him hanging out with us.

He frowned when I suggested, he meet us there. I couldn't tell him my motivation, under the circumstances. I didn't need him following me, because if he followed me to closely, he would see how much I turned out his cousin.

I must admit Benita was a natural, except, I had to show her how to pull her teeth back, in the beginning. She had only been with one man, in her life and he was beyond super nice! He was the polar opposite of me, and didn't believe in sex, before marriage.

I had no misconceptions in reference to sex in my life. I was a young, virile, pussyaholic. I guess he didn't plan on me peeling his woman before their wedding, but after a pipe fit, she was my faucet, and I opened her spout anytime I wanted to.

As we entered the Coliseum, I was surprised at how great the seats were. We sat in the middle of the theatre, just a few rows back from the front stage. The few hits of brandy I'd taken to the head earlier, worked my confidence on high. I was fooled into thinking every set of fine legs in the house wanted me. As I waited for the show to begin, I convinced Benita to relax, while I cruised for drinks.

In truth, I wanted to check what the sand was like on the beach. As I rounded the corridors of the Coliseum, I was pleasantly buzzed at how many fine women walked around to be seen. There were so many, I wouldn't have been able to choose had I been alone. I finally talked myself into going back to my seat, because I had top notch game waiting for me, in Benita.

As I approached my seat, there was a small sampling of brotha's scurrying away from Benita like cockroaches. I sat down, looked over at Benita, and suggested,

"Damn baby, they were trying to eat you alive, like the main course! Next time pull your skirt up a little and charge them mothafucka's for a show! Daddy could always use a little more bread!" I smiled.

She didn't have a chance to respond thanks to our on looking neighbor.

Sitting next to us was this sharply dressed, dark skinned, black man.

He wore a white, fur, coat, with two extremely, pretty women sitting on each side of him. His face revealed striking, African like features, as he profiled his slender frame.

One of the women sat pulling a lighter away from his cigar after lighting it. His hands were covered with diamonds and his brim was matching his white fur.

"Sit back bitch, so I can have a word with the young playboy!"

He ordered the woman.

He looked at me, pulled his sunglasses down and said,

"I'm digging that white, Godfather brim, young playboy! Only a real player can pull that off and you pullin' off some boss game, with that fox on your wing!" He smiled.

He grabbed his nose and snorted, like he had a cocaine drip.

He pointed his pinky finger, with the two-inch-long, fingernail and continued,

"Yeah, the vultures were over here tryin' to pick your pocket, but yo' bottom handled hers like a vet in da game!

I've been in da game for ten years, and it is always good to see a young Mack handle his! Stay up young playboy, because you got a boss fox on your team!"

After he spoke, he slid back in his chair. I was flabbergasted at him thinking I was a Mack but filled with pride at the same time.

In order not to have a conversation, which would reveal the truth, I found myself thinking fast. I searched for an answer that would work.

I slowly responded,

"It's all love, baby! It's all solid!"

The less I was willing to say, the safer my game would be. Benita had no idea what was going on, and was too excited to care about anything, but the concert.

She inquired,

"Okay Martell, what's going on? Did you send all those nasty creeps, over here to test me? You know I'm not falling for that! Besides, you're my honey and keepin' up with you, is already a fulltime job."

I mustered the most pimpish laugh I had in me and replied,

"Naw baby, I wouldn't do that to you! They were just trying to play you for your seat, that's all!"

I was so fortunate that Benita didn't realize how big a commodity she was, or just how fine she was.

The announcer finally announced,

"**BOOTSY'S RUBBER BAND!**"

There on the stage, in all his glory was, Bootsy Collins. He was wearing his red jumpsuit and Casper, his space bass, was booming thunder, as he shouted,

"**WHAT'S THE NAME OF THIS TOWN**?"

The Oakland Coliseum was alive and thumpin', as everybody's eyes stayed glued to the stage. Bootsy and his Rubber Band, funked the place up for a good hour and a half with non-stop boogie.
During the intermission, I pushed my chest out and had a nice conversation with the pimp sitting next to me. I was lucky enough to have a nice beard already. It had grown thick at fifteen; therefore, the only person aware of my age was Benita.
She was older than me, but no one was the wiser. I had to pull the pimp card myself, in order to keep up with my surroundings. I wasn't old enough to drink, so I ordered Benita to get us some Hennessey.
It was a straight power play. I loudly instructed her.
"Don't let any of those, bozo's get at you, unless they were ***payin' what they were weighin'***!"
Benita was dumbfounded and looked at me, as if I was speaking a foreign language. I wasn't worried, because she always did what I asked, without question. I knew she didn't look old enough to buy booze, even though she was older than me. Of course, Benita didn't drink, and my plan was playing out perfectly.
I wanted the pimp who introduced himself as Mike Love, to send his women on the drink run. They were obviously in their twenties and wouldn't be carded. He didn't let me down, as snapped his fingers and motioned at the women.
He ordered,
"The young playboy's fox, pays for nuthin', dig?
Now go powder your noses and handle the drinks!"
He quietly retrieved a small package, out of his silk, shirt pocket and handed it to the ladies.

Our conversation was short, but true to the heart, as well as very candid. Mike Love was surprised I wasn't a young pimp in the game. At the same time, I felt it important to share my thoughts with him. I made sure he knew, how impressed I was, with the way he handled his game.
He shared with me, the potential that Benita would have as a working girl. The body and wonderful goods she'd been blessed with, was a pure gold mine. The way she carried herself, was the icing on the cake. Her sexy, but square look was good for the game. Her look had money written in every language.
He suggested nothing about her needed to be changed, and if he thought I was a sucker, he would be spitting game at her himself.
Mike had no problem telling me how he liked my style and he'd noticed that Benita was totally sprung on me. It would take a very seasoned pimp a lot of time to break her down and turn her out.
Suddenly he stopped our current conversation, looked deep in my eye and reflected.
"I'm real in this izm and I think we cool enough for me to say a li'l somethin' to you, young playboy.
Looks like you broke that pretty stallion before anybody else. If that's what you pulled off, I'm telling you, you in her head for life! That is, if you handle your game right!"
Mike's gaze never changed, because he wanted to gauge whether I would pledge the truth, or not. This could make, or break my kool, and I knew it.
I took a deep breath, and got my cool swagg on, as I sat back and responded,
"Check this pimpin', that really isn't worth speaking on. As a matter fact,

it might be her that has me wide open."

I smiled.

My confidence was rising to another level as he slapped his leg and showed a mouth full of white and gold teeth with his bright smile.

"You're a rare dude at a young age, little brotha! If you ever decide to get in this game, you can go a long way! I know without a doubt you broke cherry on that vine, and the fact that you ain't sittin' here braggin' on it, makes you my type of bleed!" Mike admitted with a certain pride.

As soon as he finished his line of thought, the girls were back. The conversation between Mike Love and I left me plenty to think about.

Upon her return, I just took a long look at Benita as she sat down. I looked at her, but this time something was different. I think it was because I was looking at her in another light.

I looked at Mike's women on the slide, and realized that Benita was prettier, and better built than both of them.

I sat there and marveled at her innocence and wondered if I could sell her to the next man for money. I was in deep thought, as I heard the announcer begin the introduction of,

"STAR CHILD AND THE PARLIAMENT!"

I let all thoughts leave my head as the lights darkened and a large, life size screen came rolling downward in front of the audience.

A funky cartoon started playing. It was,

"**Sir Nose da void a funk that refused to dance**."

This was the theme of the Aqua Boogie groove that was blasting on the screen. Soon after that, a chant of,

"***Swing down sweet chariot, stop and let me ride!"***

*It b*egan to flow from a dark place on the stage, through the sound system.

It wasn't long before it wasn't needed, due to the funkateers in the crowd. This was Oakland! The home of funk and we took the chant to a higher level.

The Bay area funk mob was in full effect and ready for a concert, never to be rivaled in Oakland's story again. There was roaring thunder, along with a fire blast of pyrotechnics, and smoke from every angle.

When the smoke cleared, there was a stainless-steel spaceship landing, while hovering above the floor. Billowy clouds of smoke lay under it, slowly descending, like from the sky.

There it was in all its glory; the mothership had landed. The plume of smoke had clouded the vision throughout the whole arena, as everybody waited in anticipation.

Once the smoke cleared, there stood, Dr. Funkenstein, alias the Long, Haired, Sucka.

His real name was George Clinton. He wore a white fur hat, with a beautiful, long white, fur, trench coat, that flowed down to his white studded, knee high boots. He, like Bootsy, wore a pair of diamond studded, star shaped sunglasses on his face. He stood on the top step of the ship in a pose, as if he was frozen in time.

The band broke into the intro of his platinum selling song,

"**WE WANT THE FUNK!**" The place had become a true live funk fest as he and his boys sang what seemed like all their hits, including, P-funk, Flashlight, and Bop gun.

George even found a way to roll a Rolls Royce on the stage before the night was out.

As the concert winded down, the feeling throughout the whole arena was euphoric, without a disappointed follower. We were all feeling a bit breezy, as we headed toward the exit.

I was a step closer to the clouds, considering the wonderment of the evening.

I was also proud to be rolling beside an established pimp, known in the streets of Oakland. This had to be the case, because every ten steps we walked, somebody would pay him homage. I noticed folks would go out their way to speak. We slowed so many times for him to shake hands; it took a while to get out of the Coliseum.

I was becoming impatient, due to my hunger.

It was now about one in the morning and Mike suggested breakfast. A quick trip to East 14th and a man could feast on the best quarter-pound hamburgers in town. The spot was called, Giant-Burgers. I wasn't much for sitting inside the local restaurants after clubs.

I informed Mike; I was just going to grab a burger. One of his girls quickly pointed how good a Giant Burger would be, and Mike joined in her enthusiasm. He suggested that he would probably just see me there, because he was going to stop and pick up some quick trap money.

I was determined to beat the club crowd, that generally showed up at the burger spots after 1:30 a.m.

Benita and I were walking to the car, when we were greeted by her cousin, Mo.

Mo smiled, as if he had just struck gold, upon observing us getting into my shiny duce. He stood next to me, to show people, he was part of my posse. He had to claim his position, which made him cool. His excitement about the concert wasn't to be denied, as he hollered, "What's up, big homey? That was the shit, huh? I ain't never seen

nuthin' like dat in my life! Dem sucka's was bad as hell, huh?"
Benita whispered under her breath to me.
"Would you please say something to acknowledge him, please?"
I mustered a smile for Mo and suggested,
"Man, I can't even find words to describe what we just saw! This show was avant-garde and just too much!"
"Avant what?" Mo stammered.
I just let the conversation expire, before it really got started, so not to continue. Mo's next words would be no surprise to me, as I attempted to speak prior to him getting a word out. He beat me to the punch as he anxiously asked,
"Where y'all eatin'?"
"*Giant-Burgers*!"
I rendered, as I sat in my car.
I began defrosting my windows for the winter air.
The trip to Giant-Burgers was far too short for me. Benita didn't have time to get into a head rhythm. The secondary problem was it took a while to get a full-size luxury car warm enough to unzip. She had to be satisfied just stroking the front of my pants.
After such a loud concert, I was ready to just groove. This made me slide some, **"Earth, Wind, and Fire"** into the tape deck.
There was always something about their song,
True Devotion, that would warm my soul, and make me appreciate my fellow Americans.
I pulled into the lot, just in time to avoid the rush and Mo pulled in right behind me. I had just enough time to adjust my pants.
I found myself thankful Benita didn't dive on my tool. I walked up to the

window and ordered our food. I knew my muse well enough to know what she liked eating.

The girl behind the counter looked like a Sea-Monkey that had been rode hard and put away wet, but it didn't stop her from smiling at me. She stared at me like I was a French fry, and she was starving.

I stood outside the car and rubbed my hands together, while enjoying the brisk wind that blew through the air. I loved that time of year because life seemed so new. As I reached up to tighten my Godfather brim, I could see Mike Love pulling into the lot.

Shortly thereafter, he joined me in front of the joint. Mo was already standing at the window making enemies. He was taking far too much time ordering his food.

Mike got on his feet, while counting cash in the open like pimps do and surrendered.

"This was a good idea man; I didn't feel like giving dem white mothafucka's my bread tonight anyway! A burger and some coffee's all a Mack need!"

As I stood looking around, I started feeling proud of Oakland for having such an outstanding concert event, without problems.

Without question the hardest crews were there.

Crews like, the Tasa Rasa Projects and the 69 Village Projects. Also, in the house were the funkers from the Acorn projects of West Oakland. All were present, partying without any problems. We were all one big, funk crew! We were all too clean for fighting and messing up our threads. I was internally thanking my wonderful, black people for keeping cool.

Unfortunately, I looked to the right, and observed a short, dark, chocolate, brotha standing in front of two men.

He wore a nice, bright, red suit with a matching derby brim, posted on top of his head. His red, patent leather, Stacy Adams shoes gleamed in the night and caught my eye. But the most telling thing that caught my attention, was the men in front of him.

They were posturing in fighting positions and yelling at him, but for some reason he wasn't responding. He stood there like a statue and didn't appear to be moved by their threats.

The men in front of him wore the exact same clothes. It appeared they were dressed like twins.

I thought to myself,

"These dudes can only be doing one thing, gang bangin'!"

They both had on tan khaki's, with deep creases. They also wore Ben Davidson, brown shirts and bandanas on their heads.

The brotha standing in front of them stayed motionless. They continued to call him names and talking smack to him.

Standing next to him was another brotha, who looked to be about 6'2 and 240 pounds. It appeared; he was speaking up for the quiet brother.

A small crowd was beginning to stand around them, when I realized there was nothing, but women present. This made me approach and stand near the brotha who was doing most of the trash talking.

From my vantage point, I realized that this could be a bad move, but I couldn't help myself. My nature decided it would take over.

I figured I should at least get my gun, because I recognized them as Los Angeles, gang bangers. They were getting a lot of press lately for taking L.A. into a new decade of murder. Their concept of life seemed to bother me, as I watched the nightly news. I was bothered by the black on black

murder that followed my people like a plague.
The Los Angeles streets ran with the blood of my brothers.
I was able to be a part of the picnics in the park with the Black Panthers.
I was also proud to observe the black Muslims fight the white regime that mentally whooped our asses every day.
It was difficult to understand hordes of men, that only killed men that looked like them.
The more I read about the gangbangers in Los Angeles, the worse I felt for their misguided attempts to make their mark in modern society.
Misguided, because all they seemed to rob and kill was others with the same skin color, as offered in the mirror.
These brothers weren't even protecting their families. They were protecting the concrete streets that belonged to the white men of this country.
They would claim blocks that stained red with their blood, like the cowboys that died protecting the Alamo. Their turf wars seemed to eventually have the same end, with no winners in the streets. The only winners were the undercurrent movers and shakers who were glad to see the streets fall.
The police and prison guards stayed employed, thanks to the process. I can imagine a group of white men sitting around a round table shaking their heads in approval while asking,
"How many of them coons killed themselves today? How close are we to getting South Central, or Watts back? As long as them darkies stay in their hoods and kill only blacks, they won't be fighting our kids for college and jobs.
It'll be just like the old days! We'll be the new untouchables and

clean it all up when the time comes! As long as them coons stay out of the white neighborhoods like Westwood and Beverly Hills, we'll be okay!"

I reflected to just moments ago on how wonderful it was to see my people together in unity and splendor.

I casually walked over to Mo and suggested he keep an eye on Benita. I made sure he would take her home if I got too deep in it. I was thankful to him shaking his head in agreement without question.

He was stymied by my request, but he knew me well enough to not question my movements in the ills of the night.

I casually walked to the duce and opened the trunk. I slipped my gat into the small place between my shirt and my slacks. The word on the streets was a 380. Magnum was a bitch's gun. I said call me a bitch, thanks to it being small enough for me to remove it easily. It also held seven bullets in the clip, which would allow me enough ammo to kill whatever was coming my way. Besides, I wasn't a damned killer anyway, but heat was a needed tool in the hood.

As I approached the soon to be scuffle, I wondered what the real problem was? The brotha in the red was gleaming, with his red, silk scarf under his brim and his single gold chain, shining around his neck.

I walked directly opposite of the fool doing all the cussing, and fussing, hoping not to be noticed.

I realized this guy wasn't too bright. He had no clue if I was family to the young man in the red or not. I now stood within arm's reach of him from a side view and he was paying me no attention.

Due to his lack of respect for Oakland, and the brotha's from Oakland. This had become obvious to me as he shouted at the dude in front of him without fear.

He spewed,

"Fuck that Nigga! I'm East side up, Motherfucka!"

He threw a motion of gang sets in the air, using hands to get his point across.

"Y'all Bay area Nigga's ain't nothin'; but bitches anyway! Especially this red color wearing, assed Motherfucka here! I otta cut them fucked up threads off yo' punk ass right now!"

He slammed with disdain.

I watched the 6'2 brotha standing there doing nothing. He was flexing his hands with vigor, as they were being screamed on by the hoodlums.

I thought to myself,

"Damn, he does kind of remind me of a bitch, moving all soft and shit."

But there was something different about the brotha in the red suit, as he stood at attention, without uttering a word.

Unlike the tall dude, there was no fear in his eyes. He just didn't seem to be moved or didn't know what to say to his aggressors.

The cat with the big mouth was moments from a move, and I could feel it. At the same time the tall brotha was trying to show what he was made of, as he explained,

"Y'all L.A. Nigga's don't make me go to my trunk, 'cause I'll spray this fucka! I'm from the Freakmont and y'all don't know what y'all talkin' about anyway! Jon Jon ain't no gang banger, he just!"

Before he could finish his statement, one of the bangers shouted. "Shut yo' faggot ass up! Ole bitch ass punk! I thought you was goin' ta git yo thang out da trunk, **NIGGA**!"

He gazed over at his homeboy and continued,
“Let’s fuck these bitch made Mothafucka’s up, Big Homey!”
This round of words explained plenty to me. The big dude from Fremont was apparently a coward. This was no surprise to me, due to his body movements and the location he claimed. It was all sweet in Fremont, and more like a suburb, than any hood. The brotha in the red had been mistaken by the bangers as an opposite banger.
He was thought to be the bangers major rival, or mortal enemy, thanks to the color he was wearing. It would have been easier to tell the homey’s; we didn’t bang in the Bay. For us it was all about money and women, but I knew, I wouldn’t have a chance to inform him.
I was a changeling, moving from hood to hood; therefore, I knew the element of surprise would always be the best move when dealing with an enemy who underestimated you. I decided to just observe the action.
He was dead wrong about the Bay, and us brotha’s from the Bay. As a matter of fact, he was lucky not to be in a body bag already.
So, how could this be, these fools were right in the heart of Oakland talking smack and getting away with it? Why wasn’t the cat in the red suit getting off on them?
The answer was simple, as it occurred to me. The hot spot, night-clubs hadn’t let out yet. These young bangers had no idea what they were getting into. They were seriously putting their health in danger. A telling fact that almost had me wanting to give them a break.
The first dude looked around while lowering his voice just loud enough to be heard, and said,
“I been clownin’ in San Jose for six months and y’all Nigga’s ain’t shit out here!”

I knew then, he had no idea what was about to happen, or where he was. This wasn't Latino Ville, like San Jose. The cholo's in San Jose was into low-riding cars and smoking PCP, in joints.

This was Oaktown, and it was too late to warn them of the trouble they'd stepped into. They would have to move on and roll out before the clubs let out, because they would surely be stomped to death by us locals.

I glanced around to observe Benita sitting in the duce, and I could see she was scared to death. On the other hand, Mike Love hadn't been moved by the noise and was carefully watching me, while waiting for his food.

The air had become still and without notice the gangbanger with all the mouth took a swing at the brotha in the red. It was a wide left hook and it came hard enough to break something. The tall dude seen this and let out a scream, like a girl. If I hadn't known any better, I would have thought he was ten.

His long legs took the streets, as he left his car behind and ran like a broad.

The brotha in red grabbed his jaw in obvious pain, and was dazed from the blow, but he didn't fall.

He bent over, and spit out a tooth, while resting both his hands on his thighs. The attacker was surprised to see him take the blow as well. Before he could cock his arm for another blow, I mustered all the might, my slim, but muscular physique could gather. I released a shocking right cross to the blind side of bangers face. The thud sounded off like dynamite. Unlike my man in red, he went down in an instant. I knew I didn't have much time to react to the second dude on the other side of him, so without even thinking twice, I pulled the roscoe that rested in my belt line.

Weirdly enough, it felt as if the handle was hot, and the gun was asking to be released. I knew the code of the streets. You don't ever pull a gun unless you plan on using it. There was a strong possibility that someone was going to die tonight.

I didn’t expect what happened next. At the same time, I was putting thug number one down; the second thug had pulled a butterfly knife from his pocket. It appeared as if slow motion, as he plunged it into the side of the brotha in red. This kid was as strong as an ox, because even with his face blazing and a knife wound to his gut, he laid a monstrous blow on the bad guy.

After the blow, he toppled over, and fell to the ground.

Without thinking I took my gun and racked the dude upside his dome.

It didn’t take long for the blood to gush from his head instantly and cover my hand in a dark, red hue. He let out a groan that made me think I killed him. I was at ease as he coiled to the ground in a fetal position. I knew him to be alive, thanks to him holding his head and rolling on the ground.

I stood over him, and reared back to render another blow, so he could sleep.

At first, I held back, but in my anger all that I could really see was a replay of the brotha in red, getting stabbed. My vision at that point, was that red blur that I kept running from. I knew how bad my temper could get, and I needed to control this monster in me.

The next blow from me felt as if it was going to be lethal, as I let it fly.

As the force of anger released, I felt a presence of someone else. It was at that very moment. I felt Benita and Mo holding my arm back in unison. They were keeping me from landing the murderous blow that was the

follow up to my first strike.
They worked as a team when Mo caught my arm with both hands and held on, while Benita attempted to control my gun.
By now, the one I'd hit in the first exchange was gathering his bearings. Mike Love had his women checking on the brotha in the red. Benita was holding me back and pleading for me to stop. All she wanted to do was get out of there, and make sure I didn't kill anyone.
The first guy down was now pleading with me, while holding his homeboy's bloody head.
"PARTNA, please!"
He squirmed.
"We ain't got no straps and my homeboy, need a hospital!
He all fucked up! Come on rogue, just give a Nigga a pass, this one time! We didn't know Oakland was about da game! Just give ya boy's a ghetto pass on this one mistake, cuz! Please!"
He begged.
Benita's touch and the fear in her eyes served as medicine that soothed my soul. I just looked at the brotha, and the scarf resting on his stab wound. I was bewildered at his calm. It was like he didn't even know what had just happened to him.
Mo's proud face was gleaming as he stood near me, like a soldier in arms. I instructed the dude who was pleading with me, to roll out, before the rest of Oaktown arrived.
He looked at me surprised and wondered,
"You mean, you ain't trippin'? You gonna let me and my homeboy roll out da hood?
I let Benita hold my strap. I attempted to educate the brotha.

“Man, check this out! Brotha’s don’t do that gang shit here in the bay! We wear red, blue, purple and green, and whatever the fuck we want! We realize the color of our clothing has nothing to do with our heart, and courage. Do you think you’ll have a choice of a color when you get to hell for all the dumb shit you doing over the colors of a man’s clothes? We far from cowards! The difference is, our favorite colors are money green, backed up by pussy pink!

The cat, your partna shanked doesn’t bang! Hell, the way he’s dressed, here in the Bay, we call that G’d up. He suited and booted! It doesn’t matter what color he’s wearing!

Our gangs consist of how many women we could bump and keep on our team!

Keep that boy on boy gang shit in **your** hood, and we’ll keep pimping in ours! Right about now, you and your homeboy had better cut out! If the brotha in red dies, it’s a murder a beef!

The way that’s handled here is without police intervention. The streets will be your court, and his family will be your executioners! It’s just a matter a time, before you’ll be found dead in one of the projects.

I suggest you cats don’t stop for help ‘till you reach Mountain View, dig? East Palo Alto, and Menlo Park is part of the hood and death walks those streets, so don’t stop there.”

He snatched his comrade up from the ground, and looked deeply into my eyes, and admitted,

“Me and you okay, homey! You ever make it to my hood; you got a pass! We breakin’ out dis this mothafuckin’ Oakland!

Even though you blasted my boy, I know you coulda deaded us both! D-tray ain’t gonna forget that! I owe you one, for real!”

He admitted.
He led his bleeding friend to the blue, 68 Chevy Impala low-rider, they were rolling in.
I thought about the gangbangers landing here on occasion trying to expand their territory to the Bay. But the Bay was its own animal and wasn't going to have that kind of terror.
Killing in the Bay wasn't anything foreign. However, rarely were there any innocents in the morgue, from cowardly drive byes at the time.
We dealt with each other straight up! This meant, the best man won, and every man was aware that death was eminent, if you crossed the game.
Los Angeles during those days, consisted of mostly Crips, Bloods, and a few other gangs. These gangs had gathered a reputation for blasting each other, from the safety of their rides, and sometimes innocents were caught in the crossfire and killed. We had a soft spot for kids and declared them off limits in our Bay area neighborhoods.
Within the moment it took the two men to reach their car, Mike Love was standing next to me informing me that the brotha in the red suit was losing a lot of blood but refused to talk to anybody. Not to mention he was sure Scottie the cop and his cop buddies, would be appearing soon.
He handed me a piece of paper with his phone number on it, along with my bag of food and insisted.
"Call me young bleed! Whenever you up for it, we need to rap!"
We gave each other the latest soul brotha shake, and Mike Love was off.
I remembered Scottie was the hottest cop on the dope squad and ran through this area with his task force. He prided himself on taking down all the dope players on the strip.
Mike was right, so I decided to let Mo hold my gun in case one of

Oakland's finest decided to pull me over on the way to the hospital.
I didn't have a license to drive, therefore under the conditions, I instructed Benita to head toward, Kaiser Hospital, on the west side. It wasn't far from the Acorn projects
I helped the brotha. to the large back seat of the duce. He was slipping in out of consciousness, and still had not said a word.
My ride had a big back seat for a different purpose, but it worked as an ambulance, this night. I made sure he stayed wrapped in my beach blanket, to avoid blood on my seats.
During the short trip to Kaiser, Benita rambled off at the mouth non-stop. Her being raised like a white girl, was starting to show in her word selection. She enunciated cleanly, without an ebonic trait.
She rambled,
"Oh my God, I've never seen anything like that in my life! Martell, you would've killed that man, and they were gonna kill *this* guy!
Oh, my frigen God! What are you, some kind of ghetto hero, or something? What was I supposed to do, if something happened to you? I can't believe how close I came to losing my love! I mean my man!"
She complained.
She was nervous and unlike me, she had never experienced anything close to these actions before.
I knew she was excited; however, there was something new in her voice. I'd never seen her share so much concern and never had she declared her love for me this strongly before. But there it was now, lingering in the air, and I heard it loud and clear.
I reflected on the movie with Fred Williamson starring in it,
Black Caesar.

Thanks to that movie, I kept pressure on the brotha's bleeding wounds. It was bleeding in a similar fashion as I'd seen in the movie.

I thought,

"Damn! I hope he don't die in my ride! I would have to get rid of the duce, because I couldn't lay any booty in the back where a brotha died."

I prayed as we rode, and spit directions to Benita. I was thankful to see his chest rising up and down with a faint, but constant rhythm.

Once arriving at the emergency room. Benita immediately ran in and started screaming for help.

Within moments, they were rolling out with a gurney and people were assisting the brotha from every angle. It was obvious, he was near death, which forced the staff to rush him right in.

I was asked a number of questions. As much as I wanted to lie, it wasn't in me to do so. I labored my words, and didn't say everything, until absolutely necessary.

I gave Benita the look, which suggested her keeping quiet, due to her inexperience, as I answered the questions.

"I was getting a hamburger, and somebody stabbed him. I figured I 'd better help, so I brought him here. I can't tell you anything else.

That statement loomed truer than I could have ever known. I then prepped Benita for a long morning to come. I didn't want her involved with all of the questions I expected from the police; therefore, I'd say she was in the bathroom at the time. That way in case the L.A. boys didn't make it home, or if that cat died on the operating table, in the thick of the night, I knew everything would change.

She wasn't going be a part of court proceedings, and considering I wasn't quite 18, I was considered a juvenile.

This gave me a pass to avoid rough housing by the police. There was only so much that could be done to a juvenile in this state.

It would be embarrassing to the system that allowed my young ass to be out that late in the first place, therefore the police weren't going to talk to me too much.

Even still, I tried to make myself invisible, and told Benita to go on home and wait for my call.

She argued for a moment,

"Tell tell, you don't even know that dude! What if he dies? You can't do anything for him, with your stubborn butt!"

She added.

"Please Martell, I know your heart, but I'm scared!"

Benita admitted in fear.

I didn't have to say a word, because my facial expression relayed my thoughts, and it was obvious I wasn't to be shaken from my course.

Benita took a long look at me and reluctantly concluded; I was in it until things were clear.

"Okay, call me when you're ready and I'll come get you. Call no one else, just me!"

She insisted.

I chuckled and reminded her not to tell her mama about the events that had taken place! Benita stopped in her tracks and asked,

"Why? Are you afraid she would realize that you're not the knight in shining armor she thinks you are? Ole big head boy! Maybe she'll know her little girl really has a thug in sheep's clothing?" She jeered.

I continued to laugh at her sarcastic reaction, and shook my head, while

joking,
“You can tell her you love me, and you love licking these chocolate nuts!”
I joked, while grabbing my private parts.
Benita showed her pretty, white teeth, with her dazzling smile, and retorted,
“I don’t even like you, oh stupid boy!”
It was a pleasure to get back some of joy that was our life, even if for a small moment. Her smile, along with watching her backside turn my way, was just the treat I needed to get me through what was coming. Her arms holding me tight reminded me of my little sister’s love, and it came to me,
Oh snap, Tina!
I dropped a dime in the phone booth, and held my breath, while praying that everything was okay.
While on the phone, Veronica admitted that everything was okay, and she planned on staying all night. Her words were like a warm melody to my ears. Everything was in order at home; therefore, I could see this mess through.
I was so thankful for the emptiness of the emergency room. Besides some sniffles and probably a few cases of the clap, we were the only serious case in the place.
I had been sitting in an uncomfortable chair for nearly thirty minutes, forcing down a cold burger and fries.
It didn’t take long before a white, grey haired doctor approached me.
“I was told you’re the young man here with John Williams, is that true?” He asked.

He continued before I could answer,
“I’m Doctor Buckman. Please to meet you, young man! The admittance form says Martell, is that correct?”
I shook my head yes, as he continued.
“Well, he’s lost a lot of blood, but he’s fortunate. It looks as if there’s no damage to any vital organs. We are still having a tough time getting the bleeding to stop! It’s still touch and go. But your efforts saved his life by restricting the blood loss. Now we’re going to do our best to keep him around. He’s going to need more surgery, so you’ll have to sign some consent forms, so we can continue his care.”
The doctor insisted.
I quickly responded,
“Sorry to disappoint Doc, but I don’t even know that cat! You just said his name. That’s more than I knew about him. I just happened along, and saw someone in trouble, and it’s my dumb nature to help.”
I rendered.
The doctor looked at me oddly and replied while scratching his head.
“Well, I must admit you’re a rare one, son! We’ll try and get information on him. In the meantime, we’ll admit care, because we have little choice. Things are going to be a bit complicated, considering his disability!”
The Doctor stated.
My curiosity won the battle and I quickly asked,
“What disability is that Doc?”
The doctor looked at me with a puzzled frown on his face again, while walking away and answered.
“The fact that he’s deaf! But don’t worry my friend I’ll keep you posted on his progress!”

I had to sit down and replay the night's events in my head. At every turn of the night, I should have known the dude couldn't talk. And it hit me, "Damn, I wonder if things would've been different if his attackers had known they were attacking a damned handicap!

I then realized it would be a complete travesty if the dude in the red suit died. Most likely he was in a hospital bed fighting for his life. all because he couldn't speak, or comprehend what was being said to him, except for lip reading.

I wondered why the doctor called me rare. I'd been called that before and twice during the night. What did it mean?

I wondered if they would think the same things about me, had they seen me curl up on the nights we didn't have food at home. Or if they could see how my mama, hated me. Or if they had a chance to see the despicable things, I'd done for her with needles and dope.

The ugliness I was willing to do, to receive just a moment's caress from my dear old mother, which never happened anyway. No, I didn't feel rare at all.

I was just as bad as anyone else, except, I didn't believe in taking advantage of people. Above all, I figured all fights should be done with some level of respect.

I definitely wasn't one of a kind, when I recalled pistol whipping the gangbanger upside his head. I just convinced myself he had that coming.

Morning crept in quickly and for some strange reason, I popped up, as if were a jack in the box. The sun blared through the blinds of the hospital window.

I didn't know why I jumped up so fast, but I wiped my eyes and headed for the vending machine, for a coke.

I stretched before popping the top and pulled my watch out of my pocket. It stared back at me, revealing the time to be eight o'clock AM.

Hours had danced past me and I was still at the hospital, waiting on a stranger to live, or die. I wondered if the doctor had come out, seen me sleeping and went back inside. At that moment, without notice there was a thud. The front doors busted open with a large force, as if they were being ripped off the hinges.

After the ruckus, there before my face stood a quite large, and extremely energetic, black man.

There was no doubt he should have been playing for the Oakland Raiders, or any pro football team of his choice.

It seemed he was close to six foot, seven inches tall, and about three hundred and fifty pounds, of mostly muscle. He was guerilla black, and wore all leather, with leather gloves on his giant hands. Once I observed the obvious anger in his face, I decided to sit back down.

He rushed to the empty admitting desk and retrieved the loud bell, once silently sitting on top. He jiggled the bell non-stop as if a kid with a new toy.

The lazy clerk finally showed up. She spoke without looking up at the mammoth that hovered above the desk.

She snapped,

"Stop ringin' my bell like you the police! You gotta wait your turn, just like everybody else!"

Silence stole the room, as she looked up, and noticed her mistake. Shock and fear consumed her face. She tried to take her words back, however, I think she was aware that her word retrieval was too little, too late. The big man snapped.

"Bitch, where's my brotha? Old nappy headed bitch! I'll blow up this whole damned hospital, right along with your horse faced ass!"

The only word that escaped her untamed mouth was,

"DAMN!"

She then stuttered in a rush to get away, "I, I, I'll be right back!"

At that point, I watched her quickly run to the back of the building. I was hoping she was going to get an army, because she was not connecting the dots as of yet. This man was dangerous.

There was another blast at the door, and much to my surprise; the 6'2 soft serve dude from the nights commotion, was walking through the door.

He began to pull the arm of the giant that was standing in a huff. That's when I noticed the soft dude had a black eye. I thought to myself,

"***Damn, somebody nailed that faggot good*!"**

I began to wonder if he caught up with the banger's I'd let go and got a beat down. Fatigue made my mind slow at putting things together.

The 6'2 dude was a midget compared to the big man. There was suddenly a butterfly in the pit of my stomach as the 6'2 cat pointed at me. I thought,

"Oh no, they headed my way, and I don't have my strap with me!"

Both men turned and hurried toward me. As they neared me, I stood quickly and began to rip the soda can in my hand, in order to have something sharp enough to use as a blade. I had to distance myself in order to strike. The biggest man asked,

"What's up bleed? I got some questions for you, if you don't mind, little Nigga!"

He was speaking out of obvious aggravation.

Luckily for me, at that moment the doctor casually strolled out of the double doors and headed to me as well.

He stood there looking up and down at the mammoth sized man that dwarfed us all.

The Doctor began to stutter,

"I, ah just came to give you an update on your friend. He's out of surgery and resting in recovery."

I quickly interjected,

"Hold up doc, I think you need to be talking to these dudes, not me!"

The doctor looked up at the giant and asked,

"Well sir, may I inquire who you are to Jon Williams?"

"I'm his little brother!"

The big dude replied quickly.

"And this punk right here is our eldest brother!"

He seethed.

His shame in his older brother was obvious.

"So, what's da deal with Jon Jon and don't bullshit me, Doc!"

He continued.

The doctor smiled with pride as he answered,

"Well, it's like this young man! Your brother had a pretty decent piercing in his lower extremities; however, it missed anything major. It appears he's going to be okay, barring any complications, or infections! You can visit him once he's out of recovery and in the ICU.

In the meantime, the police are on the way and they'll need a full report of what happened. It's protocol, considering there was a stabbing involved. Good day gentlemen and good luck! I'll leave my card with the nurse."

The doctor smiled.
The big dude slapped the 6'2 on the back of the neck, and attacked, "If you woulda stood yo' ground, we wouldn't be talkin' to them pigs, you fuckin' coward! You ain't no brother of mine!"
He fumed angrily.
Before reaching the double doors, the doctor stopped and looked at me and spoke with a controlled passion.
"I don't exactly know who stabbed that young man! But I informed the police, had you not cared for him and got him here quickly, he surely wouldn't have made it! He owes you a great deal of gratitude, young man. Actually, he owes you his life!"
The doctor turned around and continued on his journey through the doors. Before I knew it, the big dude had fallen into one of the chairs and covered his eyes.
I was sure the chair was going to break, as it struggled with his weight. With both his hands over his eyes he began to cry. His quiet sobs turned to full blown tears for a moment, and then back to hurtful sobs. It was odd for me to see such a giant, man, broken down. My own humility prevented me from looking into his face.
I headed toward the phone booth to call Benita, as the huge man jumped up, and caught me. His swift movement caught me by surprise. He wiped his eyes and bellowed,
"My brother Lorenzo is a coward, and we accept that about him. I got a call from a female this morning. She said Mike Love told her what happened last night. If I was there it wouldn't have gone down like that, but I want you to know!"
His emotion appeared to cut off his words again, as he choked up, and

continued.
"You saved my brother's life! Whether you like it or not, you're a part of this. I'm Nicodemus, but they call me Nico and me and Jon, we got you for life! I owe you more than I've ever owed anybody. No matter what it is, or what you do, you got a man by your side for life, dig?
My brotha Jon Jon is the most important thing to me in my world and you just joined that circle by keeping him alive! I know you didn't have to do that shit, but you did!"
He shared with emotion.
I felt as if I was in a movie and didn't know what to say, but my words just fell from my mouth without hesitation.
"It's cool big brotha, you don't owe me anything! You seem like the type of man that would have done the same for me! We solid, just take care of your man!"
I said earnestly.
Nico just looked at me while wiping his face.
"That's my heart, and he's my responsibility, because he handicapped. I was slipping in a wet spot with this fox, while you were saving my heart. So, as I said,
"For life!"
I was too tired to argue with the thankful giant. I just shook his hand and walked outside while waiting for Benita.

CHAPTER 4

Simone

TOO HIGH FOR MAMA

"Oh my God! Dear Father, you must be trying to hurt me purposely!"

Mama mumbled, while holding her stomach.

She was trying to persuade herself that the agonizing pain was a farce.

"***I remember when you and I were friends, God! I can't believe I've pissed you off this bad!"***

She mumbled.

She had been fighting the sickness for at least thirty minutes, while hunched over by the toilet. She had convinced herself that she could kick her dope habit on her own.

She wasn't aware that in order to kick heroin, it would be a struggle to maintain her bowels.

*"**Come on bitch get up! You ain't never let nothin' in life beat you, so get up and beat this shit!***

She attempted to assure herself.

"**Lord, *what can I do? I tell you Father; I just can't take no more! I'm trying to win with all my heart!"***

She shamefully admitted.

Finally, she summoned the powers that lay deep in her soul and begged to be fixed. She had to find the strength, because Tina was in the next room waiting to be taken to school. Tina hated to be late and was already behind schedule.

"*How in the hell did I end up with the smartest girl in school*?"

Mama cursed, as she used the counter as leverage to pull herself up. She screamed through the bathroom door.

"Okay Tina baby, mama's coming! I'll be out in just a minute, I promise!"

Tina knew her pleas would be a waste of time; therefore, all she could do was wait until Simone temporarily beat the demon inside.

It wasn't like me to be missing when Tina woke for school. Usually she could smell breakfast knocking at her nostrils, and her big brother in the kitchen, waiting for her. No matter how late I stayed out the night before, I would be there for her. Since she had chosen to take this Saturday class for younger kids with college minds, I was especially proud of my little sister. So proud of her, that I never missed a Saturday taking her to class. Already Tina, at the young age of twelve was preparing to be a lawyer and she had no plans on disappointing me. She felt her success was all my doing, but I kept reminding her that God favored her.

Back In the bathroom mama finally stood on her own accord and attempted to put foundation on her ailing face. She rubbed briskly, reminding herself,

"***Wow! You used to be a fine bitch! Now you're a nightmare, disguised as a person! You can't even try to fool the world no more. Your secrets are out! You sorry excuse for a mother!***"

Mama was giving herself the business.

"**Alright bitch alright*****! Get yourself together! You gotta go, because that fine professor might be visiting her class today and you can't be***

caught short. He doesn't have to know my bad habits, does he?" She asked herself in a rhetorical fashion.

Mama looked in the mirror and continued the conversation with self.

"Okay, it's done! The mask is on and we ready to fool them all. But, if this mirror could talk, they would be committing my crazy ass!"

She admitted.

As mama exited the bathroom, she cursed out loud, "I know what that little bastard son of mine's doing! He's trying to teach me a lesson! That young fucker knows I sleep in on Saturdays!" She complained.

Tina heard the last of her conversation to thin air and responded.

"Mama, you sleep in every morning! And there are plenty of mornings you aren't even here, so please!"

Simone stepped out of the bathroom and explained. "Just wait one damn minute little girl! I'm still the mama around this camp, and I'll find a switch and beat yo' ass for talking to me like that! I know you think that dirty ass brotha of yours is a hero, but I'm here to tell you, he ain't nothin' and he never will be nothin'! That little bastard, thinks he grown, staying out all night when he wants! I got something for his ass, when I get a hold of him!"

Mama seethed.

"Well, he's ***my*** hero, and he wouldn't be late if he wasn't handling ***your*** duties, mama!"

Tina mumbled.

Mama grabbed her purse, straightened her wig and headed toward the door. The absence of her usual morning doping was taking affect and causing her personality shifts as she looked at Tina and asked,

"Did you say something, sweetie? Are you ready to go? Because I hope you know you're late! And for the record, who is that little girl that's always here?"

Tina just shook her head in disbelief, and suggested,

"Let's just go mama; at least I'll get credit for showing up!"

Mama moved slowly to the car, while digging in her purse for the sunglasses. Her energy level was low, and it took every ounce of will power she had to keep her legs from collapsing. They shook as if they were on under extreme pressure, and she was trying to keep them moving, without losing control. She began to speak to her legs.

"Come on shaky legs, stay with me! Settle down and go with the flow!" She stammered.

As her stomach began to twist into small knots during the drive, she prayed for her bowels to settle and her nose to stop running.

Although she was trying to kick the drugs, she was aware that her body still required an early morning boost. But someone at the club the night before, had stolen her morning hit. She cursed herself for not sitting on the toilet prior to rolling out. She was aware that her current condition made it difficult to gauge what her stomach and body was going to do, because it was no longer hers.

She'd been on drugs for years now, and her body reflected it. Not only her body, but her face was starting to show premature wear. The bags under her eyes bore a reflection of the many nights she decided to party, rather than sleep.

She used ass cream, preparation H, on her eyes to keep the bags away. Fashion Fair make-up had become a necessity to a woman formally known for natural her beauty.

Once arriving at the school, mama struggled with staying in the car. She felt as if the good-looking professor was there. This would be her chance to shine, because there was no telling when she would be back.

Tina realized mama was turning the car off and strongly suggested,

"I don't need you to go with me Mama; I can handle this by myself! There's no reason for you to start something you never did before! I got this!"

Mama's brain focused on finally having a doctor with some money in her life, as she insisted.

"Tina baby, mama is so proud of what you're doing that I'm going in with you! So, let's do this school thing, you and I."

She began to walk with a grin on her face.

The shock on the teacher's face was obvious, as he looked at mama, like she was an alien.

"Well, hello Miss. Fontenot. Good to see you stop in for a rare visit. I won't even complain about our star student being late, just because I'm thankful for your visit."

He sucked up.

Mama spent her visit looking around for the professor. Much to her dismay, he was nowhere to be found. She finally lost patience and blurted,

"Is that nice professor going to be here today? I've got some questions to ask him, about a paper I'm writing!"

The teachers face contorted, as he responded,

"As a matter of fact, the doctor is here today. Currently he's assisting in another class, but he'll be joining us shortly! In the meantime, maybe, I can be of some assistance!"

"No thank you!"

Mama quickly snapped.

She continued,

"I was going to leave, but I would love to watch you teach your class!"

She suggested with a fake smile.

With a splash of embarrassment on his face, the teacher turned, and went to the front of the classroom to begin his lesson.

After ten minutes of being bored to death, mama's stomach began to jitter and play games with her mind. She reflected on how much she once enjoyed school.

"***Why is it so hard for me to sit here, and listen to the aggravating voice of this knucklehead teacher?***"

She thought.

For a slight moment, she stopped thinking about her stomach. Sadness consumed her and she asked herself once again,

"***The bigger question is, how in the hell could I spend all that time in college and waste a perfectly good degree?***

Have I become so average, that I've joined the scores of people working at fast food restaurants, with their dreams stripped away, thanks to this bullshit society?"

The sad truth and the need for a fix snatched her stomach again. This time it was telling her, what it had in mind. It was twisting last night's food through her system and sending it to the escape point.

She began squeezing her legs tight in a clenching fashion, in order to move the disturbance back where it came from. It wasn't working however, as she let out a silent, but deadly disaster.

The whole class began to fidget, one at a time. Everyone began scanning the room silently and accusing each other of the monstrous gas that was circling the air. The pungent odor seemed to be choking the breath out of everyone.

Not knowing who was responsible for the explosion, the teacher held his nose as if he were wiping it and opened a window. He coughed and struggled to speak for a moment, and finally, he blurted.

"Damn! I have no idea which one of you set off the fire alarm in here, but may I suggest you are lactose intolerant!"

The students all laughed and begin pointing at each other. Mama sat sideways in her chair, praying she hadn't soiled the lace Frederick's panties, she was wearing. She spent the next five minutes trying to talk her body into, at least allowing her to get up without blasting the room again. The lack of dope in her body was beginning to take a major toll and she was feeling the effects. She was losing the battle and accepted her defeat, while preparing to head into the bathroom. A scary thought, due to it being located in back of the class.

It presented several problems, however. First, even though it was only twenty-five feet across the room, it would seem like an eternity. She couldn't control the fire, escaping from her ass. Second, it was a single bathroom and if she blew it up, everyone would know she was the flamethrower. She was the one that set their classroom on fire, and Tina would have trouble living it down. Tina was already ashamed of the way mama carried on, these days.

Third and most importantly, if she didn't make the stop in the bathroom right now, she wasn't going to make it anywhere else.

The third won, because her bowels weren't going to wait anymore, and it would be better to make the beeline to a slight embarrassment rather than losing it in the classroom.

Mama slowly rose from the desk with a fake smile on her face. She realized if she moved any faster it would be over. She gathered her best creeping ability and moved out. She wished she could have walked from a bent position, but she knew it wasn't feasible.

As soon as she was standing erect and safe to make the long, slow, journey to the bathroom, the door opened. Much too her dismal belief, there in full form was the fine, articulate, and educated professor that she had the hots for.

She cursed in my mind,

"Oh, my fuckin' goodness! Shit, damned mothafuck! What is a bitch supposed to do now? Please Dr. Feel-good, go the fuck back out!"

She had no choice, but to continue to the bathroom at this point. She clinched her ass and tried to sneak to the dope-fiend sanctuary. She tried to make herself invisible, but the teacher called her name.

"Oh Miss Fontenot, here's the gentleman you've been waiting for, in living color."

He mused.

Mama couldn't walk their way and just waved at the two men, as she continued to the bathroom.

The professor stood baffled at mama's direction and took a seat at his large desk in back of the room.

Tina sat embarrassed as she placed her head on the hard desk.

She used it like a warm pillow instead of remembering its wood composition. This wasn't new to her, because for the past few years, she'd seen mama run to the bathroom as if out of control. But it was always at home, and she would just take a walk outside for air. Usually it was the two of them, and mama would spend quite a bit of time inside.

Without any question this time was different, and after what seemed like an eternity for Tina, the door slowly opened, and Mama headed for the door without a word to Tina or anyone else.
This was probably a good idea, because the students would have hung her with a fine rope.
It was only open for a moment, but the smell that emptied from the bathroom sent some of the kids out of the room running for cover.
The professor grabbed some papers from the top of his desk and almost tripped over himself leaving the class.
The car was like a weapon in the hands of mama as she slipped sideways out of the parking lot. For what made a spooky moment, mama and Tina cried simultaneously. Mama pulled to the side of the road and dropped her head on the steering wheel.
Tears began to run down her face in streams. The picture resembled her sitting in a waterfall. At the same time Tina sat sobbing with her head buried in the desk as the children teased and called her, ***shitty kiddy***.
Mama knew she had taken her life on downward spiral, and it was way out of control. She contemplated the humiliating things she was asking of her own son in reference to her drug use.
She was also reminded of the constant embarrassment she was becoming to the only person she loved in her world right now, Tina. Something had to change right then, and there was no doubt in her mind.
She placed Aretha Franklin's, ***Dr. Feel-Good,*** in the tape deck and headed to Doc's house for some back up.
Doc lived in Oakland, at the corner of 86 and D Street, in a six plex of well-hidden apartments. The street was clean and neat with small, bright, green bushes nestled on each side of the walkway. As she looked

through the window, she could see Doc slow dancing alone through the window.

The slight, soulful sound of the Dramatics mellowed through a cracked window. The song was entitled,

"***I Can't Get Over You***."

Doc wore a scarf on his head, hugging his chemically conked hair. At first, he didn't respond to the knock at the door and just continued to dance. Mama gave up knocking and proceeded to the window and banged until it felt like the house itself was shaking.

Without breaking his groove, Doc came to the door like he'd heard the knocking from the start.

"Well hello Miss Trouble, I was just singing about you, 'cause I can't get over you. See, I know you been goin' through some changes and I been goin' through some changes myself."

He sang the words of the song, without missing a beat.

Mama was in a panic and looked at Doc without the luxury of patience.

"Look man, we need to talk!"

Mama blasted, while rubbing her arms. Doc anticipated her emotional outburst and interjected,

"Okay Slim, I'll hook you up as long as you straighten out yo' hand after your first set tonight! I already got my morning hit, but you know I'm a need my late-night boost, dig?"

He demanded.

Mama walked over to the record player and turned it off. She grabbed Doc's needle marked, bicep and led him to the couch.

She sat down and insisted,

"Look super-perm; just go get the scagg! I'm getting way too sick for the bullshit, man!"

Doc knew the all too familiar pain in Simone's face, being a fellow dope-fiend; he knew the sickness all too well. He didn't even bother to ask whether she had her tools or not, it was easier to just share his.

Besides, he knew Simone was good for the blow. She was the only dope-fiend he knew that never had trouble copping.

After dropping the package in a cut-up coke can, he said,

"I'ma let you use my tools man, but don't plug my shit, and clean 'em when you done noddin'!"

He insisted.

Mama didn't say a word; she just went right to work. She pulled off both her shoes and quickly dropped her Leggs pantyhose. This revealed a plethora of dark track like spots on each of her feet and ankles.

Doc was in the mood, which prompted him to place the most mellow, horny groove ever on the record player, ***Sweet Sticky Thing***, recorded by The Ohio Players.

Doc began dancing again in anticipation of getting mama into bed.

Simone heated the spoon of horse and fumbled with trying to find a vein for the best of five minutes, before screaming.

"You gonna help me, or watch me, you simple minded Motherfucka? This shit ain't helping me while it's in the dropper!"

She glared.

Doc's mental state was so cool from hitting earlier that it smothered his urge to punch her in her head. Instead he walked over and took the stab from her and snapped,

"Bitch! I done told you about your mouth when you talkin' to a grown assed man! If I didn't know you was hurtin' so bad, I'd fuckin' slap yo' ass!"

Simone just chuckled with disdain and replied.

"Just find me a vein, Nigga! Because you done got so skinny, I could probably blow your ass down with one pussy hair!"

She giggled.

While struggling to find a vein, Doc opened his mouth and boasted,

"Once you are ridin' high off the horse, I'm gonna fuck the dog-shit outta you!"

Mama was losing patience and demanded,

"Come on man, find some fuckin' blood! Doc baby please!"

Doc pulled the empty needle out of Simone's foot and suggested, "Damn yo' shit is lookin' bad! It's abscessing with puss and shit! I didn't know you was hittin' hard enough for all this to be goin' on! What's yo' habit these days? It's gotta be a C note, or a buck fifty a day?"

He surmised.

"I'm sorry Monee baby, but you gonna have ta hit in the arm like a regular junky, if you wanna get high! That is, unless you want me to spike you in that pretty pussy of yours?"

He asked, while drooling.

Mama mumbled complaints but pulled up her sleeve and started slapping her arm, after tying the rubber around it.

This time it was pay dirt, and the blood filled the dropper and upon seeing the heroin flow, she let out a sigh of relief.

The feeling of pleasure was almost immediate and within moments she was almost her calm, educated self once again. She was slurring bright thoughts of world intelligence and grandeur, as she started her nod.

The high was so good that Mama didn't feel anything could be wrong with the world and she was almost ready to forget what she wanted to discuss with Doc.

She was on a grand high. So grand that she sat there with her legs wide open and the brightness of her pink, lace, panties was playing peek- a-boo with Docs eyes.

She didn't even notice when he started rubbing his slacks and holding the area below his belt.

Her head began to bob up and down to her chest. She had trouble controlling her jaw movement, as it twitched from side to side. She could feel small trails of slobber drip from her mouth, but I took too much energy to wipe. Her mind would remind her of how nasty drooling was, so she would gather enough power to wipe every now and then.

Doc's mind was stuck on one thing and it was time to get at it. He slid his pants quietly to the floor and danced around in his silk boxers. He carefully slipped in near Simone, as she nodded. On an upward swing of her head, she noticed him placing himself between her legs, while he rested on his knees. He took his snake like hands and began to rub softly between her legs and thighs.

"***For a woman with a dope habit, Simone still has a delightful body!***"

He thought to him-self.

He could never forget how much he enjoyed the juicy pussy that Simone hid between her legs. As he rubbed, he spoke with a slight tone.

"Damn girl I could never get enough of that pussy, never!"

He began to salivate while licking his lips, prepping for the session that was about to take place.

Simone's mind was far away from sex, because she was on a journey flying high in a nod of relaxation and splendor. But at the same time, she remembered how good Doc was at eating pussy and she had no problem with a hot tongue playing in her heated box. She figured, his would do just fine.

"**What the hell!**"

She thought with a grin.

"He can have a little of this juicy pussy, if he eats it first!"

She hushed to herself.

On cue, he rubbed against her panties; and as he saw an opening, he slipped his hand inside to feel the honey, soft, pubic hairs that lay straight as if baby hair.

The moisture was just enough to harden his once soft penis. Doc looked downward at his now willing manhood and got excited, then yelled, "Yeah! Damn right, I'm fuckin'! I was scared my dick wasn't gonna get hard again, cuz that damn dope been killin' my shit as of late! But today I'm boss hard and I'm about to get me some cock!" He smiled.

He vigorously played with his penis and rubbed inside her panties with his fingers. Before long he pulled his dick out of his pants, no longer able to control himself, and became more aggressive with her pussy. His aggression kept him moving inward until he felt something a bit strange, and like a kid on ten bars of candy he jumped up and started shaking his hand. He screamed,

"Oh my God Simone, I felt your string! You didn't say you was on yo' period! Oh shit! That is about the nastiest thang I ever done of in my life! Doc ran to bathroom as Simone found the energy to laugh. "My period oh wow! You are so right my brotha! Ha, ha, ha, I forgot all about that plug. Oowee I bleed like a stuffed pig too!" She continued loudly as she could hear Doc cursing in the bathroom! She smiled, and stuttered with

low energy,
"You alright baby?" She then spoke to herself,
"***That's what you get! You nasty, little, fuck***!"
Doc finally returned from the restroom drying his hand with a towel and a complete sadness on his face.
He suggested,
"Well, so much for my hard dick! That mug is like Jell-O now! Just like most days and it's all your fault for not telling me you was on that thang! What if I would have put my face down south, Simone?"
He asked in disgust.
Mama laughed and saluted and slurred,
"Then I guess you would have received your red wings, Captain! Come on now, you know you've had ketchup on your mustache, and hot dog before, buddy boy!"
Doc responded with shame on his face and insisted,
"Oh, damn Simone, you one nasty Bitch! I ain't never ate no bloody stuff in my damned life! Is you crazy?"
He walked into the kitchen and cleaned his outfit as mama wiped her eyes and tried to straighten herself up in order to talk.
She began,
"Look Doc, we need to talk! I got some serious shit on my mind and I need you to listen to me. I just left my baby's school and one of the most embarrassing moments, I've ever had in my life. I am slowly becoming a worthless dope-fiend and I'm finally seeing it for real!"
Her voice rocked with a self-hate. Doc felt the mood change and hesitated as the moment quickly became somber. He sat down next to Simone while picking at a sore on his face.

The open sore seemed to attract him. He picked at it, like there was something in it that needed to come out.

Mama looked at him and realized he was completely content with his lifestyle.

It was at that moment she could see the emptiness in the life she was living. There wasn't anyone in her life worth hearing her problems, but she needed to purge.

"Doc damn you, I need you to hear me for a change! Chase inside yourself and find that person you used to be and let me talk to him please! Just for a minute, please!"

Mama begged.

Doc felt as if he had just been slapped with a cold rag by Simone. He thought to himself,

"Simone must be serious; I don't ever remember her saying please! She doesn't even plead when askin' for dope!"

"Doc, it's got to be you! Thanks to you, I'm on this shit and if you don't listen, I swear I'm gonna bust!"

Mama cried out.

Tears began to stream down her face with an uncontrollable ease. Doc felt bad for her; because this was the first time, he'd ever seen his crime partner cry. Even after all the black eyes and stomach blows, he'd delivered to this hard lady.

Most days he would hate to admit she was a game opponent, during their skirmishes. Thanks to her delivering plenty of nut cracking blows in retaliation, to his bad assed ways. But not this time, she was actually crying.

Doc rose from the couch and poured them both glasses of brandy. He sat next to Simone, while sharing a look on his face he rarely exhibited. The look on his face was compassion.

"Okay Monee, now that my high is pretty fucked up and my dick will probably never want to see daylight again, tell me what's on your mind? I'm listening."

He admitted.

He maneuvered his emotion to the front and tried his best to generate a smile. Mama sat upright and wiped her runny nose with her hand and shared,

"Check this bleed! I've gone far too many days without any sunshine. I feel like Dracula! I'm afraid of the daylight and live for the night! Today was the first day in nearly a year I was up during the day. It was the first time in months that I really looked in my little girls' face and realized how grown she's become. She's been growing up without me and I've been dying without her. I just couldn't see it.

She won't even look me in the face, Doc. She looks at me like I'm just along for the ride! I can't remember the last time I brought her something or took her shopping!"

Mama admitted.

Doc interrupted,

"But she don't really need for nuthin', Simone! The one thing that jive turkey son of yours does, is take good care of his sister! Even though I can't stand the little bastard, I've seen that for myself!" Doc retorted.

Mama jumped up and grabbed her glass and took a long swig. She gave Doc a distant stare and shrugged her shoulders.

"That's a completely different thing! That little Nigga don't need me, or nobody else! He's just too fuckin' strong for me to ever worry about his

no-good ass!"
Mama complained.
"What the fuck Simone? I can't believe I'm admitting this, but he's hell of a lot more man, than my sissy assed son! But hell, I treat Twisty way better than you treat your boy. What's up with that, anyway?"
Doc asked.
Mama looked Doc deep in his eyes sourly and scoffed,
"My boy is a cold little Motherfucka, Doc! Don't ever turn your back on him! I warn you!
Did you ever wonder how I get my hits when you not around?" Mama asked, with an earnest stare.
A look of bewilderment crossed Doc's face as he asked,
"What in the hell are you sayin', woman?"
Mama wiped her face with both hands and continued.
"It started as soon as we went from crystals to horse. I was in the bathroom about three o'clock one morning after singing at The Mokesmo club. We opened for the Twins that night and I was on fire like never before. I mean my little voice lit the place up. Even the Twins noticed me that night and no one could tell me, I wasn't Billy Holiday.
I was so satisfied with the night that I decided to take my ass home, so I could fix my kids breakfast the next morning.
But what I didn't know then, was, when you have dope in your purse, it calls for you. I didn't know what my daily feed was going to be yet, so my habit was just developing. I got up and went into the bathroom to fix and I couldn't find a fuckin' vein for nothing' in the world!
So, here I was sitting on the floor next to the toilet, butt assed naked. I had dropped my robe to the floor. I was hurting for a fix bad.

My palms were sweating, and my dropper was slipping through hands. Lord knows I was frustrated beyond belief. I had both my feet up on the toilet, and my back against the wall. My naked pussy was just hangin' with the door halfway opened.

My body was giving me nothin' but air. It was as if I had no blood in the usual spots. I was a minute away from shooting in my eyeball.

For some strange reason, I happened to look up and guess who's standing there? Martell!

This dude was able to stand in complete silence without making a single, solitary, fucking sound. My son didn't flinch at anything I was doing. He wasn't moved by the sight of the needle, or the fact that my body was wide open. His eyes were as cold as an ice cube, straight out the fridge! I mean this cat showed no emotion. He looked through me like I was transparent and never existed. It felt as if my own seed could have stabbed me ten times and not blink an eye. For the first time in my life I was afraid of somebody. I was far more afraid of my son, than I've ever been of you. You ain't got it in you to be a stone-cold killer, but my son does. I've seen it in his eyes! My shooting dope didn't move him and neither did the horror of the moment.

I was stuck in my horror at the monster standing there and I can honestly say, I didn't know what to do. Love and respect were already on vacation, so I asked him a set of questions that would change our lives." Simone admitted.

Tears began to run down Mama's face and her breath was shortened as she continued.

"I asked my baby boy! The black prince that came out of my womb, "You gonna stand there looking stupid, or are you going to help yo' dope-fiend mama take a ride?"

His breathing didn't even change. Nor did he hesitate as he asked me in the most casual tone I've ever heard,

"What do you need me to do, mother?"

The sarcasm in his voice shocked me, as he took the dropper from my hand as if he really knew what to do.

"I need you to find a vein for me, in one of these dried-up feet, or ankles!

Then shoot this bullshit in my blood stream, so I can take a ride!

Are you up for that, dear son?"

I asked.

I asked the question with half of me hoping that he would run like a little bitch in horror. The other half of me was ready to choke him if he refused to bless me.

My sweet son closed the door behind him and quietly entered the bathroom. He then asked me the smartest question a kid could ask.

He asked me, how come you don't just shoot it in your arm like everyone else does? That's what my baby boy asked me.

He deserved the truth, so I gave it to him.

Most of our singing costumes are sleeveless and although I wanna be Billy Holiday, I don't need everybody knowing I slam this shit!

Martell placed his little boy fingers against my lips, hushing me mid-sentence. Without a second question he grabbed my needle and felt around both of my feet and ankles with no hesitation.

With my frustration mounting to another level and without direction from me, he slid his hand up my inner thigh. His fingers landed not more than three inches from my vagina and he tipped a vein that bled like a fountain.

He watched the blood run down my leg to the floor.

Mama began to get emotional and began crying again as she continued.

"He watched the tool fill with blood and slowly eased it into my body, while looking directly into my eyes, like he was a man, and I was a weak, little, bitch!

His stare was cold, almost vicious in nature. It was the look his daddy gave me when I told him I was finished, but Martell's was fifty times worse.

After my float started, he grabbed me like a rag doll, and sat my naked body on the toilet, without even as much as a flinch. The only thing he told me was to clean up the place, so that Tina couldn't see who I had become."

Mamma tearfully admitted.

Doc was becoming emotional, as he unsuccessfully fought back tears.

His southern accent returned in his emotion, as she said.

"Simone that there is some of heaviest shit I've ever had laid on me in all my days. I never knew your boy had that in him, never! No damned way!"

His face was a bit puzzled when he quizzed,

"I don't know though! You always have acted like you hate that turkey with a passion, and I've always wondered why. I just never bothered to ask." He admitted.

Mama shook her head, and suggested,

"So now, whenever I can't find my slam spot, my son finds it better than me, and it's been that way for years. One day Doc! One day you'll understand everything! For now, let's just get off of Dexter's son.

Like I said, if I was you, I would stay away from his ass! You must know

he sure hates you, with a passion!"
Those words seemed to strike a nerve with Doc, as he quickly responded,
"What are you talking' about Simone? I would beat the hell outta that little jive ass nigga! He's a fuckin' coward of a brat anyway! I ain't done nothin' to you, or your little crazy assed son! Anyway, fuck him, and his punk assed daddy!"
"You really haven't looked in his eyes, have you?"
Mama asked in amazement.
She continued,
"He hates the ground you walk on, broham! He's never said it, but I know my demon child! And for the record, even I can see he's anything but a coward. He knows I followed your stupid ass into the dope game! He's also known for the last four years that you've been hitting me as well. What he doesn't know is, I like that rough house shit and half the time, I be whoopin' on your ass!" Mama giggled.
"Don't you worry, his little ass better not look at me sideways, because I will stomp a mud hole in his ass!"
Doc assured Simone.
He began to wipe his runny nose with a handkerchief and admitted,
"I still don't know what the real problem is though, Simone? Why we here trippin' off all this shit, anyway?"
Mama settled herself down and sipped the last of the brandy, then answered,
"Doc, when I leave here I'm going for help! This was my last jolt with heroin, if I can help it. Tina is the only thing in my life worth a shit and nothing personal, but that includes you.
I know I don't have the heart to kick cold turkey, but between a halfway

house and maybe a methadone program, I've got to do it! Enough is enough, and I can't stand no more!"

She bellowed.

Doc sat silently in shock, listening to the words that came out of Simone's mouth. After the words brewed for a while, he jumped up and assumed his pretend, pimp mode.

Mama recognized it when he displayed it. It was a farce that she often let him put on in front of others, in order to keep his ego intact.

He yanked on the beltline of his slacks, while twisting his lips and suggested,

"Bitch, you crazy! You know how hard it is to kick the big, bad, boy? Bigger bitches than you have tried and failed. So, what in da fuck makes you stronger than the average junkie?"

He scorned!

Doc was becoming agitated at losing a major money source and her heroin habit. He was certain he had to talk her out of this idea, for his own good.

Mama was always able to get money when there was none to be found. She had a knack for it. Thanks to the clubs she sang in and the constant suckers that gave her money, Docs fifty dollar a day habit rarely suffered.

Upon losing her bread, he would have to become a better hustler in the streets and the streets were becoming meaner. The thought hit him like a ton of bricks. He had to do something quick, before he lost his money train; it was about to run into a safe house forever.

"Hold on a minute baby girl, I can dig where you comin' from and I can help you get there. Just sit tight; I got a surprise for you." Doc smirked.

He went to retrieve the telephone from his bedroom and dropped to the bed. His legs felt weak from the thought of losing Simone's resources. His brain was working overtime.

"Damn, if she goes straight, she ain't gonna want my dope-fiend ass no mo! I gotta do somethin, right now!"

He thought.

Doc picked up the phone and made a quick call. Within moments he was back in the room with Simone. He sat next to her and tenderly grabbed her hands and peered into her eyes. With all the fake care he could muster, Doc spoke.

"Look baby, I'm your man, and I got your back! If it's clean you want, then we'll do it together. I'm gonna kick with you!"

He shared.

A renewed excitement was reflected on mama's face, as she smiled with a gleeful, girlish look.

She asked,

"Are you serious baby? You gonna kick with me for real? You know you don't have to bullshit me, don't you?"

It was as if Doc was a completely different person.

He soothed.

"No damned way I let you do it alone! I'm with you! But you know I need to hit just one more time. Then it's to the program with both of us! I called in a marker to a dude that owes me. We take this last good jolt and it's methadone from then on, cool?"

He mused with a sincere voice.

Mama held him tight and admitted,

"You just don't know how happy you're making me right now, daddy!"

Doc went to the kitchen and poured them both fresh drinks. After ten minutes of sipping, there was a knock at the door. Doc opened the door without looking through the window, or the peep hole.

A short, stout, muscular built, dark skinned man entered the apartment. Doc called him Mojo Man, as he handed Doc a package.

He had a bright smile, and a curious look.

"Here you go, Doc baby! Now, you know what this horse is, right?"

Doc cut him off before he could start a conversation or complete his thought.

"Don't trip Mojo, we'll rap later!

Doc insisted.

"Right now, I just wanna get high with my woman, dig it? Don't worry about the bread, I got you on dat!"

Doc insisted.

Mojo man looked a bit concerned and suggested.

"Just remember what we talked about, brotha man!"

His tone was firm and direct.

From the look on Mojo Man's face, he wanted to stay and party.

Doc's demeanor suggested he wanted to make certain that Mojo exited the small apartment as quick as he had entered it. At that point mama was dancing around and moving her body to Johnny Guitar Watson's, **REAL MOTHER FOR YA,** on the record player. Her skirt was playing slightly up and down on her thighs clinging to her appetizing onion shaped booty and dropping at her whim. She swung her wig around with strong, but controlled motions. She moved like Tina Turner on stage. Mojo could feel his member starting to stand at attention. Mama was so happy to have a kick partner in Doc, that she paid Mojo no attention and acted as if he wasn't even there.

Doc sat down and laid the package on an Ohio Players, "**Honey**", album cover.

Simone noticed it was in a balloon and not the regular waxed paper used for the heroin. It wasn't the china white that had been their claim to fame. It looked more like a piece of sticky tar, or hot pavement.

She wasn't about to slam a black, sticky substance anywhere in her extremity's. However, she really wanted her last time getting high to be a memorable one. She looked away as best she could, until the strange substance caught her attention and she decided to sit down and check out what Doc had on the album.

Simone picked up the sticky stuff and looked at it long and hard. Much to her pleasure she could feel the potency of the dope entering through her pours. She then suggested to Doc,

"This looks like some sticky **shit**! I mean literally, bleed! What in the hell is this?"

Doc began to lick his lips as he spoke and smelled the dope. This here is the latest and greatest horse to hit the streets baby! Let me introduce you to the almighty Kaddafi! Black tar is what it's called!"

He boasted.

"This shit is the coolest high on the planet right now. This is our special high together, before we play the monkey! It's the Rolls Royce to the heroin game right now baby and we are getting some of the first batch to hit the streets."

Doc revealed with a great sense of pride.

Mama just looked at the tar with a puzzled face, but the anticipation of a new trip was enough to make her prepare for a hit in her foot.

"What you doin' that shit for, girl? You gonna be kickin' this bad boy anyway, might as well take it to the head and tie off one of those pretty arms. Hell, ain't gonna be enough tracks to show anyway! That is, if you can kick!"

He teased.

As she watched the needle on the cooker, she confessed.

"I've gone from a prime catch, to a bitch who can't control when she needs to squat on the toilet. My nose runs all fuckin' day!

I get hot and cold flashes all day and I play with life all night! I've become a vampire for real, sucking the blood out my body! I've got a habit that I spend my bread on, while not giving anything to my kids! I swear this will be my last hit of this life!"

Mama surrendered.

Doc acted as if he was being kind by stabbing Simone first. It didn't take much convincing, considering her anticipation. After he hit her, she saw him get up, and get the remainder of the old dope from under the counter. She remembered the stash place for his scagg, because she recalled the two of them trying to deal, at one time. They dealt until they realized selling dope was a full-time job. Neither of them had the temperament for the job, therefore they quickly quit dealing when they became their own best customers.

"What are you doin' Doc?"

She stammered.

An aggressive heat ran through her body or was it cold? she couldn't tell. Her eyes ran into the back of her head. It seemed they were trying to run and hide. She could hear Doc in the background, like she was dreaming.

"Oh yeah, I forgot to tell you, that shit is as pure as that pretty assed daughter of yours, bitch!

You ain't neva leaving me, or the dope world if I can help it! I made you bitch and you gonna always be my dope-fiend, girlfriend, bitch!"

Doc spurned.

"I gotta put somethin' on this shit before I can slam it! It's just too damned pure!"

Doc complained.

Mama's head began to jerk out of control. Her feet, along with her legs began to dance, with fire.

Doc dropped the tools that were now in his hand and snatched mama up from the couch and shrieked,

"Naw bitch! You not supposed to O.D. got damnit!"

He carried her into the bathroom and placed her in the shower. He ran cold water over her head and body. The color of mama's eyes was still absent, while the cold water cooled the fever, that seemed to overcome her. Now, her body was limp and appeared to be freezing.

Doc left her in the tub for moment, while the water ran. He rushed to call Mojo on the phone. He was counting on the fact that Mojo went directly to his apartment. Mojo answered the phone and informed him,

"I tried to tell yo' stupid ass! This shit ain't been danced on and is pure as hell, like you asked! You thought I was bullshittin' about the tar, Nigga?

You gonna end up killin' that fine assed woman and then yo' ass goin' to the fuckin' hoosegow, Jive Turkey! And if you snitch, you one dead, pretty boy, I swear! Your best bet is for you to take that woman to the hospital and save her life, while saving yours! I hate punks like you, that can't handle your bitches!"

Mojo insisted.

Doc hung the phone up in a panic and sat on the couch, trying to decide what to do.

Ideas hit him suddenly.

"Fuck it! If the dope don't kill her, I'm a drown the bitch!"

He thought out loud.

"***Oh lawd***!"

He shouted and freaked as he ran to the bathroom.

"Shit! *I don't think she breathin'*!"

He frantically revealed.

"I gotta do somethin' quick; this bitch can't die on my watch! I'm a con-man, not a killer! She's gotta find a way to live; I need her far too much to let her go, one way or the other!"

He admitted, while rubbing her body.

Once the ambulance arrived at his front door, Doc explained that Simone was a disgruntled lover that showed up at his doorstep. She was torn up over their breakup.

He began to explain how she turned to using drugs when he split with her up over a year ago.

He boasted about informing her that he'd moved on with his life and how she was no longer a part of it. And she confessed her life wasn't worth living and she couldn't be without him. He suggested, she got a hold of some bad stuff before she showed at his place. He said he hated dope and dope users and never wanted people like that near him. Simone was the exception.

He had no doubt that all of his ravings hadn't convinced the white E.M.T.'s that worked tirelessly on Simone. This meant it would be a smart move for him to stay at home, instead riding with them to the hospital.

The elder of the two men gave Doc the look.

“The police are going to have some questions about this, especially if that woman dies. I guess it’s up to you, whether you’re going to await their visit, or come to the hospital and answer the questions. No matter what, it’s going to happen, the decision is yours.”

He suggested with suspicion.

It was obvious that he was trying to inform Doc to avoid the cops coming to his house. He would be better off meeting them at the hospital and avoid a search of his premises.

Doc had to think on his feet and prepare to lie good to the police.

He knew once entering the hospital, it was official. Especially since mama was in a full coma, with no way of knowing when, or if she’d ever come out of it.

CHAPTER 5

Martell

LIFE WITHOUT MAMA

Getting oranges out of Mr. Thompson's tree had become easier; thanks to me growing into good sized young man.

I was the ripe age of seventeen, but my life experience showed the marking of an older man.

I didn't live my life anything close to a typical seventeen-year boy, and by all accounts I didn't act like any seventeen-year-old kid that I knew. The only thing I would have in common with a teenager my age, would be my choice to remain in high school.

I had already grown a full beard and my body was muscular, with defined biceps. My appearance tended to fool people on a daily basis. The problem was simply that I also looked too damned old to be in high school. The one saving grace in reference to my looks, was Castlemont High School was hood fabulous.

This translated into no one there having time to worry about me. The drop-out rate was a major problem in Oakland and if things weren't bad enough, they were starting to describe our linguistic twang worldwide. White folks were beginning to teach it, as well as trying to understand it. The language had been handed a name made purposeful by the societal giants.

They called it a language within a language: Ebonics. What a mess! But somehow, I felt untouchable, thanks to help from God up above.

Only he knew that every day, before I started my day, I prayed to him. I asked his forgiveness for the dirt I did wrong and for whatever, I was slated to do wrong.

Considering the difficulty of the past two years, I was forced to be fearless. I had already become dangerous to those who posed a threat to me, or mine. But now that Jon Jon and big, brotha, Nico was always somewhere close, people were paying attention to me in the streets.

Mama was in a coma, so not letting the welfare people take Tina required a lot of work, along with intimidation. Thanks to my new friends, all it took was following the case worker home and to her kid's school, and we were able to scare the dickens out of her.

Nico made sure she reported good things, without harming her. Since the crazy night I'd saved Jon Jon's life, I couldn't get Nico, or Jon Jon to give me a day off. Who would've ever thought that Jon Jon would have the heart of a Lion?

The fact that he couldn't hear or speak put him in the realm of the truly fearless. I had no doubt that he would kill for me, with just one word. I was beginning to believe Nico, when he said, he was my man for life.

Mike Love and I kept in touch and flourished in a fresh, meaningful friendship.

Fear was a foreign concept to me. The only thing I found myself afraid of was God's wrath. Although, I wasn't afraid of going to the white man's prison, it wasn't high on my list of things to do.

I was aware, I would be tried as an adult, if I got jammed up doing dirt. I couldn't get into any trouble because I could ill afford being locked away.

I knew mama couldn't take care of Tina, considering her current condition and I was the only person Tina really had.

My little sister was a becoming a beautiful young girl and a tremendous student.

My one trip to juvenile, was a setback for her. She had stopped being the star pupil and lashed back at her teachers. She even missed two days of school, which was not a reflection of her personality. Unfortunately, I wasn't given much choice in the matter, because this cat decided he liked Tina quite a bit more, than Tina liked him.

As a matter of fact, she didn't like him a bit.

The problem was simple, taking no for an answer wasn't his thing. He decided to follow her home for three days, which was a big mistake, because it sent me into motion.

I couldn't believe they made stalkers at such a young age. But here in my sister's face was a teenage stalker, prepping to be a stalker once he reached adulthood.

I found myself in the position of setting him straight. My move would be harmless enough, but hopefully a life's lesson. I felt for him. It wasn't all his fault. I got the street breakdown on his life. I was made aware, he didn't have a daddy at home, just like most of us ghetto boys. I got the run down on his mama as well and was informed on her habits. This would assist me in handling the situation.

There was no question that she loved her son. Word on the street suggested all she really cared about was him being a good kid. But even so, my move couldn't be soft, if it was going to save his life.

I kept an eye on their house for a couple of evenings and noticed his mama was a looker from a distance. The best intel I was able to get from my spying was to observe she didn't have men swinging in and out of her pad.

I had to admit she appeared to be a fairly settled and strict mama. This made me respect the way she handled her lifestyle.

I always believed that women that brought club men home to meet their kids, were dumb. They would pretend there was no sex involved and convince themselves their kids were naive.

Not realizing they were creating boy's that often-lost respect for women, as well, as losing respect for their own mothers.

These mothers counted on their son's love, but refused to accept, love and respect as two different things.

It didn't take me long to come up with a plan. Although, it was bold, I had to trust my instincts.

I would also have to pray that jail wouldn't be the outcome. Thanks to the street information I gained, I was sure I had the upper hand. Truth be told, I had enough on her little confused son, to put him in juvenile as well.

I was thankful for an extremely cool late night, as I put on my black clothes. I climbed through a slightly opened window. As I entered the foreign domain, I automatically felt comfort for some odd reason.

My first thought was,

"Damn I'm hungry!"

I found no reason to remain that way, so I made myself a sandwich a poured a glass of red Kool-Aid.

I walked upstairs and looked into the first bedroom and observed two little, lovely, black, kids sleeping. They were just so cute; I wouldn't bother to wake them.

I traveled through the hallway to the mother's room and there she was sleeping soundly, with the covers rising to the tip of her pretty caramel thighs. The blanket was raised enough to show a teaser of the kinky pubic hairs of her vagina. Her hair was tied down by a nasty little scarf, wrapped around her head.

I thought to myself,

"Damn! She's good looking! I wonder why she put that nasty assed, scarf on her head."

The sandwich tasted so good that I hated to sit it down, as I removed my razor out of its usual hiding place. It didn't really make sense to wear gloves, due the fact I wasn't wearing a mask anyway.

I struggled internally about using my razor, but I didn't know if she was tiger or cat, so I had to have it. It would emit the fear needed for the task. All the hours of me practicing with razors paid off. I had become deadly and efficient with the old school slice. I could pull it out, and slice three ways before anyone knew I had it in hand. A perfect weapon, I'd learned about watching old movies. It was perfectly legal and just as lethal.

I took a moment and enjoyed looking at the pretty lady smile, as she slept. It appeared as if angels were visiting her. I recalled mama telling Tina, that beautiful angels visited her and made her smile during her sleep. I inched up close to the sleeping beauty and held my razor in one hand and grabbed her mouth aggressively, with the other.

Her eyes flew open, as if they were being blown up and she began to shake frantically. I quickly placed the blade near her nose with a slight, but firm tense. I made sure it never touched her.

She was in terror, but I could tell shock was her first feeling and it

proved to be my ally. It kept her from fighting or responding in violence.
I whispered.
"Please lady, I know this is scary and feels odd, but believe me when I say, I'm not here to hurt you. And I would never hurt your babies!"
I was as assuring as possible.
She took a deep breath and gave up her struggle. I took a deep breath along with her and found myself surprised at how natural it all came to me, to be the bad guy.
"If you promise to listen to what I'm gonna say without screaming, I'll promise to put this ugly razor away. At which point, we both can be breathe, without any problems, dig?"
She still hadn't made a move and her breathing was easier, as I continued.
"I'm going to give you my word not to hurt you, if you give me your word, not to scream! If you promise me that I'll put this blade away, and remove my hands, because I know this ain't cool! If we're on the same page, nod your head yes, please!"
I calmly asked.
She nodded in agreement and I showed her the blade. I put it in my pocket. I slowly removed my hands from her face.
The first thing she asked in her deepest concern was,
"Are my babies okay? You didn't hurt my kids did you, you bastard? Please tell me they alright, please?"
She inquired frantically.
I sighed and asked,
"Miss Lady, if I said I'm not here to hurt you, why would I hurt your babies? They're lovely!"

"Thank God"

She sighed. Then she looked me up and down, and implied,

"You a good-looking young man. Why would you be here to take some, old pussy? I know you get plenty of that! I ain't got no money, so it's gotta be rape, you nasty bastard!"

I guess my facial expression gave me away, as she began to plead.

"Please, young, black, brotha don't do that, please! It must be a control thing, huh? I ain't gonna fight you, so you don't have to cut me, or mess up my face, or none of that, shit!"

She surrendered.

"I sat up in her bed and informed her,

"You sure talk a lot lady! Look, I'm not going to rape you! Even though you kinda fine! You give yourself and your old pussy too much credit. I tell you what, you put on your nasty assed robe, or house coat. I promise I won't do anything to anybody in your house! But keep in mind, I always keep a gun, so be cool! We can go to the kitchen, away from your kids and talk about our problem, dig?"

"No money, or pussy! What the hell you want in my house, nigga! She frowned.

"Don't call me that, please! I said sternly. She had the look on her face that suggested, as soon as she could, she would clock and stab me.

This made me quickly warn her,

"Dig this Miss Lady, my boys are just across the street and they're no way as cool as I am. As a matter of fact, one of my boys hasn't bathed in a week and I had to stop him from trying to mess with a woman just yesterday! He's been checking you out. So, it's important that you be cool!"

I lied.

It pained me to lie on my friends, but I found myself needing something to make my night easier.

It worked like a charm, as she put on her ugly house robe and led me through to the kitchen. As we approached the kitchen, she stopped and asked,

"Who ate a sandwich and Kool-Aid this time a night?"

I shook my head and replied,

"I'm sorry! I'll give you some money for the grub! I hadn't eaten all day!"

I pulled out a 20-dollar bill and sat it on the table. She looked bewildered, as she surmised,

"You 'bout the strangest, nicest, crook I ever met! I can't imagine what you want from me! And right about now, a bitch very curious!"

I grabbed my sandwich and glass and suggested she sit. The first thing I did was make sure she'd seen the 20-dollar bill on the table and relayed,

"This is for the food, lady. I'm sorry to be here like this, under these circumstances. I didn't break anything, and I apologize for startling you! I made sure not to touch you anywhere that you would feel compromised! At least that was my intention!"

I surrendered.

Her face contorted once again, and she was totally perplexed as she sat in a chair watching me finish the sandwich.

The tension was leaving the room and I was relaxing. "Boy, I love turkey ham"!

I admitted.

"Okay lady, here is my dilemma; I'm here to do **you** and **I** a favor. I don't know if you realize it, but your little, Teddy is a baby stalker. If we don't stop it now, he's gonna end up dead, or in jail. As a matter of fact, instead of being here I could have had him arrested or beat down! I have seen too many of our kids in the system, so I took this drastic measure, believe or not, to help."

She placed her hands over her face and became emotional.

"Shit! What his little ass do this time?"

Her movements suggested, she was not surprised. She began to tear up.

I continued,

"Well, I have a little sister and it's my job to protect her and right now your son has her afraid to leave the house, due to him stalking her, like a grown man.

I wouldn't have gone through these extraordinary lengths, except I snooped around the school and he's been beat down three times for the same thing. The three prior girls he scared, all went to other schools, out of fear.

Know this, I'm from the hood and could have had him fixed for life, by my boys. But I figured, if I gave him a good scare, it would help his future and yours as well.

I admitted.

"Now listen pretty lady, breaking into your home was the only way I could let you know the severity of the situation! To cover myself, I have 5 people that would say, I was them tonight. I say that just in case you wouldn't listen."

She sat back in the wooden chair and wiped tears from her face, and admitted,

"Yeah, he's been kicked out of two schools because of it, and I've been

afraid he's gonna get in real trouble and I would lose him.
I guess its possible God sent you here to help me deal with this." She cried.
She wiped and continued,
"This ***is*** some scary shit, but I am relieved it's somebody like you! You must be in a good college somewhere the way you talk!"
She assumed.
"No. I just believe in black men being different than what they expect of us!"
I admitted.
"Even though I'm here breaking into your house, I am here to try and help your boy, because I think he's young enough to be helped."
I suggested.
She looked at me with genuine care in her eyes and earnestly asked,
"Now, if you hurt my boy, screw your plan. I may decide to just call the cops and put your ass in jail?"
I smirked and suggested,
"Well, as I said before, I'm the nice guy out of my crew. Let's just say, if they got word you crossed me, I would have to beg them to behave!"
The curiosity disappeared from her face.
She asked,
"So, what's your plan, crime partner?"
"Well, I was hoping you would go back to your room and go to bed. Of course, I'll need you to trust my motives by now and realize, I've got your best interest in mind. I'll sneak into his room and scare him into changing his ways, but I promise not to hurt him.
Most cats that stalk women, are cowards, or future killers; I figure we

need to find out, either way!"

I held her hand and asked,

"Are you game for this action? Someone has to help your son"

I suggested.

She stood up, scratched her head and replied,

"I guess if you were gonna hurt us, you could've already! If it was pussy you wanted, you could've taken that too! So, I guess I can trust you're not gonna hurt my mixed-up baby."

She surrendered.

Okay I'm in, just be sure you don't hurt my boy! We're good on that, right?"

She asked with intensity.

I stood up and assured her,

"I promise, just to rattle his cage, without really harming him! But it has to be serious, in order to save his future.

I must admit one thing, you are way fine! Get rid of that ugly robe, and that nasty scarf and next time maybe."

I laughed without finishing my sentence. She looked at me and laughed.

"Negro please! I'm buyin' a gun after this shit! Just hurry up and get your crook ass out my house!"

The smirk on her face suggested she wouldn't have minded if we would've laid down for a little pipe fitting.

I turned off all the lights and crept into Teddy's room, as quiet as a snake in the covered grass. He lay there sleeping like a gentle Prince, without the motivation to do anything wrong. Of course, I knew different, because I believed in my heart anyone and everyone was capable of malice, or bad behavior.

I lay next to him and quietly placed my blade against his throat, while shaking him, until his eyes opened.
When I placed my hand over his mouth, I looked him deep in his eyes and I began to feel moisture at my knees.
The little fucker had peed on himself. This was a perfect time to warn him about Tina and little girls like Tina.
I passionately informed him of his reality. Which stated, next time he wouldn't have to pee on himself, because if I had to come back, he wouldn't have a dick to pee out of. I made him understand the wages for stalking little girls, was death. I assured, I wasn't the only one watching him, so he'd better stop now!
I ran my blade across his little dick to let him know how real this was. I was out the door and, in the wind, as quickly as I had entered the place.
When I returned home, I was greeted by Tina and Veronica dancing around the house like they had just received a million dollars.
When I walked into the room Tina jumped on my back, like she was still a little girl. Veronica was jumping up and down in excitement and I noticed something I'd never noticed before.
Veronica had a wonderful set of girls, jumping around, as if they wanted to escape the confines of her thirty-four "D" bra cups.
Tina was on my back and all I could think about was, how I could I have missed those things Veronica was bouncing around, before me. Was I losing my edge?
Tina rubbed her hands through my short curly hair, while smiling. This made me look at the joy on my little sister's face, and ask, "What's up kid? What are you knuckleheads so jazzed about?"
She jumped down and grabbed both my hands.

She asked if I was ready for some great news. I stood silent awaiting the news.

"Tell Tell, mama moved today, and she actually opened her eyes!" Tina said with joy.

She began to jump around again in wonderment. But, for some reason, the news felt odd to me and my stomach took a dive into the depths of nowhere.

It felt like it found the deepest part of my soul and hid there. I was just stuck in a timeless blur for a moment.

"You know what that means? It means she's basically out of her coma and we gonna have our mama back, big brotha!"

Tina sang.

It was at that very moment, I realized I still didn't like, nor did I respect my own mama. My emotions made me ashamed of what I was feeling. I should've been happy my mama was coming out of her coma. It had been two long years and we still didn't know what happened to her, except for an overdose.

According to the police, we were too young to deal with the information and we couldn't handle the truth. But they didn't have a problem sharing the fact that she was a dope addict with the local newspaper.

Tina was much too busy celebrating to notice my confusion and dismay, but Veronica observed my twisted face.

She approached me and gave me a hug. It suggested love was in her heart. As she held me close, she whispered in my ear.

"Someday, I would like for you to explain the mess between you and your crazy assed mama! She can't see what I see in you, Martell and I don't understand it.

My heart tells me, you're a hell of a man and I'll wait for you, in more ways than one! Because I have, I do and always will love you. You're everything to me! You know life is crazy when a girl wishes her father could be more like the man in her life!"

She admitted on the sly.

I felt so wrong for feeling this way about my own mama, that I could barely hear her words.

I grabbed Tina and gave her a hug, while pretending I was joyful.

"That's the best news I've heard in two years li'l sis! I guess you better get yourself together."

I suggested.

Tina hugged me back, while crying tears of joy.

"It's okay Tell, you can cry! I promise I won't tell anyone! I promise!"

She smiled.

I smiled back to her and headed to my room.

The one good thing mama handed down to me was a strong appreciation for great music. Music from the old days to the new; therefore, my music knowledge was extensive and was a big part of my person.

During tough times I felt as if the current music could never express my deep emotions.

I dug out my, ***Sam Cooke*** album and played,

A Change is Gonna Come! I played it over and over again. I was hoping something would jump out at me and make me recognize what I was feeling, but it didn't.

I wanted my mother well and would do anything to see to her safe, but it was a lot like watching an enemy enter my life again.

I wondered why she hated me so much. I wondered why I was beginning to join her in sharing those same despicable emotions, she consistently displayed to me.

I struggled with emotions, mostly because I rarely felt any good, or bad. I couldn't think of anyone I really loved, but Tina. For Tina's sake, mama and I would have to find some equal ground. I hadn't seen my sister that happy, except for the higher education program that came looking for her.

I soon drowned out all the negative thoughts by zooming in on the woman Veronica was becoming. Her acne was clearing, and she was rounding out just beautifully.

I couldn't believe the words she'd just uttered in my ear. As I reflected on the moment, I thought to myself,

"That little girl doesn't love me! She's just going through one of those puppy love crushes!"

I continued to ask myself, what kind of man could I be, not to like my own mother? And if this was my reality, what could I do about it? I now had to ask myself an even better question,

"How was it possible to live and not be in love a woman?"

I dug Benita in a major way, but I knew I wasn't really in love in an unconditional way. I longed to look deep in the eyes of a woman and see heaven.

At least through Benita's eyes, I saw an angel. I was getting older it seemed. In this transitional period of my life, it was becoming difficult to observe the glow of an angel. Anything short of a miracle wasn't going to change my spiral downward, into a cold, callous, self-serving shell of a man.

Thank goodness for Malcolm X and his teachings to assist me in holding a glimpse of morality, in my person. Because, up to this point, even the preachers I'd visited in the churches shorted me with **their** truth, instead of God's truth.

The next morning, I did my usual and prepared Tina's breakfast. I poured myself a glass of orange juice and sat down to read the Oakland Tribune, along with the Wall Street Journal. The brotha's always laughed at me for reading such esteemed papers, as the Journal, but I considered myself fortunate to have that torch inside of me.

That torch had served me well, because I loved knowledge and the quest for it. They had no idea about the politricks of the Un-United States, but I was blessed enough to have a decent grasp of it.

I was aware that all of our lives were being affected by the suits and the lobbyists that helped to drive policy in our worlds.

I followed the teachings of Malcolm X in reference to politricks and most of his teaching financially and idealistically. His belief in being black helped to make high school a breeze for me, due to my yearning for learning.

Good grades came with very little effort, and the teachers loved me, as I kept my hand raised in class. I really loved the psychology of the mind and how it played out in our lives. I was very extroverted at school, thanks to my appreciation for it.

Somehow Mike Love had been informed about mama's recovery and called to wish me luck with her.

He sensed the problems that worked like an ugly magic between my mama and me.

I later found he kept a direct pulse on the happenings in the streets and kept his eye on the town.

I started buying, selling and fixing cars while mama was gone.
The money was slow, but consistent and I was fortunate enough to meet a couple of young girls at one of Mike's parties.
They really seemed to dig me and got pleasure from spending their money on me.
Along with their contributions and Benita's financial assistance, we really did well in my household.
At first it was strange receiving gifts from the new women. I turned them down a few times, even though I knew Tina could use the gifts. But, observing the glow in her face, after trying on a few outfits, I relented and gave up my opposition.
Nico, and Jon Jon often teased; I was already becoming a pimp through my dealings with Mike Love.
Nico made no qualms about being jealous of the time I spent with Mike.
Veronica was there often. She seemed to liv there and cooked dinner for me, like a wife would.
She hated being home with her drunken daddy and made sure to give Tina anything she wanted.
Money flowed into our house very fluidly, during mama's absence. I found it odd, how it flowed so effortlessly, but it was wonderful.
I still fell to my knees every day and every night and prayed for direction.
Although God never answered me, he took good care of me and I knew it was his arms that kept me safe. I continued to ask him, if I was wrong for accepting the gifts and the love I was getting.
Somehow, I knew in my soul, I was taking advantage of the situation.
Even Benita was right there in place, giving me anything I breathed for.

Most times I wouldn't even have to ask for it. If I mentioned anything in conversation, it would just come my way.

Mama's rent was paid on time every month for two years in a row and the landlord loved every minute of it. The cabinets were full of food and the house ran as smooth as a dream.

I took one more look around the place, as I waited for Tina to exit the bathroom. She was all smiles and she joined me in the duce. She talked like a virgin man, begging for his first sex, for the duration of the ride. Her anticipation of mama's return consumed her. As we entered the parking lot of the hospital, Tina finally looked over at me and realized there was something bothering me.

"What's wrong big brother? You look like you got a lot on your mind? You aren't worried about mama, are you? The doctor's say she's gonna be fine when she comes home! They said she's got some kind of trophy, or something like that. She has to work through it."

"It's called atrophy girl!"

I snapped.

"It settles in your joints when they lay dormant for a length of time."

"How you know all that? I've never seen you interested in medical stuff?"

She wondered, while mumbling.

I just shook my head and exited the car. Tina was in a hurry and I noticed myself dragging, as if I was waiting for something.

Once we were through the hospital door, an odd feeling came over me as we stopped at the gift shop. I grabbed mama a large bouquet of flowers and let Tina pick out a card for her.

I recounted the plethora of cards; I'd purchased for mama over the years and struggled with the thought of her actually reading them. Instead of leaving them out, I placed them in the medical cabinet that sat next to her bed. I gladly wrote them, because up until now she was unable to read them. I was afraid they would make me look like a punk, if she read them now.

I was having trouble placing a label on my emotion.

I didn't know if it was melancholy, or depression. Could it have been anticipation, or desperation? I couldn't recognize what it was I was feeling. The only thing that was certain, was the emotions were there to stay.

With all that I'd seen and gone through, I realized something was happening to me and I was different. I was a changing into a man and I couldn't tell if I was to be a good man, or bad. I was leaning toward bad with traces of good, because I was at home in my new mind. I was slowly killing the other side of me, so the new me could make its presence felt in a world that was afraid of the black man.

I would find a way to hide what I didn't want mama to see somehow. I painted an emotionally convincing smile on my face and stepped into the elevator with my little, sister. I wondered if she could see the different me, standing beside her.

The ninth floor was full of people rushing about, doing their nursing duties and chatting away.

The people were doing just about anything within the means of sanity for a paycheck.

"***This was the will for survival and the struggle for money!***"

I thought to myself.

These ladies were cleaning grown folks' asses, removing diapers and wiping fluids for money.

Men were cleaning toilets, along with vomit and kissing deep in the asses of the men in charge for money.

Wow!

I began to think.

The power of that paper money is beyond comprehension.

A confidence consumed me as we walked toward mama's room. It was if I was moving in slow motion and every one of the women within eye shot, was wondering about me.

Mama's room was a sobering experience for me, on most days.

On this day it was empty, except for the weltering flowers I brought a few weeks before.

Until this day, there was no reason to breathe life in the room. The room wasn't as cold and damp as it had been, but it still carried a distant feeling for me.

Tina stared at mama for a moment, before saying anything. I think mama either felt her presence or felt the hate in her heart for me. She slowly opened her eyes.

Tina's eyes filled with tears, as the two looked upon each other. Mama eyes began to well up and display tears as well. Tina ran to the bed and grabbed Simone, as if she was raised from the dead. She wrapped her arms around her and held on tight. It was as if she was holding mama down from flying away in a hot air balloon. There was love in each of their eyes and it was now clear to me that loving was a foreign concept to me, except what I felt for Tina.

I looked into mama's eyes, while she held Tina and I saw generations of hurt and pain.

The drugs had taken a toll on the woman as she sat there without make up, or years of sun. His face was bleached by the nothingness that had been her existence for the last two years. It was void of the mellow color it once had. Anyone would've thought she would reach for me in order to close the family circle, but she didn't.

She cuddled with Tina and softly whispered,

"It's okay baby, mommies back! I ain't never gonna leave you again, I promise! As soon as I get outta here we're gonna kick start our life, I promise!"

Mama smiled, and wiped Tina's tears.

She laughed,

"Wow, little bit, look at you! You sure haven't been missing any meals, have you?"

"Naaa, I eat far too much thanks to my big brotha!"

She admitted, while rubbing her belly.

She had pride on her face, as she spoke of me, which seemed to bother mama. Mama took a deep breath and looked at me with contempt. She appeared distraught by my even being there. Her eyes looked toward me, but they were looking beyond me. She surrendered,

"Yes! Your big brotha, the frigen superhero!"

Her gaze turned my way with an ugly scowl and her words speared the air.

"Looks like you've been standing in the gap pretty good huh, black? I guess I owe you a debt for handling all the business, while I've been laid up, huh?"

She spurned.

She took a deep, troubled, breath and continued.

"Well, I'm thankful for you being there for Tina. I guess I truly owe you now, huh Martell?

Come give your dear old mama a hug!"

She insisted with a conjured tone.

I could tell I was dealing with the same old mama when she began to speak to me. She had the same dislike and contempt in her voice for me as always. It was all familiar and I felt it deep in my gut. The hug was for appearances and a gift to play into Tina's happiness.

As I embraced my mama, I could feel the two of us sharing a forced, false emotion.

My mother appeared to be angry at me for surviving, instead of falling. She wanted me to fail so that she could lavish in the glory of my inability. I could feel her in pain to hug me. It prompted me to pull out of her grasp.

In the midst of my confusion, she suggested,

"Damned boy, you look like a grown ass man! You think you're a big shot now, huh?"

I quickly responded in anguish,

"No mother, I'm just Tina's big brotha and your black assed son! That's what I am!"

I observed the look on Tina's face, and she looked at mama in a peculiar fashion.

That was the day, Tina finally accepted a truth that had escaped her for so many years. She was perplexed at what she could see through mama's eyes. But whatever it was, it wasn't the love, or appreciation, it should've been for my support of mama's household.

"Mama, what's wrong with you!"

She admonished.

"Martell's been the only one to keep **you and me** holding on! He's spent countless hours in this funky place, reading to you! Sleeping in here, while staying on the doctors, assuring everyone you'd be okay!

He made sure everyone knew you were a fighter, so they would help with your care! And now that your back, all you want to do is fight the one person that's been by your side! I don't understand Mama!"

Tina snapped in displeasure.

It was all true, but I didn't want mama to know. I couldn't discern why I did all of those things. I didn't want to be forced to tell mama whether it was out of obligation, or love. Unfortunately, I didn't know the answer.

"So, you did all of what your sister just said, black?"

Mama asked in surprise.

"I guess I did some of this and some of that."

I calmly admitted.

"Why'd you do it Martell? So that I can owe you? Is that why you did it?"

She spurned.

"Naw old lady, it's not that at all! The one price-less thing I can offer the people in my life, is loyalty! Personally, I'm good with that! I have nothing else to offer."

I smiled, as I was beginning to learn myself.

"Hey, why don't I let you two share one those mothers and daughters' moments, while I go get you something sweet out of the vending machines? You look like you could use a boost, mother. I'll be back in a minute!"

I continued.

I needed a moment to breathe. The new high I'd been feeling was gone and replaced with wondering. I wondered how long it had actually been ugly between my mother and me. How long had I been blind to it? I wondered if she was mad for birthing me. Or was she more upset that my father was a nothing, according to her?

How could Tina have not noticed it before? Was it hate, or what was it? And why was it there, hiding in mama's every glance? It was all too mysterious, but I had no plans on spending my lifetime trying to find the answers. Finally, I wondered, had mama created a monster in me?

I stopped and stared at Mama Simone, along with Tina through the glass and was thankful to see my little sister so happy. She acted as if mama had been there as a mother the whole time, instead of the invisible drug user that was never home for her.

Tina was satisfied with the vision she wanted of our mother instead of the truth. There was one thing I wasn't sure of.

I wanted to know which kind of mother was being handed back to my honor roll, sister.

Mama seemed to be winded by our visit, which prompted me to go back inside the room. I handed her the candy and placed my hand on Tina's shoulder.

"We don't want to be the ones to putting her back in a coma, now do we, sis? Let's give mother a break and let her rest!"

I suggested with half a smile.

Tina returned my smile and replied,

"No, we want her well!"

She hugged Simone again and admitted,

"Mama, I love you and I promise we'll be back after school is out, right

Martell?"

I pointed Tina toward the door and told her to wait for me, while I had my moment with mama. She accepted my direction and stepped outside. I closed the door and handed mama the remainder of candy bars, and the cupcake I had purchased for her.

She looked at the sweets long and hard and said,

"Guess you been able to put food in the house regularly, huh hustler? Looks like you've been maintaining all the bills on time as well, huh? You turned out to be nothing like your dope-fiend mama, or your no-good daddy did you, boy? If I know you, there's even a phone at the house as well, huh?"

The contempt in her voice was clear.

"I can't recall, the last time I was called a boy, mother! Yeah, we eat alright! In case you need us, the nurse has the phone number in your chart. You can call Tina whenever you want, until you get out of here."

I responded.

I noticed mama's nose began to twitch, which meant her anger was rising.

"So, come out with it and stop bullshitting me, Nigga! Tell me what fuck you want to tell me! Ask me what the fuck you wanna ask me and get it over with!"

She demanded in a raised tone.

"First of all, don't call me Nigga!"

I said calmly.

She interrupted,

"What tha fuck you mean, **Nigga**? I had you!

I call you what I want! You came out of my womb! What, I'm supposed to be, scared of **you**? Why, because you big and buffed now? You're supposed to be tha boss dawg, or some shit?"

She argued.

"Wow mother, you got a lot of pinned up anger! Has that been simmering in the bed with you, waiting to surface for two years?"

I asked, while making certain the door was closed.

"I simply don't find the word as a term of endearment! Nor do I find it acceptable vernacular for a strong, black man, with the vocabulary to express himself!

I can and do talk ghetto with the best of them when it's necessary, but even then, I don't use that word. And guess what dear mother? You'll never hear me call anyone that word, unless it's all that they understand.

So, I ask you to respect me, the way I'm willing to respect you. Plainly put Simone, I'd never call you a Nigga!

Now, if we've got that out of the way, let's talk about some real issues."

I pushed.

Mama's face was priceless, but her energy level was depleted, which limited the fight in her. She was losing her mind with control, as she yelled,

"Damn you Martell! Who in da fuck do you think you are? Jesse damned, **fuckin**' Jackson?"

I calmly chuckled, and responded,

"Look Simone, I need you to listen for a change! No disrespect intended, but Tina's on her way to be great lawyer one day.

I believe in her and need to know you will too! I need to know you're going to be a muse for her and get her through the rest of this schooling.

I've been there and frankly I've done my best.

I don't want you on that junk no more and I think I've done enough to be able to say that.

With that being said, I know junkies need a lot of sugar when they're hurting and if you ever get that feeling again, try candy. That'll be better than you thinking you're Billie freaking Holiday. I don't know how many more, ***good morning heartaches,*** my little sis can handle.

She's a strong girl, but her weakness is you. I just wanna hear that you're ready to be her strength, instead!"

Mama's anger slowly dissipated, into the air. She sighed and adjusted herself in bed and responded.

"Listen boy, I don't need no sermon from your triflin' ass. Especially in reference to the merits of motherhood! As a matter of fact, why don't you get the fuck outta here and let the doorknob hit you, where the dog should've bit you! NIGGA!"

She said bitterly.

My frustration was all too familiar and I was already losing hope that she would do the right thing.

"I see, the same old selfish mama, acting in her same old selfish way!"

I responded.

She balled her fist up and slashed,

"Boy, if I wasn't sick, I would be beating your ass into a whole new century, **Nigga**!"

Unwilling to relent my position, I quickly responded.

"Check this out mama; I'm doing my best not to disrespect you, but you're making this difficult! This isn't about me! As a matter of fact, it's not been about me for almost eighteen years and I've still not complained! I didn't complain when you showed up home, drunk,

nightly, or high off your ass every night!
I didn't complain on the countless nights I went to bed hungry, due to your unwillingness to provide! I didn't complain when it was me, that made sure the daughter you delivered ate and made it to school every day!
I haven't complained about one damned thing, in this shallow existence you'll left me, called life! Not one single time! I didn't ask to come to this unholy Earth!
Like you said, you put me here and then abandoned me. I still haven't asked you for anything, except to stand up and be a mother to your only daughter! A daughter with a heart of gold, who despite every attempt you've made to destroy her, loves the ground your ass walks on!
So, right here and fuckin' now, you tell me, what's it gonna be, Simone? Blame me, a kid half your age for your misery in life, or stand up and be a mother?
And know this, dear mother, on your strongest day, you couldn't whoop my ass! That day has come and gone, with me slamming dope in your body!"
I scolded.
My words burned through the air, with deep emotion and I waited patiently for an answer. At the same time, I wanted to explode inward. I didn't recognize the person admonishing Simone; because this was the first time in my life I actually felt this kind of rage. For all of her posturing, mama knew I was right.
She bit her tongue, until a spot of blood was present and asked me for some water. After taking a couple of sips, she pulled the nurses' cord.
I scanned for Tina and found myself thankful that she was on the other

end of the corridor and not listening to our conversation.
"Look Martell!"
Mama said in a commanding voice.
"Life usually walks us around the block quite a few times and leaves us sweaty. Some of us stop to take showers three times a day, because we don't know how to move forward, without one. And then there are those of us who just keep walking and deal with the stickiness, until we finished our day. We become afraid of taking too much time.
That's you, the consistent shower taker and for better, or for worse, I'm just the opposite. And whether we like or not, we're stuck with each other.
I knew I was fuckin' up before I ended up in this mad house. I know you'll find it hard to believe, but I was on my way to kick before I came here. I was going to a program that morning and that asshole Doc, hit me with a hot shot of pure tar, heroin. He was set to keep me on his team. That shit almost killed me, so I will not be slamming any more dope.
I realize I'm lucky to be alive and when I get outta here, I'm killin' that Motherfucka! So, you can go plan whatever future you want for yourself, because Tina is going to be alright!
I'm gonna take care of my baby!"
Mama said, for the first time in her life, with confidence.
The nurse opened the door and mama requested medicine for an intense headache. I said my goodbye's and was headed out of the door. She stopped me in my tracks, while I was facing the door. She blasted,
"Hey black! Remember, I asked if you thought I owed you something! Well I do and I hate I do! So, one day I'll pay my debt!"
Without looking back at her, I responded,

"If I've learned anything from this short span of life, is no one owes anybody anything, except what we owe God, mother."

I opened the door and exited into the hallway.

Tina had spent her time asking a million questions about Simone's recovery. The nurse's face was becoming irritated at the aggressive inquiry from such a young girl.

I wanted to warn her ahead of time, that she was dealing with a future attorney, but Tina got to her before I could. The nurse was ready for me to save her when I cut into their conversation.

I'm sure she was expecting a spark of joy from my face, instead of the doom and gloom that loomed apparent.

"Is there something wrong, Mr. Martell?"

Nurse Jennings asked, with her typical middle aged, white lady tone.

"No, it's a happy day, because my mother will be coming home!"

I lied with a fake smile.

"Well, let's not get ahead of ourselves, okay? There's still plenty of work to be done before she'll be ready for home. The important thing is she's back with us!"

The nurse smiled.

During the drive home, Tina was so excited I thought she would never stop talking. She had already planned shopping trips, and nights out to dinner for the whole family.

I was convinced she had no idea how difficult maintaining a relationship was, for the two closest people to her in her young life.

CHAPTER 6

Martell

ONE GROWN ASSED MAN

As we parked in front, there was a surprise waiting for me. Tina and I noticed a police car. There standing was an officer at the door and another near the grass, resting his hand on his gun.

Tina wondered why they were there, but I knew why. My night trip hadn't exactly produced the results I'd hoped. I never wanted jail to be the answer, after my visit to the baby stalkers house, but I didn't plan on running.

I parked my car and was happy that I had attained a driver's license. I informed Tina that more than likely, I would have to go with the cops, but it wasn't a problem.

I told her of the hollowed book in my room that contained some money. An embarrassing truth, the best place to hide anything from most black men, was a book. I made sure she didn't ask the police any questions and I promised her I'd explain thing later.

I suggested she make the usual call to Veronica, until my return. It was a good thing I had given Veronica a car to get around with, because it put her in a position to take Tina anywhere, she needed to go.

It was only a Chevy Vega, I traded for a stash of refer. Although, a little, cheap car, it ran well, after being tuned up.

I gave Tina my keys and empowered her to be my personal soldier, which translated into being strong.

There was no way of knowing, just how much trouble I was in, but for Tina's safety, it was worth it.

I would be allowed a phone call and at that point, I would tell Tina what to do.

"Tina, promise me you won't look outside while they take me, promise! Just go in the house like it's a normal day. I want you and Veronica to do your thing 'til I call, promise?"

"I promise, Martell!"

Tina said, while putting her head down in a sign of emotion.

I walked to the officer standing in the grass and asked,

"How can I help you officer?"

The cop clutched his gun, as if I were three hundred pounds.

"Are you Martell Mackie?"

He asked nervously.

"Yes, that's me!"

I answered in anticipation.

"Well Mr. Mackie, I need you to put your arms behind your back, because you're under arrest."

He said, with a slight smirk on his face.

I responded by turning around and allowing the cop to cuff me, without incident. Within moments both men had hands on me, feeling me up like I was Janet Jackson. They asked the familiar questions, as being recorded by every black man being profiled in America.

"Are you on parole, or probation? You got any knives, guns, weapons, or dope on you?"

“No officer, none of the above!"

I quietly responded.

"Mind if we look inside your car?”

The other cop asked quite nicely.

“With all due respect sir, yes I do mind. My car is parked and locked and my sister has the keys. Of course, you’re welcome too if you have a search warrant for my car specifically.”

I responded.

“It’ll be easier on you, if you cooperate, son!”

He sternly pointed out.

“Cooperation doesn’t mean giving up all my rights, sir! Unless you are arresting me for contraband, my car isn’t evidence.”

I offered, like a law school student.

“Just get in the frigen car, smartass!”

The cop seethed, in frustration.

We began to drive toward downtown Oakland.

“You’re one of them extra cool Negro, black power brothers, huh? You haven’t even asked why you’re being arrested, Broham!”

Cop number one chuckled.

He continued,

“Don’t you want to talk about the little bastard that snitched on you when he was crying to his principal?”

The cop joked.

“Yeah, the little, black, fucker said you broke into his house and damned near cut his fucking neck off! Said you’re one bad mother fucker! Boy I tell you, if we were in my hometown of Jasper, we’d show your ass some fucking justice! These white brothers of mine in California have gone soft on you negra's!"

He bragged.

I observed the Broadway turn off and wondered what these two were up to. We went under a tunnel and I wondered to myself, ***"Okay, they're going jump on me now.***"

I realized at that moment the sign actually read, **Oakland Police Department**.

They placed their guns in a lockbox located on the wall, outside the station. Once the guns were safely tucked, the cops yanked me out of the car and walked me into the station. A metal bench rested in front of the booking desk and a man was sitting there in handcuffs and leg shackles. He reeked of booze and was screaming at the cop, sitting at the desk. The two sat me down next to the apparent drunk and informed the desk cop of my status.

"Hey Lieutenant, got another one of ***them*** for booking! Don't you hate you decided to help your brother in law and take over his shift?"

The cop smiled.

The lieutenant seemed to disregard his words, as he looked at me. He questioned the big mouth cop.

"What's the charge on this one and what kind of disposition does he have? Because I'm about to take this other asshole on an elevator ride! And Sister Theresa knows I got room for two!"

He offered in frustration.

The drunken white man sitting next to me, spit on the ground and yelled, "Fuck you pig! I ain't done nothing to be in this pig pen! Fuck you, and your wrinkled assed mother!"

The cop responded,

"Okay that's it, dickhead! My mother's a sweet old woman, who doesn't deserve you bad mouthing her! You drunk son of a bitch!"

The offended cop looked at the three cops that were working deeper in the building, and summoned,

"Hey guys take this bitch for an elevator ride and show him my love! He's drunk, so watch it! I can clearly see this asshole falling on his head!"

He chuckled.

The two cops responsible for my arrest were pouring themselves coffee.

The first cop suggested,

"Book this one on, breaking and entering and assault with a deadly, on a kid!"

His smile was sly and wicked. He chewed his gum and popped it loudly.

The lieutenant looked at me somewhat bewildered and asked,

"Are you sure about this guy? Did you boneheads read him his rights and get a statement?"

Both men looked at each other and shook their heads, as the first cop responded.

"Aaah no, we didn't read him his rights and he wouldn't give us a statement without a mouthpiece present; we figured we'd wait until we got here!"

"Okay, did you do anything before bringing him here? Damn, did you even search him! He might be packin'!"

The desk cop rendered.

The second arresting officer's face contorted, as he answered "Yeah, we searched him sir!"

The desk cop looked me up, and down and said,

"I'm Lieutenant Beene and I'm gonna book you and take your statement."

He then read me my rights. Afterwards he asked,

"So then tell me what happened?"

I looked at him and replied,

"Didn't you say that anything I say can be used against me and that I had the right to remain silent?"

"That's what I said but help yourself and talk!"

He strongly posed.

"Well, silent it is! That is, until I'm appointed an attorney!"

I mused.

The cop took a deep, labored breath and suggested,

"I would be doing myself a favor and told all that happened, if I was you."

After, about thirty minutes of trying to change my mind, he finally gave up and asked my name and age.

"My name is Martell Mackie and I just made seventeen years old!" I admitted.

I observed shock in his eyes at my response. He then asked again, "How old did you say you were, young man?"

"Seventeen!"

I replied, with attitude.

I was a bit surprised by the look on his face. He jumped up and screamed,

"Got damnit! Stupid sons of bitches!"

At that moment he glared at the cops that arrested me. They were sitting, laughing and drinking coffee.

"I can't understand why you morons didn't get the kids ID, or nothin'! This guy's a minor and you brought him here! Are you fucking crazy? He's supposed to be at the juvenile facility! What a major screw up! You idiots just gave this guy a pass once he talks to mouthpiece!"

He yelled.

The first cop walked within arm's reach of us and tried to whisper to the lieutenant.

"I think it'll be alright! This kid has no idea of his rights. I think we can slip him right in."

He attempted to speak, as if I wasn't there and couldn't hear him.

Lieutenant Beene looked at him with a crazy stare, and responded,

"What, are you stupid?

The young bastards already invoked his right to counsel, and from what I'm hearing, he's already turned you knuckleheads around when you wanted to search his car!"

The surprised cop asked,

"He lawyered up already?"

"Yeah, now get him the hell outta here, and go find a real collar to make up for your stupidity.

Hell, as a minor he could've went home with his mommy and we prevented that possibility. Just get him to the hall, with no stops on the way and I mean no stops! He'll be free bout time you get him there!"

He slammed.

He turned his gaze to me.

"As for **you,** soul brother, don't get too smart for your own good! This isn't my daily job, booking assholes. My ears are to the streets and I'll be keeping an eye on you!"

He informed me.

I chuckled and said,

"You can keep both eyes on me, sir! As a matter fact you can come to my baptism. I'm a good ole church boy!"

I never knew how much he meant by the eye comment until later in my days, thanks to two unsuccessful attempts to take me down in the streets, of Oakland.

The drive to the Coco County Juvenile Facility was a quick one, considering Beene warned the officers not to sway off the beat and path. I was sure he was informing them in a covert fashion to refrain from finding a cozy comfort spot and whoopin' my black, ass.

Unfortunately for me, it was getting late. That meant going to court on the same day, wasn't happening.

Booking went fast and within two hours, I was fingerprinted, clothed, and housed. The whole process seemed to be ugly at every turn. I couldn't imagine the daily thought of a grown man ordering people to spread their butt cheeks daily.

I wondered what kind of man could literally check nut sacks and assholes for under aged boys. To make matters worse, if a kid hid something in the anus; it would have to be retrieved by finger force.

I was able to make a couple of collect calls once housed. I called Nico first and explained the situation. I suggested he go speak to the lady. I made sure he heard me when I told him to be nice. I asked him to explain the gravity of the situation to her and I was sure she'd change her direction.

Next, I called Tina, and informed her that everything would be okay. I explained that it was my first arrest and along with a mistake the cops made, I was probably going to be released on my own promise to appear. I knew jail would be a bad trip for someone with my background, and my appreciation for life. It was clear why the outlaw cowboys ran from the law and were willing to shoot it out 'til death.

The door swung open and the funk released into the air of the large room, which happened to be built like a large gymnasium. There were bunks and cots wall to wall.

Boys were packed in there like cattle headed to slaughter.

I fiercely concentrated on just trying to keep my face stoic and not letting the smell, or the surprise of the mere numbers show on my face.

The guard led me to a small bunk with a thin mattress and an even thinner pillow. As I looked at all the black faces looming about with smiles on their faces, I felt a lockdown on my soul. The guard told me to make myself at home, as I placed my small need bag on the bunk.

The jailers were nice enough to put toothpaste and a toothbrush in the plastic bag. Another guard came through the gym and did a head count. There was a group, lifting mop buckets full of water, like the buckets were a first-class weight set and some were flat out exercising, until the guard showed up.

There were scores of boys' playing cards and dominoes. But the middle of the room received the vast majority of the attention.

In the dead center of the chaos sat a T.V. with a large group of boys watching it. I was amazed at their ability to listen to the unit with all the noise that was present. I could hardly hear myself think and I could feel something was amidst.

I knew there was a test coming for me, but I didn't know what it was just yet. After the count, the guard left the room. At that time, the room became louder and more raucous as the inmates lit cigarettes and began to curse each other out in jest.

There was even a dice game going, with top ramen noodles as payment.

Then came the challenge. Some knucklehead felt like I was going to be his dinner, for the night. He stood about three inches taller than me, with a stout frame. However, there was nothing in his eyes that said he was menacing. He was no way more dangerous, than I'd become.

Little did he know, I didn't fear anything but, God.

"That's my bunk, punk! And if you want to use it, you gonna have to pay taxes, Nigga!"

He insisted, as he threw my stuff to the cement floor.

"Of course, there's a li'l' sumthin, sumthin we can do, to work this out!"

He smirked.

I took a few steps backwards and replied,

"First, I got your Nigga hangin' at the end of my nuts! Second, I'm wondering if you asking me to fuck? 'Cause I thought you was faggot as soon as I saw you! Anybody tell you, you got a pretty mouth, just like a li'l' bitch in heat!"

I grinned.

"On second thought, I'm sure I can find a lot nicer ass to hit in here than yours! That is, if I was a batty boy like you! So, I think I'll pass on that one, ***Partner!"***

My words caught me assuming a side stance, preparing for his blow. Just as I assumed, he turned his back to me in order to have a fighting advantage. He thought his prehistoric moves would be a surprise to me. As if an orchestrated dance, the fool suckered punched wildly at my head, not realizing I had changed my vantage point.

I was an experienced fighter.
"I hate bitch assed Nigga's!"
He sounded off, as he rounded his fist by the side of my moving face. As planned, he was truly predictable in his attack to my face. I never understood why it's always been so important for black men to land one on the face, or chin. I guessed it would be the bragging rights of the knockout factor. What he didn't expect was me changing my direction, which made it easier to escape his punch. My complete flurry was already calculated in my mind, which gave me an advantage over him. One of my favorite books in my personal library was,
"THE ART OF WAR."
I learned quite a bit in reading it and put the teachings into use regularly. Therefore, I slipped his punch, with a slight bend of my upper body. As soon as it was thrown. My knee blasted him in the groin area without thought. It never failed; black men refused to cover their nuts. as if they were sacred in battle, but in truth nothing was sacred. No matter how big a man was, a shot to the nuts would bend one over in a pain. This would send his hands to cover his nuts like a magnet to steel.
Needless to say, his hands were indisposed as I finished him with a powerful right cross to his nose. The sounds and agony of his pain could be felt throughout the entire gym. His nose cracked like hot grease to a skillet. I could see several boys in the gym cringe, at the sight of both blows. I even felt my nuts cry for him as he fell backwards to the floor. The next move was to immediately grab for my need bag and retrieve the frail toothbrush.
I couldn't help wishing I had my butterfly knives, or a razor. But only the brush lay inside the plastic bag. It had to serve my next move, when I

broke it in two pieces. I placed my back against the wall and maintained my fighting stance, as one of his enforcers walked up to me.

He got in a stance ready to strike a blow, but I could see in his eyes he wasn't hard at all. He was just trying to save face in front of his boys. I prepared to throw down for the second time, a voice filled the gym. It was rough, strong and commanding.

"Leave the new dude alone! Y'all gonna fuck up and make us loose the T.V! Then you'll have to deal with me!"

The voice sounded off, from a sitting position in front of the T.V...

"Shit, he den already kicked Boo's ass and you can't fight no better than Boo, Elroy! Just let it go! He den showed y'all, he ain't no sissy! The way I see it, y'all lucky he ain't bustin' a hole in Boo's ripe ass, right now!"

The voice rumbled through the noise.

The other boy's in the gym began to slap each other five, laughing heartily. Elroy listened like he'd heard the voice of God and slowly backed away from me.

"This ain't over sucka!"

He whispered in a southern tone.

"Mitch ain't gonna save yo' ass next time!"

He whispered, while back peddling.

I smiled and responded,

"Bitch please! He just saved your punk ass!"

I relaxed and laid on the bunk I was assigned, with my ass to the mattress and my eyes wide open.

I observed my new surrounding and there was one thing that was certain, I no longer had to ask where the black boys had gone in this society.

They were all there, locked up like failed animals and I could only imagine what the grown-up prison was like.
But I was near being sent there, if this was a real case in front of me.
I recounted looking in the lady's eyes after my unscheduled visit to her home and they didn't suggest jail and the eyes never lie.
I could hear Mitch giving orders, as if he wasn't a prisoner and it left no doubt to his running things. I heard one of the boy's refer to him as trustee instead of his name. I put two and two together and figured it meant flunky or smart enough to play the game. Either way, he was top dawg and I had to thank him for his intervention.
All I could do was pray for some intelligent reading; however, I was thankful to my ghetto upbringing, while visiting this Juvenile Facility.
It made it a lot easier having the so-called Ebonics as my second language, because my usual diction would have labeled me a square, instead of the chameleon I'd become.
Most of the brothers didn't believe it was cool to enunciate, considering there was so much slang being spoken.
After meeting Mitchell, I could see why they listened to him. He was only five foot three, but he was a mass of pure muscle. He was built for competition, even though his glasses and crossed eyes made him look like a stone-cold killer.
I was certain he was picked on as a kid, due to the misdirection of his pupils. When he looked at me, I couldn't decide which eye to concentrate on. He had those cold eyes that didn't care about stabbing you. It seemed, he also had a sense of fair play and that would be the side for me to stay on.
He picked up on something in me, that he respected, during our 3-hour

conversation. He was hungry for the knowledge I shared, as I broke down how we as black men should have been capitalists. We should have been taking advantage of the American dream. Instead we allowed ourselves to be victims of a society that refused to see our worth.

I broke it down to him who the true homeless in American society were. We were a people ripped from the bosom of our homeland and redeployed in a world refusing to recognize us as human and we were starting to believe it.

I also informed him how we had no concept of our home and no matter how long we remained in America; our ethnicity would always be accomplished with a hyphen in the name.

He was curious as to why I spoke English so clearly, but he heard me break the language barrier when handling Boo, with the basic hood in my speech. I expressed to him how the white man had been our enemy, but thanks to his supreme knowledge of deceit he'd tricked us into thinking that the brotha on the next block was our enemy.

Even during the slave trade, he manipulated us into enslaving each other. The real enemies were causing us to battle, without getting dirty. I expressed to him the mastering of your enemy's language always put you in the position to seem transparent, but able to strike without them knowing they had been infiltrated.

That's how the police infiltrate organizations, with their undercover cops. They are always trained to sound, and act like us.

I promised him I would send a book that would make it all clear, entitled, "***THE SPOOK WHO SAT BY THE DOOR***" written by a brother named, Sam Greenlee.

It would explain a good portion of what I was saying.

"Damn, we gots to stay in touch, bleed!"
He demanded.
"You 'bout the heaviest young brotha I den met in this joint!"
He admitted out of admiration.
"But to keep it real with you, young Mackie, I can't read a lick! I never could read or write, just like most of these fools in here. But keep that on the low.
I just bullied my way past shit, whenever I was challenged. Even my teachers, just pushed me through!"
Mitchell admitted with shame.
Our conversation fascinated him and generated a new interest in reading and writing. He complained that reading was something his hard life never offered him. I found myself in an odd position. Should I keep it real with this hulk of a man and take the chance of pissing him off? Or maybe try to say something that could spark a difference in his life.
He was in transition to Vacaville in order to be screened for Penitentiary life in fifteen days. At which time he would turn eighteen, therefore I felt I had to step out on a limb of faith.
I surrendered,
"Check this out Mitchell, I'm not trying to brag, but I see your future too important for me to continue a lie. I'm scheduled to graduate soon and that's even with having a dope-fiend mama and an invisible daddy. But brotha it's been just like a burglary, I had to take it.
Dig this, my white teachers worked for a paycheck most of the time and was willing to send me through to the next grade regardless of my work or effort. And then there was what I thought was a mean, old, black teacher. Her name was Mrs. Lewis, and I thought she hated me, because

she stayed on me every day. But I think I can identify the moment that changed me. This may come off corny, but real.

One day I sat in her class and crossed my hands. I had decided to shut down. When the class went out for recess, she made me stay in with her. I figured she was going to send me home. Instead, when the kids were playing, she sat in the chair next to me and slapped me upside my head. As I got angry, she shared some things that would change my life.

She said,

“Remember them tears you’re fighting back boy, because that’s what the white man wants from you, and the way you acting you’re giving him what he wants. Now get up and come here!”

As I stood next to her she wrapped her arms around me while rubbing my head and told me,

“Martell your life is going to be very difficult son, because you **are** so bright. White people are going to try and kill your spirit. You see young man, if you learn to move in the shadows, while taking every piece of knowledge not meant for you, you’ll be in prime position. You will have to fight their children for schooling and jobs. I’m afraid for you, because you are a beautiful black prince, and they don’t want you to know your potential! So, you have a choice to make today, Martell. You’re either going to learn to beat them by learning everything you can! Or you’re going to let them beat you, as you accept defeat. You are not typical young man and I watch you every day. You learn faster than any student I’ve seen, and people follow you. I will not allow you to just be nothing! Be your best baby!” She said.

She took a deep breath, and rubbed my baby face with her hand, and continued,

"Martell, I promise to teach you son, and you can learn from them white teachers as well. You got to take it all! You come from kings, and that makes you a prince! Remember, it's never given to the black man, but God will make sure it'll always be there within your reach. One day you'll find out why you were chosen to be black and made to endure the toughest life on this planet!" She finished.

I was impressed that I'd almost remembered her words like she had just said them as I was sharing them with Mitchell.

I took a deep breath as I recalled her words. I continued my lecture to Mitchell.

"Mitchell my brother, I had a tough time seeing myself the way she saw me. But she put a cloud of pride in my heart that day, and I've never cried inward or outward since!

I also realized my worth that day, thanks to her and it's been that way since we talked. Man, my own mama didn't think I was worthy, but that lady did!"

I admitted humbly.

Mitchell lowered his head and replied,

"Speakin' of mom's, that's why I'm doin' this bid. I stabbed the cat that was beating on my mama. Truth is, I always stayed in trouble, because I didn't like me much. Maybe if I would've had somebody like yo' teacher, I coulda learned how ta read!"

Mitchell submitted.

"When I see words, they backwards chicken scratch!"

He continued.

"Aw you're dyslexic!"

I blurted.

"Huh, dis what?" He asked with major curiosity.

I peered deep into his eyes and suggested,

"Dig this man, there is learning disability out there that causes people to read and see words backwards! You're not dumb, or alone in that game! There are millions of the smartest people in the world with the same problem. It's just like you can't help it if you get sickle cell. You can't help dyslexia and they have ways to teach you with it. Just ask for help, because until you do, you're cheating your life, man!"

I admitted.

My words were as real as I could muster.

I was aware it was time to break up the heavy session. It was automatic for a man to want a friend to stay by his side in jail. I informed Mitchell; I was just passing through. He smiled, as he truly enjoyed his time to teach. I listened and learned about the prison system and the do's and don'ts of living in it.

He had been incarcerated most of his juvenile life and was going to be with relatives in the penitentiary as a grown up.

He informed me, that even at this level, booty bustin' happened regularly to the weakest. If I had just given in to Boo, he would've tried to have my ass, literally speaking.

He shared with me how he'd never had a man, but there was a dude waiting for him in Vacaville who looked just like a broad.

He was fine as new wine with little tits and a big ole ass. He was going to down for fifteen years with no wife, so he needed a substitute. He admitted that upon meeting me, he wished he would have learned how to read, because his man-girl loved to write him.

I didn't have time to react to the different atrocities, he expressed that occurred in the system. I just knew it wasn't for me, but I would always do whatever was necessary to protect the people in my life.

After listening to the story of why he was incarcerated, there was no doubt, I had to handle Doc. But unlike Mitchell, I had to use my head.

I already knew it, but this trip just helped me to see it more clearly. After explaining my mishap with the police to Mitchell, I was thankful for their making such a blunder. He suggested I would get kicked out as soon as I talked to the Public Pretender and we chuckled at his play on words.

By five a.m. that morning the guard called my name,

"Mackie, roll up! Your ugly ass is going to court!"

He yelled, after calling ten other names.

I was excited at the thought of getting out. I realized it had only been one night, but jail just wasn't for me.

Mitchell lifted his head from his bunk and whispered with a deep voice.

"Hey Mackie, when they spring you, don't forget what we talked about."

"I got you Mitchell!"

I responded.

As I hit the door, there was a voice in the void. I looked around and it appeared if all the boys were sleeping. The voice crept in the darkness.

"Punk ass, betta not come back! Because, I got something waitin' for yo' black ass, Nigga!"

The voice whispering through the morning was Boo, informing me it wasn't over between us!

"Next time you might be called Boo the bitch, cuz it looks like Mackie coulda had you suckin' his dick by the way he spanked that ass! I suggest you shut your mouth, fo' I put something it, Boo!"

Mitchell interrupted, while chuckling.

I had made a friend in case; I was coming back, and Boo was hushed.

The court holding cell was worse than the gym and I never thought that was possible. There were stainless steel benches for us to sit on and cement walls surrounding us. It was cold and drafty and revealed no signs of humanity.

There were blotches of dried blood along the benches and the walls. One could only surmise the stories behind the dated blood. I just looked at the stains and accepted them as testimony to my current situation.

Ten of us, stood waiting to be escorted through the steel door that led into the courtroom, with one Mexican cholo in the mix. The mere numbers gave mention to the cultural numbers behind bars. On the other side of the door, was a cage that separated the normal folks from the inmates, while still allowing interaction.

I was wondering where the public pretender was, that would be taking my case. Mitchell had informed me, of how it all was supposed to work. The public pretender was supposed to talk to me, submit my plea of not guilty and ask for my release with a promise to appear on a later date. The deputy finally called my name and I was a bit worried, as I stepped into the cage, without talking to any counsel whatsoever.

I stepped out of the first cage and a young white boy in a wrinkled grey suit accompanied by an ugly pink tie approached me. He was also wearing some worn black loafers that had worn heels. I thought to myself,

"He can't be making any scratch dressed like that, or is that typical young lawyer's regular gear?"

I scanned the courtroom looking for any signs of Nico.

I was surprised to see Teddy's mama sitting in the room next to Nico's large frame. The young lawyer explained to me, I would be getting out today, because it was little Teddy who told the school a lie.
He told them he was afraid for his life, because I'd broken into his house and threatened him. However, once his mother found out about his lie, she called the district attorney and informed them her son was bi-polar and delusional.
As he was explaining the deal to me, the Judge called my name.
When it was all said and done, the lady stood up for me and informed the judge that there were no charges to be filed and it was all a misunderstanding. The judge told me; I would be released. I had to go back to processing, in order to be released from custody.
I gave the lady and Nico the nod, as they hustled me back to lockup.
Court completed at 11:30 a.m. and was still in the system at 10:00 p.m. that night. The small comfort was the chance to put my clothes back on and drop the juvenile clothing into a basket for the trustees to wash.
It wasn't until midnight that I was able to hit the street and become a free man again.
I couldn't wait to get a Nation's burger and a milkshake.
Nico picked me up in his ride and had the burger and shake in hand.
I could have sworn he was becoming like a girlfriend, as his gold tooth reflected in the night.
He smiled with a strong appreciation for my presence, once he saw me walk out of the facility. He pulled a bottle of brandy out of his leather jacket.
"Here ya go Mack! A little erk and jerk to warm you up before you kill that burger!"

Nico shined.

Nico was twenty-three, therefore drinking to him was a daily treat. It was always strange to hear the giant talk with such softness. Drinking booze never fazed me, one way or the other, but I felt as if I could use a swig after what I'd been through.

"Teddy's mom is fine as fuck! And she like yo' young ass, brotha man! You must've hit it, cuz she came runnin' when I told her you was locked down!"

Nico smiled.

"Naw, I didn't mess with that lady, dude! She was just cool that's all!"

I replied.

"Bullshit! If you broke into my crib, I wouldn't be getting you out of jail! I would be puttin' a hurtin' on yo' ass, black! But I'm telling you, she gave me her number and told me to give it to you. She said call her, when you have time. That broad wants you to shag her mate!"

He teased with an Australian accent.

"Alright, slide me the number and I'll see what's she's about. But for right now, I got business to handle man!"

I said solemnly.

"Business, what's da lowdown, Black?"

Nico inquired.

I took a deep breath and shared.

"Dig this man! My mama told me why she ended in the hospital in a coma. The dude that's been whooping her ass since I was kid, gave her a hot shot of pure, uncut boy. All because she decided, she was ready to kick. He's had a pass for too long. It's time to exercise him out of the picture, man. I'm truly tired of this cat and it's time to lock him in!"

Nico's face contorted at my words. I had grown to notice, a stranger would have an easier time messing with Nico, than me. He never took it well whenever he found someone messing with me.

"How do you want him served up, ham or cheese?"

Nico angrily inquired.

I observed the larceny in his face. It was death, no doubt.

"No, he's not worth a jacket like that, Nick!"

I said quickly.

I took a long look out the window and continued.

"I been thinking about what to do since I was inside, and I have a plan."

I insisted.

Nico became upset and blasted,

"I know that you are your own man, Black Mack! But you five minutes safe from juvey! Let me get this while you sleep?"

Nico insisted.

"Don't vex big man! My plan is nothing nice! This cat's not going to say anything when it's all over. I refuse to fool myself however, I have to be knee deep in this one. He needs to see my face for almost killing my mama and for the years he's caused me and my sister hunger pains! If it wasn't for this dude, my mama might not be an addict.

I know my mama still cares for this dude. It's the black woman's code to stand in, so we won't kill him. But a debt is owed, and poetic justice is way past due!"

I confirmed.

My words were spoken with a firmness that meant business.

"I ain't never in my life heard a young Nig, I mean a young brotha talk like you, man!"

Nico admitted.

"But it's a welcome change for a brotha like me to listen too. Especially, since I have one brother that don't talk and another that's a straight booty poundin' faggot!

Hangin' with you, I'ma have to practice correcting my speech!" Nico continued seriously.

I interrupted,

"Speaking of language, did you bring my tapes? I could use some mental food, prior to putting this work in on, my mamas soon to be ex old man! Drop that "**Last Poets**" in, so that I can get fed, please!"

I insisted.

"Man, you about the only dude I know under twenty-five listening to them militant assed Poets and that black on black loving stuff! I gotta admit most young cats in the streets, messing over other black youngsters, while you still on a black power trip."

Nico swelled.

After placing the tape in the deck, he continued,

"You a strange dude, Martell Mackie! But I got you, so let's roll this junky to the grave!"

Nico exclaimed with conviction.

As I began to whisper the poetry on the tape, Nico inquired,

"So, what's the plan, my brother? What you wanna do with this little punk? You know, all we have to do is go and pick up Jon and he'll kill at your word! And that's for life Martell!"

Nico admitted without hesitation. And I knew he was one hundred percent real in his assessment.

I thought out loud,

“I only know of two things Doc’s afraid of and one of them is typical for a dope-fiend and that’s running out of dope. But I feel I would do better exploiting his other fear.

I can remember my mother playing a trick on him, with a toy one morning and dude pissed on his pants.”

I reinforced.

I thought about my mama in that hospital and wondered if Nico had it right and maybe I should take Doc out of the game altogether.

I considered all the things I’d done wrong in my lifetime thus far, and I couldn’t think of one cowardly act. Anything short of dealing with Doc face to face would unacceptable. But after tasting being locked up, my strike had to be calculating and effective. Most importantly, mama couldn’t know about it.

I couldn’t take the chance that she would turn on me.

If Doc was to end up dead, she would know I did it for sure.

I recalled my visit to juvey and made it a point to send some children books to my new acquaintance, Mitchell.

CHAPTER 7

Martell

Call the Doc

The sun was on the creep, playing peek-a-boo with the clouds, as we rounded my street. The trees were blowing slightly, and the beautiful colors of spring caught my attention.

I sat on the steps, outside of our place and enjoyed the air brushing against my beard. For a moment, I tried to imagine what it would feel like to actually live as a young man, my age. Those thoughts were so foreign to me, it made me feel strange.

My mind had taken my curiosity to another level. I was imagining what it would feel like to really know my father. Up to this point in my life, I had given him a pass. I could not remember a day missing the man. I chalked it up to not missing something you never had. I figured, the way mama felt about me, had to be his fault and I needed to figure it out.

I would consider him my enemy, thanks to his choosing to leave Tina. From what I gathered; he showed no remorse. Or did he have remorse and my twisted mother, was the reason he never contacted my baby sister? I was going to figure it all out, but for right now, I had to finish my revenge with Doc.

It was too late in the day to go to school, but school was what I needed to settle my nerves. My head was still a little cloudy, because I couldn't

find any logic that would sum up my life thus far.
There's something to be said about a trip to jail and the way it makes you wonder about your life. I decided to put all thoughts off until I finished that one piece of business.
I had a stack of files I called my personal, Co-intel-pro files. CO-IN-TEL-PRO, was a coined phrase, or acronym named after the infamous FBI files. These files were used to bury every good, black organization, that attempted to make a positive change in the black communities.
The Feds began a program, consisting of counter-intelligence profiles to infiltrate the Black Panthers and other, black organizations, legally. I stole the name, like they stole me.
My life was beginning to take on a theme. A phrase coined by a black, esteemed leader, Malcolm X.
Malcolm used a phrase that stayed with me for life. ("**By any means necessary.**")
The words were implanted in my brain and for some reason it meant family to me. These things led me to believe that no one should be able to mess with your family and get away with it. However, in order to stay clear of prison, I had to deal with Doc with a level head.
There was only one thing that would clear my mind and I knew I was due. One good hour of relaxation and I'd be good as new. I watched the brotha's drink, until they could barely walk. As well as blaze that Thai stick weed, until they could barely say their names. But there was only one fix I used to relax me, and I was sure there would never be a shortage of it.
I would be a pussyholic, until the day I died.
I had to release the pressures of all the ideas, exploding in my brain.

I entered the house and retrieved the phone number in my pocket, given to me by Nico. Nico was absolutely correct in reference to, the way little Teddy's mama looked at me. It was pure lust, and I needed a moment to take advantage of it.

It took all of ten minutes to break down her lies, that suggested she wasn't interested in a young buck, like me. She was afraid I couldn't keep up.

I could tell in her voice and the levels of the conversation that she was ready to see. My sexual confidence had never taken a hit or been in question before. Although, I had never been with a woman as old as she, I was looking forward to the experience.

She had to be thirty-five or so and I was beginning to wonder if smashing was going to be any different with her. Or, would it be the same as Benita. Would it rival, my sexual conquests up to now, I wondered?

I tended to fair very well sexually, due to my mentality, and everything else God blessed me with. At least that was one area I was thankful for, when it came to my biological daddy.

I treated sex like I did everything else. It was more of a mental competition, instead of a physical one and I refused to lose.

I always accepted my position and never made excuses for being what society labeled me, a male chauvinist pig. I was a bit and made no apologies for it.

I took a nice, long hot shower and slapped on some of the latest craze in the cologne, Giorgio.

I looked in the mirror and smiled at myself while boasting out loud, ***"This old chick has no idea what's headed her way! I don't know if it's a disease, or a blessing, but this dick has girth and stays hard for***

hours. And it really doesn't matter how many times I achieve, it'll stay that way, until I decide to let it down.

I'm like the Bunny commercial, I just keep going."

I said to myself.

I found myself thankful, that I wasn't hung up on orgasms. I truly just loved being in control of multiple vaginas, or at least fooling myself into thinking so. It was like a sport to me and I loved winning. I always worked hard to find the right combination for my sexual situation. I'd been in her house already and observed a good portion of what she had to offer, so I didn't expect any surprises.

It was morning and I could remember Uncle Jamie. I also recalled the times I ran with him, but I was different than he. I couldn't imagine paying for a piece of woman, even with a pocket full of money.

I rounded the corner in the duce and at the same time, I played sex games with the lady in my mind. I had to concentrate on the lower part of my extremities to keep my bulge from stiffening.

This was a little unusual for me. I'd always taken pride in my unique dick control. Maybe she was something special, I thought as I stood in front of her door.

I was tempted to just enter the premises, considering I had already broken into her residence. But instead, I chose to knock like normal people.

There was always something about sex that would cancel all that sweetness that everybody observed in me. She opened the door and immediately fell back into the house without waiting for me. She didn't utter a single word, but it was obvious she wanted me to follow her into the house. I could hear the song,

Maze, featuring Frankie Beverly's, LOOK AT CALIFORNIA.

It was mellowing in the background.

She had no idea of how soothing it was for me to be moved by the soulful groove of the music. My soul felt an automatic ease, at hearing some of my favorite music.

She was wearing a skintight, black, and white striped dress, that revealed every curve she had to offer. The cotton looked as if it were weaved while she was wearing it.

This time her hair was tied in a seductive bun, held together by bobby pins. Her hips protruded, just enough to reveal that she was a woman and not a girl.

I followed her through the house, eagerly. I felt hypnotized by the sway of her hips. She had the seduction side of things down to a tee. Her ass swung in a way that sent my passion to a boiling point. She knew exactly what she was doing, and she was my personal temptress at the moment.

As we walked through the hallway, I could smell an aroma soothing through the air. She had obviously cooked breakfast sometimes during the morning and it smelled as good, as if she had just finished it.

She led me directly to the kitchen without delay and I followed like a doe in the headlights. I was stunned by the sexiest stimuli ever placed in my face.

There was nothing impeding the lay of the dress on her body, which led me to believe, she had no panties on. She rubbed my neck and carefully sat me at the head of the table. She placed a plate of food in front of me. The food smelled great, but the aroma of her perfume seemed to surpass the need for food.

I held the fork in my hand and gazed at the same thighs revealed to me just a short time ago, under different circumstances. They were even more luscious this very moment, then they were that night.

I didn't know how she pulled off the limited light throughout the house, but I was than thankful for the trick. She opened the refrigerator and grabbed the orange juice. To this point, neither of us spent a moment saying a word. When she bent over to get my drink, the dress she was wearing lifted like there was a magic hand working for my personal interest.

As she bent over, a mound of dark, thickly formed hair, could be seen. It covered her large space completely, but not enough to prevent it from revealing a very profound box It was so appealing, I was certain it could hold its own, under any kind of pressure.

By now, I almost needed a straitjacket to hold my dick back! She turned to face me with the orange juice and my stick was beyond noticeable. She noticed the rise in my pants and I promptly dropped the fork on the table. The temptress held the glass in her hand and slowly fell to her knees, while holding the glass in her hand, like a magic trick.

She took a moment to look in my eyes, which I'm sure was dripping the vision of her fat pussy. She carefully held the glass in one hand and began rubbing the scale of my heated part with the other.

Once her hand began to trace the lines of my penis, I could see the smile of pleasure on her face. It was a smile I had seen before, that signified that I passed the dick size test. At this point, she made it obvious, she was in a hurry to release the beast and I was feeling the same way.

She quickly unzipped my pants right in time. If she hadn't, I was sure my button would have popped at any moment.

My dick jumped out of my pants, like a wolf trapped in a cage. She grabbed it with the speed of a running train, as if she was afraid my jimmy would run away.

Once it was in her hand she began to moan, I realized she was in love with the shaft of my man stick. It stood hard and firm, with a perfect helmet riding on top. Then she shined it up and down with the stroke of her hands.

Her lips began to moisten, and her groans became more evident. As the rubbing of her hands became more pleasurable, she stopped and took a sip of the orange juice. She held a nice sized swallow in her mouth and continued to slide her mouth over the shining head of my dick.

The working of her mouth concentrated on the helmet of my tool with an intense concentration. It was a natural reaction for me to place my hand on the bun that rested on top of her head. To my surprise, a mane of brown hair fell to the side of her face and it was real, instead of a wig.

I gave her head a slight push to gain some leverage and she choked immediately, which prodded me to back off. Once she choked, I knew she didn't have the Linda Lovelace deep-throat skills, but she was still licking me like a lollipop.

I soon caught myself and realized it was my turn to put work in. I guided my hand to the hairy mound that I remembered earlier in front of the ice box. I knew if I'd broke her back until she couldn't take no more, I wouldn't have to follow suit and eat nothing.

It had never failed me, so I was sure it would work now. While she was playing, I reached down to examine what I was in store for. I took my complete hand and began rubbing the lips of her fresh, slippery, diamond mound.

As soon as my hand touched the lips on her south box, she let out an “ooo” that would have awakened the sleeping neighbors.

Her legs began to tremble, and her pussy started gushing with moisture. I worked my two fingers around her lips as if it was a martini glass.

My grip was firm, but seductive. I was showing no doubt that I was the one in charge. I felt her complete body tremble vigorously. I slowly slid my index finger right through the center of her dripping V. I pushed until I was full fingers deep, within in her vaginal walls. It was like my fingers had a mind of their own, searching for the soft spot.

Within moments, I found the pearl that awaited me. It lay hot and sticky, in middle of her ocean crest. I began to tickle it, in order gauge whether she was controlled by the honey of the pearl, or was she a “G” spot woman?

I had already encountered girls that wouldn’t give in, until you found their spot called “G”. I didn’t have to wait long. I soon uncovered the correct rhythm and exercised the pearl, until she was frantic.

I had unlocked this combination, without using much concentration. She grabbed my shoulder with a firm grip and her body twisted from one side to another. Her breathing become deeply erratic, without notice, she was shaking and quaking in fits. I felt her blasting sex juice all over my hand.

I thought to myself, **one down and at least two more orgasms to go**!

I worked the pearl until I thought she was spent. I knew she was done, as she fell back to the floor, smooth out of breath.

There she was, on the floor, lying on her back, after an explosive orgasm. Her fat, juicy, wet, hairy mound lay there soaked, dripping and depleted. A grown-up twat with plenty of experience and I hadn’t come close to finishing her off yet.

I looked at her lovely legs just waiting, bent at the knees. Her split was

spread open, while covering the top of her Southern V.
It reached all the way to the back of her tantalizing ass.
I remember thinking,
"Damnit! There's no end to that juice box!"
I dropped my pants and pulled them off, with the quickness. I didn't dare hesitate and lose the moment.
I reached down and grabbed her hands, as she attempted to catch her breath.
She asked,
"What you doin' daddy?"
I felt a bit strange to hear such a sentiment coming from the lips of an older woman. However, it felt good to hear it and I felt like I deserved it.
I stood her up and wrapped my arms around her for a moment and danced with her for about four minutes.
I positioned the chair, so that it would serve as her final resting place, as my mind figured to beat the brakes off her melting vagina!
Once she caught her breath and realized what I was about to do it was too late for her to back out. My hand started running across and deep within her mound again.
From the rear I got a real idea of how big her box was, and it was amazing to me as it stood there pink and dripping. I wasn't wasting any time, because my dick would have jumped up and slapped me in the head if I was to make it wait any longer.
I grabbed a firm grasp of my pole, and aimed for the center of her space, knowing I couldn't go wrong. I reminded myself, this didn't have anything to do with love, so she wouldn't be like her son, and stalk me.
I had it in my mind to beat this beautiful piece into submission. Her age

was a personal test and would be my personal best. Once I found the tootsie roll middle, I played until I got more of her juices flowing. I expected to slide in, without much effort, but that wasn't happening. She was alive, and back with me finally as she surrendered, "Easy big daddy it's been awhile!"

I struggled getting my dick into her dripping pussy, and I couldn't believe a woman with kids could be so tight, even though her juice was plentiful.

"I see why they say it's like a rubber-band, damn! Maybe the doctor placed extra stitches in her vagina after each baby."

I thought to myself.

I mumbled sly complaints while working my way into her crevice. Within a few moments of wicked work, I got my head in, and probing. At every stroke the juice began to cover my shaft and I wanted to scream like a girl in ecstasy at every inch that entered her wonder box.

I started off slow, and in control, and her warm precious was grabbing me like it couldn't live without me. By now she was screaming, creaming, and cussing in an entirely different language of pleasure. I thought,

"*This pussy should've been gold plated!*"

I knew I had conquered a new victim, as her body began busting orgasms over, and over with pleasant moans throughout the house. I had worked her pussy for almost two hours until I knew she was raw, and couldn't stand any more dick, or orgasms.

I was lucky, because I didn't have to think of ugly girls, or baseball to hold my nut, like average men. I had exceptional dick control by now and wouldn't bust, until I was ready.

The muscles in her beautiful gleaming legs, began to stiffen as she finally gave it up said those familiar words,

"Baby, I can't take no more! You killin' me! I ain't got no more pussy juice left and my stuff can't handle no more! Ole greedy bastard!"

She pleasantly praised.

Her breathing was depleted and broken down for the count.

"Okay lady just hold out one minute! It's my turn to fill it up"

I passionately pleaded, in a whispered beg.

"What? You ain't done yet?"

She cried.

I refused to answer and changed my speed at that point. It was good timing, because the tape had played both sides and the music was over. My strokes had a personal mission now and I controlled myself into the long stroke. I purposely had to give her more stick now in order for me to blow. Once I started this process, I pressed her with more dick than she knew was there and she let out a loud,

"Oh my Lawd! Your young ass gonna kill me! You, big, dick, Motherfucka!"

She loudly moaned out of pleasure and pain at the same time. I concentrated intently on my explosion. Her words prompted me to lay the long stroke on her and I instinctively covered her mouth and told her she had to take the dick for one more minute.

I finally felt the pressure reach from my toes and move through my body. The thunder hit my head. The music was off, which made the thunderous claps on her ass sound off throughout the whole house. Her breasts were bouncing about violently, as if they were in concert and were having trouble staying in the bra that held them at bay.

If anyone had been in the house, they would have thought I was trying to kill this woman, rather than destroying her pussy.

As the orgasm hit her, it felt as if it filled her throat and I was now good to go. I was sure she felt all my cream inside her as she moaned so hard, that she couldn't talk, or utter a single word.

Although still erect, my tool and I were extremely happy, because it all came to a head. I would never underestimate the power of a seasoned, pink grenade again. I wanted to beat my chest and lock her sweet pussy in a room, just for my own personal use. Once I let her go, I realized I was holding her up and she fell to the floor, like she was dead.

I lay next to her for about ten minutes, in order to work through my high. I got up and tried to talk to this beauty, but she was in a daze and not to be stirred. I could only get one word from her, as I reached over and gave her a soft kiss on the forehead,

"What's your name?"

I whispered.

"Anita!"

She struggled.

I just grabbed a couple of bites of food and headed out the door, feeling like a new man.

I had a feeling; I wouldn't be soon forgotten. I also knew from that moment; I tagged that drained body with my message. It read, "**Martell was here**! **He killed this pussy**"

My mind and my pipes were clear and thinking clearly was no longer problematic for me.

Upon washing my now empowered body and peering into my conquest bathroom mirror, I searched my memory to replay my visit with my mama.

So much had happened in just a two-day period, it was surreal. I attempted to recount the conversation with mama. In truth it was like it had just occurred.

The cat was out of the bag and most of my questions had been answered, during my visit to the hospital. Although, mama and I shared a strained love, it was still love as far as I could tell. I was compelled to feel some warmth when it came to her.

Care was filling my temple and it was obvious to me that anger was definitely a big part of this new person I was becoming.

The story mama shared with me about Doc's antics resonated deep in my soul and was snatching my every thought like a thief in the night.

I attempted to make this a beautiful morning, but I envisioned choking the life out of Doc.

I disliked Doc with every inch of my person; therefore, he had to be dealt with quickly.

Falling short of murdering him, there was no doubt he needed to know how serious things were. He needed to know, if he refused to take heed to my message, I would have to pull his card for good.

There was an advantage to handling a dude like him. He had no grip on his life and his crew had become deeply immersed in using dope. They were all in the penitentiary, or dead.

Next, I spent time at the kitchen table making calls until my plan was in motion.

Thanks to Doc having a large ego, he had no idea what was in store for him. I'm sure he fooled himself into thinking he was in the clear after two years without a single mention in reference to his heartless attack against Simone.

This would be a vivid lesson learned from a man he once knew as a boy.

My heart was hardening, and that day I chose to make anyone pay that would cross me, or my loved ones.

I found it very satisfying to make my word stick to the wall, since it was the only thing I really owned.

I was forced to accept Doc not giving my warning any credence, as I warned him that his time was up for fucking up my mama's life.

I promised him and gave him my word, that I wasn't going to watch it anymore.

Long ago, I told him it was time to move on, because I was no longer respecting her wishes to keep the gloves off him.

He didn't believe me when I informed him that mama's arm no longer reached far enough to protect him, from her young foolish, jive turkey son.

I remember it all like it was yesterday, although it had been five years since the conversation. I clearly remember him laughing like I was playing. It was obvious time hadn't been good to the pretty boy and it showed on his now blotchy skin and unnaturally, pocked face.

According to the streets, he'd been trying to stay in the game by retrieving the same three suits out of the cleaners and wearing them thin. His alligator shoes were wearing on the side of the heels and beginning to look like frog-skin. His face had dark spots from dried sores he'd picked, until they bled. He was running simple cons like stealing from Mervyn's and Newberry's and returning the goods. He, however still had a little zip in his game and retained the ability to con women.

I really hoped my mama just happened to be one of the women in his past, with no hopes of a future connection.

The trap was set, and I had one of my trusted contacts tell him that mama was back from the dead and headed to bingo.

I had to see if he was going to reclaim his money source.

Without trepidation, he was briskly moving to get Simone. Thanks to my bourgeoning reputation as a hustler, I was setting an example by my willingness to put work in, on the streets.

I enjoyed being the chameleon for those who were unaware of my propensity to be a gangster. To the untrained eye, I was a pawn. When in truth, I was truly the lead man, pulling the strings in my posse. I was blessed with the ability to get things done in the background, until I was right in your face with it.

Midnight approached, and it was time to put on my black clothes, and head into Richmond.

The Bay was quiet along the shores, due to it being a weeknight. Things were pretty much business as usual during the week. Highway seventeen was going through a construction change, which made driving the highway difficult. I loved running across the Cypress Overpass, because the duce would rise and fall on the stretch of freeway like on waves in the ocean. The highway was built with breakaway sections that swayed, until the day it was buried in a Bay area centered earthquake.

I dared to look over to the hills, in order to regain the memory of when we lived there, at least according to mama.

As I headed into Richmond, I was reminded of the AC transit bus days. Those days I rode the big rims of the seventy-two P, into Richmond from Oakland. If you didn't hit Richmond in time, you came up short trying to go to North Richmond. Nothing public was willing to head into North

Richmond after dark, including the bus lines.
There wasn't a bus driver in the world that would be caught dead driving a bus into North Richmond after hours. It would mean taking a chance with your life! But that was part of the legacy of my extended hood.
I had things to do in the hood and I needed the flavor of desperation that came with it.
I hit Cutting Boulevard and took in the night air, along with the struggle into my nostrils. I felt the pain of the streets and knew I was home.
The vampire I observed running dope, as well as the two freshly painted Cadillac's let me know I could breathe. I turned left on Harbor Way and headed towards North. There was work being put in on every street north had to offer and life was living and breathing money.
I pulled up on West Ruby and blew at the door with the only porch light blazing through the darkness.
Dr. Strangelove got in the car with a smile on his face. He was as skinny as a rail and his smile revealed the three teeth he had left in the front of his mouth.
He was one of the very few white boys in the projects that lived to tell about it. His ass had been whooped so many times in the hood, that at an early age he started practicing black magic.
He would read palms and give out spiritual advice in the hood. Strange also had one of the best Mexican connections for the Thai stick weed everyone wanted.
I was aware of him making a nice piece of money selling weed, but you would have never known it, due to his constant spending on ghetto pussy.
Oddly enough, Strangelove enjoyed my personality, because we could

talk about political issues and psychology. The hood seemed to be short on intellectuals for conversation, because it was replaced by hustlers. He also appreciated my innate ability to transform under any situation. Whenever we were together, I observed him marveling at the fact that I had a spiritual center, even though I continued to remind him I didn't play in the black magic realm. He also could not believe my mind was so deep at such a young age.

I pushed the button to the trunk, and he placed the burlap sack inside.

"What's up Cool?"

He asked.

"Strangelove, how's tricks my brotha?"

I chuckled.

"Everything is solid, just been diggin' this ghetto gold, baby! I've been getting polished on the regular from the big booty Judy's!" He admitted.

He began to observe the plush interior of my car and continued,

"It took me a couple of fishing trips and dealing with a down low witchdoctor or two, but I got everything you asked for, Black.

I gotta tell you bleed; your boy came through like a gangbuster, taking no shit and took care of everything else! And black, you coulda warned me, you were sending a fuckin' monster! That's one big assed, soul brother! Are you sure you can control him? Cuz, he looks like a fuckin' cannibal to me bro! Like he wouldn't mind eatin' an arm, or leg with dinner, or some shit"

He smiled.

"Nico is a true brotha!"

I replied.

Dr. Strangelove's tone changed, as if someone tapped him on the shoulder.

He shared,

"These streets are hot too! If you do any shootin' out here, the pigs will roll hard! You know they got it in for us Negroes!"

"Hell Strange, why do you think I picked you up? I need you to pretend to be white and deal with your brethren, tonight!"

I said laughingly.

He quickly replied,

"Awe that's fucked up, Black! You know I was born with a pork chop in one hand and a bottle of thunderbird, with a ripple chaser in the other! Ain't nuthin' white about me, but my nuts!"

He jeered.

"It's important that we stick to the game-plan Doc, with no spells, or black magic, you dig?"

I demanded.

"Come on Mack, I know how you is 'bout yo' bizness! I den left all my potions at da house, daddy-o! But you know, I got some shit from New Orleans's guaranteed to make this dude's dick fall off, right?"

"Naw Strange, dis Motherfucka already gonna wish he didn't know me when I'm through! But straight ahead, here's yo scratch!"

I ventured, while handing him a small bundle of money.

A patrol unit rolled past us usual but paid no attention to us. I found myself not concerned with them stopping us. I had my stock wheels on my duce. Along with a refusal to paint the duce a bright color helped to avoid some cops. It suggested me a sports fan, instead of a money man. Police in the inner cities of America would always use a black a man's ride to help determine his ghetto standing.

Black men had the tendency to buy the most expensive rides without owning a house.

A black man rolling the streets anywhere in California with candy paint, rims and a blasting stereo with no job would be an automatic follow and stop. And rarely did the police leave empty handed. This was simple mathematics. Even if the brotha didn't have warrants, there was a seventy percent chance he didn't have a license and or insurance.

This would allow cops to search your car, without any other reason. Therefore, most black men pulled over, would translate into results at least most of the time. And the other small percentages of black men drove normal cars, because they usually had normal jobs.

Between gas, car payments and insurance, one couldn't afford gold spokes and three stage, candy paint.

My car represented the Oakland Raiders, which made it unique, but not flashy.

The Brother's Johnson*, *Get tha Funk out of my Face, was streaming from my tape deck, as we crossed the train tracks into North Richmond. The difference in the maintenance of the town was easy for the eyes to observe. It appeared there was no budget in the books to keep North Richmond up with the times. The small stores appeared to be dead, on the Main Street. They were old and tattered.

North Richmond's biggest landmark stood erect to let everyone know they were in the hell zone.

The pink color of the North Richmond Baptist Church jumped out at anyone passing it.

It was one those landmarks that left its mark in your brain. It also served as a beacon, for the drunks that stumbled around the area. They appeared to share the same routine every day of their existence.

North wasn't the place for newcomers, due to it having one of the highest murder rates per square mile, in the United States. However, in my mind, the struggles were like wine to a wino. It gave us all a reason to fight for life every day. Whether your reason was alcohol, or murder, death was always a possibility.

Alamo Street became interesting, once you passed the big, pink church. The street was a throwback from the past, because black folks owned their homes. These same blacks knew the game and played house with the white men running things, until they obtained their own homes and thus independence. They were unlike the new hordes of blacks, who suggested not working for the white man, but willing to go to his prisons and slave for pennies.

We found ourselves stopping in front of a small, puke purple, house with sheets over the windows. I parked my car and blinked my lights twice in the darkness and within minutes, the silhouette of two figures quickly worked their way to the back seat of my car.

The door closed and, in my vision, it had become obvious that one of the men had a pillowcase over his head. I also noticed his hands were bound, as Jon Jon had a stronghold on his arm.

I slowly pulled away from the curb, so not to get any attention from anyone sneaking in from the clubs. Jon Jon tapped me on the shoulder with a devious smile on his face.

I made a slight noise and pounded my chest to show my approval of his work. Strangelove sat quietly next to me, without saying a word. The one understanding I made clear with everyone doing dirt with me, was the less said on any caper, the better.

I had a true belief, that a good portion of the brotha's locked up, were in that position, because they just talked too damned much.

Jon Jon tapped my other shoulder again and I looked back to gauge his face and I knew exactly what he wanted. His face prompted me to ask nicely,

"Twisty, you don't know me, but if you do as I say, you'll live through the night. Now, lay down in the seat and my brother back there won't pistol whip you! You got my word on that!

I know you're gagged, so I'm gonna ask you to lie down in the seat, dig?"

Twisty dropped in the seat, as quiet as a church mouse.

We made the careful drive out of north, doing the speed limit with Jon Jon sitting in the back seat and Twisty lying, beside him. We were not as big a target, with a black man and a white man rolling easy.

Over the tracks, the duce bounced with the full load in the car and we made the right turn out of north Richmond. There was always a feeling that I shouldn't be driving out. I always felt like I should be staying to help my people rise from poverty, whenever I drove out of North.

Cutting boulevard, was still alive this time of morning, as the heads were running around trying to find the scratch for their morning hits and the drunks were doing their normal peek a boo for a drink. I made the block at the Fullerton Brothers Funeral Home.

I was waiting for Roscoe to give me the signal, that everything was in place. Roscoe was a strange cat, willing to do anything for a dollar. Although he was a hustler, I found him to be extremely loyal and true. He was put in jail on three occasions. All for being involved in some sick stuff, but never snitched on his trap partners, even with the D.A. offering

him amnesty.
He looked like a mad man, because he wore a large afro and a heavy, scraggly beard, with crossed eyes. He thought he was Sugarfoot, lead singer from the singing group, **The Ohio Players** and always walked around humming, ***Skin-tight***, recorded by the same group. I guess the brotha's brain was running amuck from working with dead people every day.
He oversaw filling deceased bodies, with formaldehyde.
I couldn't tell if it was the chemicals, or the dead people that made him crazy, but tonight it didn't matter.
I needed him in order to get my job done and I was taking no shorts.
He stood outside the front door, with a piece of fried chicken hanging out his mouth, as if it were a cigar.
I pulled into the private parking lot of the funeral home and he slammed the gate closed behind me. As we pulled in, I observed Nico standing at the back door with a large smile on his face.
I shook my head in appreciation, being glad to see him, as I turned the key and shut the motor down on the duce.
Strangelove stepped out of the car and I pushed the yellow button inside the glove box to release the trunk. Jon Jon snatched the captive like he hated him and pulled him behind me.
Once I reached the door, Nico shook my hand affectionately. He held it tight. It felt like, he wanted to hold me hostage and revealed,
"Mack, your boy is fuckin' crazy as hell, man! I thought he was gonna run out of chicken and start eating one of the dead folk! I'm glad to see yo' ass, brotha!"
"Yeah, he's a different kind of dude, but he's a warrior and he's true!"

I responded.

"Is everythang cool, Superfly?"

I continued.

"Did you say, Thang? Did I hear you say Superfly?"

Nico mused.

"Oh yeah we gonna have fun! You got Ebonics going on tonight! I'm gonna have a wonderful night! And yes, my brotha, the casket is on the rollers and in the Hearse. I'll get it when you're ready. And can I say, I'm proud to work with you, black! 'Cause this shit is fuckin' brilliant!"

Nico continued, while pointing both his hands toward the sky like pulling triggers.

We walked through the back of the funeral home as a team, with my plan on everybody's mind.

There were two bodies prepped in the back of the funeral home, as Roscoe grabbed himself another piece of chicken. Jon Jon looked at him in disgust and Roscoe scoured,

"What? You ain't neva been ta Roscoe's chicken and waffles in Los Angeles? Them's my folks! I gave 'em the idea!"

The funeral home maintained a strange odor, as we entered. However, it was spotless. Roscoe turned on a tape of pre-recorded organ music and motioned for Nico and Strangelove to move forward with the casket. They began pushing it forward.

It was settled on a rolling cart, like a real funeral. All of the men had put on black blazers and white gloves, with black ski masks over their faces. Jon Jon sat down with our captive and yanked the hood off of his head and his gag as well.

The removal of his hood revealed a pink Mohawk and four earrings on each one of his ear lobes. His skinny face showed signs of running mascara and eyeliner, as he screamed like a woman.

"Ah! What y'all want from me? Please! I'll do whatever y'all want! A bitch just ain't ready to die! He told me he was eighteen, I swear he did!" Twisty cried.

I had to hold in a laugh, as I gurgled,

"Miss Twisty, this is a funeral home! That means it's soundproof, so please stop screaming! All you gonna do is piss me off!"

He took a deep breath and responded,

"Please Mr. Fine ass, you promised! Just tell a bitch, what y'all want! Cause, I got the best head and jailhouse pussy in the Rich! I just want to live!"

He pleaded.

I looked at him, while holding in a hearty laugh and suggested, "Booty is not gonna help you tonight! Like I promised, you'll be alright gurrrl, if you just get a hold of yourself and sit down, dig?"

Twisty took a deep breath and replied with fear.

"Okay Mr. Fine ass, but remember I'll do anything you want, if y'all don't hurt a bitch!"

"Twisty, you gotta be cool, because my boy, over there don't like little, frail bitches like you! So, it's best for you to sit da fuck down and play your role."

I said using my man-sized voice.

I let the organ music play for a while, before I decided to open the casket in front of me.

I looked at it with a deep appreciation and pleasure for what I had to do, along with its beauty. I had a thing for beautifully finished wood, since I was a little boy.

I slowly opened the casket, with as much mystery as I could. There, bound, gagged and struggling for air, was Doc. His perm was all over his head and his face was drenched with sweat. His nose was running from an obvious lack of dope and he was sick. His lips were white, and tears were streaming from each side of his face. His skin was very dark and blotchy.

I searched internally but couldn't find any compassion in my heart for the man. The surprise in his face, was worth a million photos, as he looked at me.

I looked over at Twisty with a devious smile and suggested,

"Now Twisty! Now you can scream!"

Jon Jon released his arm and Twisty ran over to the casket as if he'd been bolted from a cannon and yelled,

"Daddy! Oh no daddy, what you do dis time?"

Tears began to flow heavily from his eyes, as they dropped on his daddy inside the casket. Jon Jon snatched Twisty's arm and pulled him away from the casket.

Nico looked on laughing and holding his gut. He lauded,

"This is fuckin' lovely! Just fuckin' lovely!"

I looked at Doc, lying in the casket and asked,

"Hey Doc! You doin' a'ight in that box, cool breeze?"

I smiled and took a deep breath. I continued,

"I must say, you don't look very comfortable!

My buddy over there was nice enough to drill a couple of holes in it, so you could breathe! At least, until I finish talking. Now, you should be taking real short breaths, in order to spare the air! Don't want you to die,

without paying your last wishes to your daughter! Oh, I mean son!"
I surrendered.
"You know what, Doc, or whatever yo' real name is? This is beyond being your fault! I did warn you! I can remember a day you were in the room beating on my, one-hundred-pound mama. I was in the room watchin' Popeye. He said to Bluto, ***enough is enough and I can't stands no more***!
I stood there looking at you, while holding a hatchet in my hand! All I asked you to do was get off of my mama and you knocked me down to the floor, like a man with no heart! I was simply a little boy, protecting his mama!
Now that the tide has turned and your bitch assed boy, is over there watching you be the victim. Wow! It feels very different huh? But I'm doin' the beatin' this time. Talk about poetic justice, this shit crazy huh?"
I smiled.
"I realize in all fairness; you should be able to share your feelings. Tell you what; I want to hear what you have to say, because honestly man, you look like shit!"
I teased.
I gave Jon Jon, the nod to release Twisty's arm and he ran toward his daddy, falling all over the casket in hysterics. I couldn't stand to look at Doc, as I gestured to Twisty,
"Here, wipe his face before you remove his gag! It looks all kind of nasty in there!"
He took the handkerchief from my hand and with uncontrollable tears; he began wiping his daddy's face and nose. Twisty's face reflected laces of shame, as well as caution. I knew he was afraid of his daddy's words,

once the gag was removed. "MOTHAFUCKA! YOU YOUNG, SNOTTY NOSED BASTARD! YOU DON'T KNOW WHO YOU FUCKIN' WIT! YOU BETTA GET ME OUTTA THIS FUCKING DEATH BOX, NIGGA!"

Doc yelled in complete anger.

I motioned for Jon Jon to grab Twisty again. Without needing much effort, I felt the hate rise to my eyelids, as I blasted at doc with pure emotion.

"IF YOU UTTER ONE MORE WORD, YOUR BITCH ASSED SON OVER THERE IS GONNA BE SHITTIN' POCKETS OF BLOOD! YOU SIMPLE MINDED SON A BITCH!"

After a couple of deep breaths, I regained my composure and continued. "Fuck Doc! You're so stupid and unbelievably predictable! The thing is, I've been around you long enough to know what you'd say! The bad thing is your dope-fiend ass, still said it! My man is over there is one half inch from sending your son to faggot-land forever and you're still talking shit!

Despite the fact you're dead wrong! My mama told me you tried to kill her, just because she wanted to clean up. You gonna fuck around and have me kill you, over your lack of personality.

Damn Doc, you called me a Nigga! I hate that word about as much as I hate you! It's never used in my vocabulary, but neither are the other words I'm using now. Words like **fuck**!

You put me in the mind of "**THE LAST POETS!**" They did a poem about brotha's like you. It was entitled,

Die Nigga! That's what I think of you Doc."

I slammed.

Slobber bubbled and formed around his mouth and he shouted.
"FUCK YOU MARTELL! I KNOCKED YOU DOWN WHEN YOU WAS A LITTLE, PUNK ASSED BOY, AND I'LL GET YOU AGAIN! YOU AIN'T GONNA GET AWAY WITH THIS!"
His words spewed with anger and as his nose began to run again. I took a deep breath and replaced his gag, as he jerked his head from side to side in the casket. I bitch slapped him with a thud, until the pain of the slap kept him momentarily dazed,
as I admitted.
"Well, like I said, you are way too predictable, but you haven't learned who I am just yet! However, I have a feeling by the end of the night you will. I gave Jon Jon the nod and within seconds he was standing in front of the casket, holding a pistol, pointed at Twisty's head.
"Oh, baby Jesus, Holy God please! Please Mr. Fine ass, you promised!" Twisty cried in total fear.
Jon Jon clicked the gun one time and I could see Doc was twisting in the casket with, uncontrollable rage and fear. I looked at Doc and recalled,
"Oh yeah, I did promise not to kill you today, didn't I?"
I looked in the face of an impatient Jon Jon, and ordered,
"Sit the gay boy down and let him catch his breath!"
I then turned my gaze back to the casket.
"Okay, Doctor dope-fiend, it seems as if we are at an impasse, but somehow, I figured we would be. Therefore, I prepared for it."
I admitted.
I pointed to Strangelove and motioned for him to bring me the burlap sack, which was resting on the ground next to him. At this point, it was slightly moving in a creepy kind of way. Strange approached the casket,

with the sack in his hand and I instructed him to lift it toward the casket. I knew Doc would leap out the casket to his death, if he could, due to his thorough fear of snakes. He didn't prove me wrong.

Strangelove opened the bag and dangled a snake above the casket. Doc's eyes grew three inches, as he screamed to the top of his lung. As he screamed, the sound was muffled by the gag. But his energy level was raised beyond belief. We watched him squirm and vibrate himself into a frenzy.

"That my good brotha is, a Coach whip snake and it moves so fast. Oh boy and his venom is oooh! Well I better let that go for now!"

I shuttered.

Strangelove let the snake wiggle and squirm, before dropping it into the casket.

Upon seeing the snakes, Twisty began to scream at the top of his lungs.

Roscoe laughed until he began to grab his side from laughing pains.

Strangelove slowly lifted another snake and showed it to Doc.

The second snake was wiggling, while the first snake was cruising somewhere in the casket with Doc. Doc appeared to be in shock and tears were rolling off his eyes like a river.

Strangelove was enjoying himself so much, that he lifted the second snake without my ordering it. This snake was even too much for me to look at.

"Look at that one Doc! His colors are sure vivid, with all that yellow and orange and oooh what's that smell he's giving off? Is that some type of poisonous venom or something?"

I mused, as Strange dropped it into the casket.

He quickly dug into his bag again and pulled out a cold looking black snake, with a menacing head and a death stare. His two fangs were large and protruding, as Strange held it up over the casket. The snake was six-foot-long as my buddy languished with it in both hands it was a scary sight.

I tried to muster some compassion for Doc, because I knew he was so close to a heart attack. Strangely enough, my heart couldn't find any.

I insisted.

"Now Doc, the first two snakes represent a snake for the two years that my mama was in a coma."

I could see him squirming and losing his mind, but the heavy glossed casket was so heavy that it barely moved. His mind was gone now as I fought for his attention.

"Be still while I'm talking to you bitch!"

I yelled.

"Oh yeah, you can't huh? You got snakes about to creep into the crevice of your ass! I guess it's kind of a fucked-up feeling to have someone about to kill you, huh! I guess you are wondering about this third, mean, black Motherfucka right here, huh?

Well this one's for all the nights you made my little sister sad. You remember Tina don't you, Doc? Well, this black snake is called a racer. I call it an eraser, cuz it's gonna erase yo' ass from my family forever!"

I scolded.

Strangelove grew tired of holding the snake and admitted,

"Shit, I can't hold him no more Mack!" The snake dived into the casket. The sound of Doc losing his bowels could be heard through the funeral home, thanks to the organ music falling silent. I was becoming leery of Doc having a heart attack, but I was going to stay true to the task. The racer dominated the other snakes and rolled across Docs face and head, until his eyes began to run amuck and appear crazy. Doc began foaming at the mouth and passed out. Nico held his nose with his hand and admitted,

"Now, that's just foul! I could do without the smell, Mack!" Strangelove grabbed the snakes out of the soiled coffin one at a time and stuffed them back into the sack.

I sat next to a slobbering, crying Twisty, as he asked,

"Why did you kill my daddy? God don't like ugly and two wrongs won't make it right!"

I looked at him empathetically for a moment and then reminded myself of my mama's pain, as I slammed,

"Stop cryin' punk ass! Your dope-fiend assed daddy ain't dead! He's just passed out, like the bitch he is! But always remember, he could be dead. Now it's your turn to do your part in this. You gotta let yo' daddy know, if I see him near my mama, or my family again, I'm going to kill him! Tell him, even if he sees my mama out, he'd better act like he doesn't know her. Lastly, If I go to jail for this party, the men in this room is gonna fuck both y'all up and that's a promise! Y'all got a pass this time! But you only get one!"

I relayed, with obvious disgust.

Twisty wiped the tears from his eyes and replied with passion and fear at the same time.

"I understand and I know you coulda kilt me and him. I promise you'll never see us again. Although, I don't like what happened, a bitch understands why it happened. Thank you, Mr. fine ass! I thank you for not killing my daddy! I know he can be a bastard sometimes, but all the

papa I got!"
I brushed my shoulder and replied.
"The only thing worse than not having a daddy, is having a bad one! And girl you have got a bad one!"
He looked at the ground and muffled,
"Well, he talked about yo mama a lot, so I know he cared about her. He just doesn't know how to show people love. I know he did y'all wrong and I'm sorry!"
I grabbed Twisty by his shirt and fumed,
"I never said I wouldn't kill him. I just said I wouldn't do it now! Get him away from me, while I'm in a good mood."

CHAPTER 8

STREET ED 101

I opened the window and allowed the sun to bless my face, while finishing the last of the French toast. Tina was late coming down for the awesome breakfast that I had prepared and that wasn't like her. She'd never slept through my tasty, French toast and even more importantly, she was never late for school on her own accord before.

I reflected on my night and figured she'd better get her tail downstairs, because I was sleepy as hell. I couldn't help but laugh, recalling the look on Doc's face, once he'd seen the snakes being placed in his casket. I don't think it would've made a difference had I told him the truth. The snakes weren't poisonous and just happen to be Strangelove's personal pets. I went to the stairs and made the call for Tina to come down for breakfast. After ten minutes Veronica began to walk down while rubbing her eyes.

It was a task to look away from her, I was blessed as she was changing right before my eyes.

Her acne seemed to disappear overnight, and her sheer nightgown revealed nothing but body. I tilted my head sideways and noticed the firm, beautiful breasts that bounced, as she walked down the stairs. The shapely V between her legs had slight laces of fine hair and much to my surprise Veronica appeared in my eyes for the first time, as a sexy woman. A woman with a body shaped by the heavens and I was truly amazed.

I had to concentrate to remove my lust and asked,

"Hey gurl, where's your playmate? It's time for her to eat breakfast and take her lawyer brain to school. As Veronica reached the bottom of the stairs, she wrapped her arms around me and began to kiss me on my neck. Before I could respond, she had one of her legs wrapped around me and the space between her legs lay pressed against me tightly. I felt ashamed, as my dick began to rise, without my consent and I commanded it to relax.

"Come on gurl, stop playing and go get knucklehead from upstairs! Tell her to hurry! I have other things to do, today!"

I surrendered, while peeling her away from my semi hardened tool.

Veronica grinned and admitted,

"I felt your shit, Martell, you know that's mine, right? If you don't know by now, one day you will!"

She demanded.

She was insistent, as she began grabbing my ass.

"What makes you think all that? You too ugly for me. Now where's your play sister?"

I asked light heartedly.

Veronica rubbed my head and replied,

"I thought you knew! I took her to the hospital earlier, because she wanted to see your moms. As a matter of fact, she's been acting a little strange since you went to jail, baby."

I gently grabbed her soft hands from my head and asked,

"What do you mean a little strange?"

"I don't know Mack, it's like she's depressed about something. I tried to put my finger on it and get her to talk about it, but she wouldn't!"

Veronica admitted, with concern.

"Okay I'll head to the hospital and figure it out!"

I said, while sliding out of her grasp. I tried to walk into the kitchen, but my mind wouldn't allow me to forget what she was wearing. I had to sneak another peek, as I looked back and asked,

"You need anything?"

"Just some of that lovin' that you keep away from me, daddy! I felt what you packin' down there, and oooh, I want what's mine!"

She insisted jokingly.

"Man, stop playing, with me! Just lock up on your way out. You got your key, right"

I asked, while dodging cupid's arrow.

"Hey Martell, look at this!"

Veronica said, while lifting her gown and revealing a perfectly mounted, luscious, and hairy pussy. There it was the perfect diamond placed directly above her vagina. Behind what laid pretty like baby hair, was a heart shaped birthmark. It was breathtaking and her young body was flawless, without a defect. This left me momentarily dazed. She had no idea how much will power it took to keep my dick in my pants, even though, the passion I was feeling was a bit weird. If she was a regular chick, I would have hit that ass with reckless abandon. But I had to get away.

I couldn't imagine what could be bothering Tina unless mama started some mess. But Tina was the only thing mama cared about in this world, so it couldn't be that.

By the time I reached the hospital, a million things were running through my mind. I was sure none of them touched on what was itching at Tina and I was correct in my thoughts.

I stopped at the gift shop and purchased mama some flowers and a Jet magazine. The little donkey, looking chick, beyond the counter was beginning to feel comfortable flirting with me. I didn't have the heart to tell her, that it was against my rules to feed the animals; therefore, we would never make it out to dinner like she wanted.

As I arrived at mama's door, I could hear someone heaving some serious vomit and I hoped it wasn't Tina. When I opened the door, Tina was standing next to mama, holding her hand, while mama vomited in a plastic container. Tina's face was red, and her eyes were swollen. I knew the look in her face. It was a reflection of her having a real crying spell.

It wasn't something she did often, but whenever Tina did cry, I always made it my personal challenge to find out why and figure a way to help.

I walked into the hospital room and sat the magazine down while exchanging the wilted flowers for the new ones.

“What’s going on ladies?”

I enquired, with a fake smile.

“Mama looks like she doesn’t like that yellow blouse you are blinding her with today, Tina!”

I smiled in jest, to break the sadness.

“What’s up big brother? How’d you know I was here?”

Tina asked.

“Come on Sis, who else but rash face, is going to tell me where you’d be?”

I laughed.

“Ooh, that’s not right Martell! That girl would die for you and you talk about Veronica like that! You’re just not right for that!”

Tina giggled.

“Do you even have anything left to throw up mama?”

I asked.

“You try being dead for two years and wake up to what seems like hundreds of different medicines boy and see how you feel!”

Mama revealed sarcastically.

She continued,

“So, what’s up Miss Tina, you want to share with your big brotha the big secret? The secret to why you’ve been crying this morning? And tell the truth with no B.S.!”

Mama demanded.

After a few moments' mama looked at me and frowned,

"So, the Doctor told her I may be in here for a month or two, because I need to get therapy and learn to use my motor skills again. That includes learning how to walk right all over again. Wait until I see that Doc, I got something for that bastard!"

Mama exploded.

Mama did something a little weird at that point. She began to bite her lip until there were traces of blood, as she cut her eyes to Tina. She wiped her face and suggested,

"Anyway, this little heffa over here feigning for that no-good daddy of y'alls! She's thinking, she's missing something in life by not having his no-good ass around!"

Her sarcasm filled the room and Tina responded.

"That's not true mother! I just wonder why he doesn't love us. I can't see a man leaving his only son and daughter! When Tell went to jail, I just wished I had our daddy to talk too, or even take me to see Martell in that awful place."

Tina cried.

Tears began to roll down her red face again. Mama adjusted her gaze to me and slammed.

"They finally caught you in some of your shit, huh, Mr. no Good? Who bailed your triflin' ass out of jail?"

I had a difficult time accepting her words, which made scoff,

"Not you! Because you were in this fabulous hotel, due to good habits huh, mother?"

"Please! You two stop it, please!"

Tina seethed,

"I can't handle it today! Please! Just act like your mother and son just for a little while!"

Tina begged.

I could see the anguish in her face, and it made me feel a bit guilty.

I rubbed my little sister gently on her head and pointed out.

"Alight sis! I'm 'bout to blow this pop stand anyway!"

After looking at the contempt in mama's face, I wanted to leave. I turned to my suffering, little sister,

"Tina, I'll send Veronica to get you."

I walked toward the door and without looking back at Simone, I surrendered,

"Umm, I hope you feel better and get past that vomiting, mother. I'll come back a little later to check on you."

She twisted her nose upward,

"You just keep in mind, I won't come see a fuckin' jailbird in no damned cell, boy! And I'm not playing!"

I closed the door behind me and headed to my car, with my mind stuck on what to do about Tina's dilemma.

I knew the only saving grace, to not having a daddy at home, was having a bad one. It was confirmed to me through the eyes of Twisty as he looked upon his pathetic daddy.

He loved him without any doubt, but I wondered if his life would have been more worthwhile, without the drag of a loser like Doc as his daddy.

I couldn't ever remember a day; I felt a need for my worthless daddy. But Tina was different than I. There were lots of days I stood outside her room and listened to her cry, while I pretended, I had no idea as to why she was crying. In truth I knew why and hoped the longing for him would go away never to return.

The shame was, mama never found it within the confines of her heart to show Tina one single photo of him, therefore we didn't even know what he looked like. All we knew was, what mama often said,

"Your daddy ain't shit, so don't ask about him! As far as life goes, I'm y'alls mama and your daddy. Hell, if you need more than that, we can say he died in Vietnam!"

These words were like a speech.

As I rounded the block, there was Benita sitting on the porch. She attempted to hold back her smile, as she observed the duce making the corner, but her happiness was reflected in her pretty, pink lips.

As I parked, I remembered I hadn't serviced her lately and she was due for a sexual tune-up.

I hadn't done much hustling and needed some scratch for my pocket, which made her visit a benefit to the both of us.

"I was just about to leave!"

Benita teased.

I grabbed her and began to fondle her from every angle within my grasp, while standing on the porch.

Knowing her shyness, I exploited it to the fullest and she enjoyed coming out of the bag that had been her life. Her very controlled life and environment was sexually manipulated by me and my ability to push her buttons.

Once I finally opened the door, she was hot, wet and dripping with desire. I had Tina and her issues on my mind, but those things didn't stand in the way of my completely servicing Benita.

After she achieved her normal amount of multiple orgasms, I had to fight to keep her from falling asleep. I lost the battle and fell asleep alongside of her. We both slept off the sexual high which made me come to grips with how tired I was.

As we lay, I felt a presence in the room with us and was awakened by Veronica standing over me as we slept. I immediately rose from the bed at the surprise of her looking down at me with a smile glowing from her face. I thought, I must have been dreaming, but I soon found I wasn't.

"What's up, slim? Why are you in my room with me laying here butt ass naked with my girl?"

I whispered, angrily.

"I told you, ***I'm*** your girl! She's just playing a temporary position!"

Veronica lauded angrily.

I stood up as quietly as I could, while Veronica stared at my business, as it hung down satisfied with the work it had just put in.

The smirk on her face told me she was not shy. Just as I was forming my thoughts, she grabbed my tool and rubbed it gently. I pushed her hand away and reached for my pants.

I hushed her out of the room as quietly as possible to avoid waking Benita. If she opened her eyes, I wouldn't be able to convince her that I hadn't laid pipe to Veronica.

I crept downstairs, while keeping Veronica under control with a tight grip of my hand.

"Why in the fuck would you do some shit like that, slim?"

I argued angrily.

"If that broad would have come too, it would've been all kind of shit started! If you screw up my ends, I'm going to be pissed off! Now promise me, we have an understanding, and you won't do that shit again, Veronica!"

I demanded.

"Dang Martell, I was just coming to get you, because I made you some sandwiches! I don't care about that bitch! She doesn't know you, like I know you!

Damn, I ain't ever heard you cuss like that, Martell! Where did that come from?"

Veronica asked, while looking downward.

I worked on calming myself and replied.

"Dig this Veronica; you promise this'll never happen again and that you'll continue to listen to me, or you won't be welcome here no more, dig?"

Veronica's demeanor took a back seat as she moaned,
"Okay, I promise! Just don't be mad at me, okay?"
"Cool! Now make it into Tina's room, until Benita splits!" I commanded.
Veronica could see how pissed I was and left the house after bringing me a plate of food.
"I'm glad I didn't mess with that girl, she's crazy as hell!"
I stammered to myself.
Benita slept for about thirty more minutes and woke up all smiles. Mission accomplished, I thought with a sly grin on my face. I had no doubt she was satisfied, as she asked if I needed any scratch. After laying a yard and a half on me, she headed home to help her mother with her foster children. I sat at my thinking place, which was the dining room table and tried to figure out Tina's problem. I was quickly learning that good sex had the ability to keep my pockets swollen, whenever I put my work in.
The last words I recalled my drunken mother share about the man she called our daddy, was he stayed between Richmond and Vallejo. According to mama, his drug and alcohol abuse kept him homeless and thus without a phone.
Benita had called and left a message for me, informing of a gift she'd placed in the duce, that would help her stay close to me. After checking the message and showering, it was time for me to put some work in, trying to find this daddy person.
I was dialed in with all of the best, ghetto snitches and it was time

to swing my influence.

I realized the thing Benita put in my glove box, although a nice gadget, was just another attraction for black folks to lose their minds and spend money on. They called it a pager, or beeper thanks to the sound it made. This beeper thing was also just another way for Benita to find me, like a like a dog on a leash. If I dared to answer it, she would always know my location. If I refused to answer it, she would have a reason to say, I was dodging her.

My mind began preparing for beepers to be purchased with welfare money and for everyone in the hood to have one.

On a normal day, upon jumping in the duce and driving to Richmond, my mind would be occupied with the flavor in the hood. But this day was a different day, because of my mission. I kept wondering if my parents were victims of a man-made experiment of cultural destruction or were they willing participants in their own demise.

Something didn't add up, from what mama's stories suggested. It was hard to make sense of their separation, considering mama used drugs, as well as my daddy. I couldn't find a reason why my so-called daddies would leave such a beautiful daughter like Tina. Lord knows, if it weren't for her broken heart and her tears, I wouldn't have given this journey a second thought. The mere thought of this cat was buried for me a long time ago.

I often wondered why mama didn't have one single photograph of him. If he was that bad from the start, why did she sleep with him and have two kids, by such a cad? He had to show some bad signs from the start of the relationship.

I wondered why so many of the black women had sex with men, with nothing to offer them, but the sex itself. These were the same women hollering victim, once a baby was born, but spreading their legs to whomever was good looking, or fine. These were the thoughts that consumed my mind, as I drove.

Driving into Richmond this time was like driving blindly, because my mind was in a trance for the complete drive.

I headed directly to the ministry of information, Roscoe.

This time I parked my car directly in front of the funeral home and entered through the front door, which stood open.

Roscoe was inside dancing to the sound of, ***Kool And The Gang's hit record, "Jungle Boogie***."

He was munching on an apple, while manipulating a body that lay in a casket.

The funeral home didn't have the same effect during the day, as it did at night. There was something about night and death that just seemed to be a little more intense.

Roscoe took one look at me and let out a hearty laugh.

"Boy, I still trip off dat shit you did last night, bleed! Dat der was some creature feature shit!"

He laughed.

This time watching him eat in front of the dead bothered me.

Maybe it was because, I was hungry.

"Come on Roscoe, let's go over to Petaluma's across the street and get some fish, it's on me! We can chat while we wait for our food!"

I suggested.

Roscoe took the apple he was eating and placed it in the dead man's outstretched hand that lay in the coffin and said,

"Here ya go bleed! Hold dat for me and if you get hungry, don't slobber on my shit, wit yo dead ass!"

Petaluma's wasn't known for their speed, considering they employed an all-black staff. And for some reason, black folk never seemed to acclimate themselves to customer service. The lady at the counter sat chewing gum, while holding the phone to her ear.

"Yeah, can I help y'all?"

She asked lazily.

"We want some food bitch! Get off da phone Hazel and take our order, before I tell your uncle!"

Roscoe scolded.

"Fuck you Roscoe! What y'all want ta eat? Ole black ass bastard!"

Hazel blasted back.

Roscoe laughed and responded,

"You member the last time we fucked girl? You shitted on yourself, when old dead Fred, farted from the casket!"

Roscoe laughed heartily once again.

I grinned, in desperate need of the comedy relief provided by the two. Once Roscoe did away with his hearty laugh, a different look consumed his face. Any sound of the laughter was dissipated into the air and he looked at me as serious as I'd ever seen him look before.

He scowled,

"A'ight Martell, I was thinkin' bout what you said on da phone. I don't know if you really want to know the story behind Dexter Mackie. I recognized the name, but couldn't put it together, how I knew the name.

It's a trip, with all the years I've known you, I forgot y'all got the same last name. But he got some shiesty family and they nothin' as cool as you.

You know, he was once a righteous dude, according to the word on the street. He was known as a stone-cold ladies' man and sharp as an alligator's tooth. They say he had a couple of li'l kids, and he was a good daddy, which is rare in the hood, of course.

He once ran with the Panthers, until a dirty bastard crossed him by screwin' his old lady.

She was supposedly some high and mighty society chick. The dude was a junkie and went tender dick and fell for the broad.

While Dexter was hustling for the family, the dude was coming through the back door and introduced her to getting high in order to keep her on his team.

When Dexter found out, he gave the dude a good old fashioned, Bay area ass kickin'.

Word on the street was Dexter really loved the chick too. But this cat's family was from the same hood and vowed to kill the broad if Dexter didn't get lost for a while, 'because Dexter had really put a hurtin' on dat ass.

They dug Dexter and respected the game. It was said they didn't want to kill Dexter, because they were all part of the same crew. They understood why he whooped on their relative, but Dexter didn't get permission to whoop him. Besides, Dexter's woman believed the bullshit and let blood run the game on her in the first place.

In order to save the broad, Dexter split to South Carolina for about six months. When the funk cleared Dexter returned, but the chick didn't want nothing to do with him.

She was a cold piece. After he split to save her life, she still dropped him like a bad habit. It made him lose his mind and he started drinking and finally using dope, himself.

They said he ain't never been the same after that. But I'll tell you what; he ain't never gotta worry about having bread, thanks to his son.

I hear he's usually up in San Francisco in Hunters Point, or Daly City with Teddy Shine! I just found out, that's his boy."

Roscoe stopped and paused for a few minutes and looked deep into my face, as if seeing me for the first time. He slowly removed a flask from the inside of his apron and took a sip of brandy and made a strange statement.

He said,

"Well, I'll be dipped in buttermilk! This is the first time I put y'alls last name and y'alls face in the same brain. Why you wanna know about this cat, anyway? What da hell is goin' on? I'm knowing, right here and now y'all related or somethin'! This Teddy Shine cat, I just realized y'all sho favors each other! Is he your uncle, or sumthin?" Roscoe scoffed.

I took a deep breath and informed Roscoe,

"My life would be a lot easier, if he was my uncle."

I admitted.

"Dexter's actually, the father I've never met. And the story you just relayed to me, was about **my** mother! I have stayed clear of all this, but it's time to be introduced!"

I coldly admitted.

Roscoe downed what was left in his flask and responded.

"Damn Mackie! That's some more buttermilk! You mean Dexter yo daddy? Ain't that some shit! That makes Teddy Shine yo' brotha!"

Roscoe said, lowering his gaze.

"I shoulda known tha whole time! Hell, y'all look just alike!"

Roscoe reinforced.

"Who in the hell is Teddy Shine, Roscoe? I don't know anyone by that name!"

I enquired, in utter shock.

Roscoe held the flask up and tapped on its bottom and admitted,

"Well, if Dexter Mackie's your daddy, brotha man, I'm here to tell you there's a dude in the hood makin' major scratch and he look just like you! To put the icing on the cake, he's Dexter Mackie's son!

This dude owns tow trucks, ice cream trucks, and all kinda shit in the city! I mean this cat, got a bad assed house in da Southern hills of Daly City and he be drivin' a funky royal blue, Bentley! And the hoes dat be hangin' with him, oh my goodness! He keeps some of the finest women on the streets!"

Roscoe admitted, practically creaming in his pants.

Due to the things Roscoe was saying, I quickly interjected.

"Whore's? Are you saying he's pimpin?"

I asked, with much surprise and major interest.

Roscoe blurted,

"That dude is a whole bunch a shit, but if he ain't nothin' else, he a pimp! And I'm talking 'bout hoe's, not Whores!"

Roscoe jeered.

He snapped his fingers,

"Wait a minute Mack, if you didn't know about him, he probably don't know about you, either! Wow, that's some heavy shit! How you gonna handle that one, man?"

Roscoe asked, with a twisted look on his face.

"I don't know how real any of this rhetoric is, but I guess I need to know. Give me the rest of the 411 on all you know and keep this whole deal to yourself, dig?"

I insisted.

As I pointed my car away from the busy weekend streets of North Richmond, it was hard to imagine my direction. I was engrossed with more thoughts now than I started out with and it was eating a hole through my brain some-what like an acid bomb.

The problems were far from simple and I needed some form of closure. Or would it be a beginning? I really didn't know. There were more questions than answers and I didn't know what to believe.

I'd dealt with Roscoe for years and he'd never lied to me before, which made these tales even more difficult to accept. Because they were probably true. At least that's what my gut told me. The biggest question being, why would mama keep so many secrets from her kids? Why wouldn't mama tell us we had family within the miles of life in which we traveled daily?

I also wondered what this brother of mine was like, and was I ready to share Tina with another man?

The pager vibrated in my pocket continuously for ten minutes with Benita's number. I began to wonder whether this pager thing was a good idea. As long as she was paying for it, I guessed it was all good.

I pulled the duce over in the first gas station that entered my path and called her. She was upbeat as usual and excited to see me using the gadget, she had purchased for me. She immediately took note of my lack of patience and after asking me several times what was bothering me, she finally gave up. It was to her advantage to give up. My mental load would have ended up far too heavy for her shoulders to carry. She informed me, that Mike Love had called her looking for me and she was seeking permission to give out my new pager number.

My mood was extremely intense, due to my mind running all over the place. I was snapping at her, which made her anxious to get off the phone with me and I couldn't blame her. After doing my very best to spare Benita my wrath, I took it upon myself to call Mike Love. I hadn't talked with him in days and I needed an ally to help me settle this influx of new information.

Mike was trying to get a hold of me, to show me the new pad he'd rented in Tiburon.

This was just the call I needed. I had to figure out my next move, in order to best satisfy my baby sister. Not to mention I really needed a break.

It was early evening, and the darkness began creeping through the town like a quiet demon.

I hadn't realized how many hours I'd spent learning the news that dazzled my day.

I drove near the Richmond Bridge and was energized, thanks to the beautiful mist hovering above the waking ocean. Listening to crashes of the waves, as they hit waters of the Bay reminded me of God's most precious gifts and how fortunate we were to reap those awards.

The smell, the color, the sound, and the feel that moves through you when you're driving above the ocean is unique in itself.
Once again it served my soul well. The lush and lovely coastal drive was like it was personally laid out just for me. I once again passed San Quentin Prison and my heart sank a bit, as I thought of so many of my brotha's living in this place, like the walking dead, with life's years moving on without them.
The truth being, there would never be a chance for them to recapture the days, or years back. Yet here I was on the topsoil enjoying a pleasurable coastline. I had to shake these feelings, if I was to be any good.
Tiburon was beyond the borders of San Rafael and exemplified the world's, power, money, status, and vanity.
On any day it would be no surprise to see a Bay Area celebrity, or a well to do judge, shopping in any of the local stores. If money wasn't your ally, you couldn't live anywhere on these shores.
The parks and wondrous walking areas were set aside for the rich and required that special look. A look that showed through in the clothes you wore and the car you drove. Since there was a plethora of Raider's players, owning homes in the area, my duce would be looked upon as a possible player's car.
The Loch Lomond area contained a flurry of hills, reaching across every inch of the area; I just couldn't clear my mind enough to be envious of the mini mansion that was in front of me. Mike Love was right, he was moving on up like George Jefferson.

The three-story house was a colorful array of burgundy and pinks and laced with salmon colored windowpanes and it was truly a sight. One would have to guess if the occupant was Prince or a pimp.

After parking in the circular driveway, Janette greeted me outside of the door. She had on a sheer, pink housecoat, with matching house shoes. It was slightly dark outside, but not dark enough to hide the fact that she had nothing on under her nighty. Her perfectly round areolas were showing through, like she was shirtless. I knew it was a purposeful ploy. It was designed to draw the married neighbors into spending money, on the nicest trim around, thanks to Mike Love.

Once outside, Janette reached for me and waited for my hand to reach hers. As I stood watching her body with extreme lust, I made sure to take my time. The colder it got outside, the prettier her breast appeared to me and I was beginning to feel a pulse in my dick.

I was blessed to disguise my erection. I had an automatic limp.

I knew Janette was a loyal working girl and played by the rules of the game. Luckily for me, I'd been watching closely and listening to the rules of the pimp game. It was becoming easier to accept the gifts and favors given to me by the women in my life and they were coming fast.

Mike Love had his purple Rolls Royce parked in front of his new crib for all to see. It looked like money, even though the color was a little bodacious. The color stood out, but the car didn't in the neighborhood. After finding the strength to control my erection, I headed inside.

There was something special about this Janette woman. I took pride in my dick control, but she was testing me to the hill. She was older than me, with a high golden sheen about her face. The way she eyeballed me, made me realize she dug me more than she would ever say out loud. There was something about the look in her eyes, that lit my fire and I had to kill the feeling before Mike noticed it.

The music playing in the background grabbed and spoke to my soul. I'd heard the song before, but after listening to all the things Roscoe shared with me, it took on a special meaning.

It was a song recorded by Marvin Gaye entitled, Trouble Man. As he crooned the words to the tight drumbeat, it was all me. I stopped in place and listened, as if my life depended on it. Mike approached me in a pretty, purple, smoking jacket, while puffing on a nice Cuban cigar. His smile was lighting up the room with a glow that generated an ambience on its own.

"Martell, my brotha, what's up, pimpin'? I've been trying to catch you for a minute, mane."

Mike said happily.

"This pad is what most black men dream about, Love baby! What! You think you Rockefeller or something?"

I asked, as we embraced like brothers.

“Naw Brotha mane, I’m just taking lovely bodies on loan from the big man and selling the hottest commodity in this man’s world, orgasms and hourly dreams!

If nine out ten of the men in the world could choose something to go with their coffee in the morning, it would be pussy! And the rest would be happy with the hourly dream of a broad telling them how good their mediocre dicks felt!

A white man’s life would transform if he could actually believe he’s fucking the lining out of a pussy!”

Mike suggested, with a sense of contentment.

He asked me to follow him, and he led me to a room laced with books from wall to wall. I felt like a kid in a candy store, surveying the room.

“This is what I wanted to show you, Mackie! This is what the white folks call a study. Of course, I don’t read shit, but bitches faces!

I had you in mind young Scholar! I know you love books, and I got some heavy shit over there on the workings of the mind, including the shit you be talkin’ about.

Stuff like Freud, Maslow and Piaget and all the fancy cats you be talkin’ bout. I’ve been getting into the whole scene since you started hipping me to it. That’s what I’ve wanted to lay on you and it’s been helping me with my Mack game. After reading that knowledge, I see this game ain’t nothin’ but mind study and man. Yo’ ideas fit the pimp game like hot honey, sliding down a big ole hairy broad!"

Mike scoffed.

He snapped his finger and Janette appeared from nowhere.

"Hey bitch, bring young Pimpin' some yak!"

He ordered.

"Okay daddy!" She answered. And she was gone within a snap of the finger without a peep.

Mike and I settled in and sipped on some Hennessey, while I listened to him speak on his progress in the pimp game. He was totally comfortable in his situation and I noticed him relaxing before I hit him with the question.

"Check this Mr. Mike Love, what rap can you give me on a player out of San Francisco, named Teddy Shine?"

I asked while sipping.

Mike Love's face contorted, and he took a big sip and puffed his cigar and suggested,

"Damn Martell, it just hit me who you reminded me of! I been trying to figure it out all time and now I'm not happy I did. Teddy Shine ain't no player, mane! That dude is a stone-cold Mack, with a secondary pedigree in dope dealing!

As a matter of fact, he's the only Mack in the streets to ever peel a bitch from me! I wouldn't say I hate him. I surely respect his pimpin'. But he peeled the bitch by slippin' tha hoe some dope, while she was on the track helping his bottom broad.

This was after I had her quit that shit cold turkey and she was rollin' clean as a baby's ass!

Listen here young bleed; the pimp game is a full-time job with no shorts! Every good, money makin' Mack does a little con work on the side, as part of the game, but that dude is a full-fledged dope boy!

He got that same charm and charisma as you! He plays at pimping, but make grand loot it in the dope game, so I can't like him!"

Mike admitted.

His face suddenly changed within a moment's time and I noticed the same perplexed look on his face that crossed Roscoe's face before.

Mike downed his drink and continued,

"I just realized that cat could be your twin all day! This means he could be your brother in looks, Martell. Why you askin' about that jive Turkey anyway? You got a beef with him?"

He asked, knowing the truth was on its way.

"No beef my brotha, but you wouldn't believe what was just handed in my lap today. Today, I found out for the first time, I have a brother and he just happens to be Teddy Shine. Can you believe I never even met the cat, Mike?"

I emotionally admitted.

"Oh, damn Mackie! I shoulda known something was up. I'll be a Motherfucka! I'm usually way sharper than that! You and that cat look just alike, and it just hit me that y'all have the same last name! What the hell! I don't know what to say about this, mane!

You know what though? This pushes my agenda for the day to a new level. I was gonna sit you down and talk to you about this pimp-ism. Know this, it ain't no pimp's job to pull another's coat about the game, unless it's like your son, or some shit."

Mike said while sipping.

He continued,

"Well mane, you're like a little brotha to me and you got the skills to be in this game. Damn bro, judging by your new bloodline, it's a mothafuckin slam dunk!"

Mike admitted.

He took a deep breath and calmed his voice to a whisper and admitted,

"If you can keep a secret, I want to say, I kind of care about what happens to you, young Mack. Beside my stable, you're about the only family I have. But if anybody ever asks, I never said that weak shit! I would deny it with my last breath!"

He smiled.

He relaxed in the large, purple chair, made for a king and continued.

"But listen to me close, mane! Your new-found brother; Teddy Shine is a snake from every angle! Whatever you plan on doing with him, keep it slow, with eyes wide open! I'm a pimp, not a soldier, but I got your back if it comes down to it."

Mike suggested with pride.

I sat back in the chair and began to rub my head, and much to my

surprise Janette slipped behind me and took over the rubbing.
I was totally immersed in what she was doing, when I heard Mike casually speak.
"I think my young bitch kinda like you, Mackie! But she payin' what she weighin', so stop giving her that little hypnotize shit I've seen you do!"
Mike turned his gaze to Janette and gathered a gruff tone, while demanding,
"Bitch go refresh our drinks and send China in here to put work in! You take a fuckin' time out, Bitch! Go on now!"
He scolded.
After ten minutes, China Blue came into the room. She was a long legged, dark black, almost blue, twenty something chick, with a high ass and well-rounded lips. She had light brown eyes and the hair that stuck out of each side of the bathing suit, struck me as truly sexy.
Mike looked at me and handed me fifty dollars I held it in my hand, I asked,
"What's this for?"
He smiled and answered,
"That's for the massage, China about to give you. It's just a massage mane and no fuckin' goin' on. I don't allow my broads to fuck darkies. And the reason why I gave the scratch is, you never allow a hoe to do nuthin' for free. So, you give her that scratch and she'll do her job. Once she is done, she will bring me the scratch.

So, you just got a gift from me. But remember, my broad's ain't never free!

China will help you relax for a while, before you go and tackle that giant, called family.

Keep in mind young broham, you might not like what you find out there. It's funny, you makin' me glad I don't have no family! I like keeping my heart hidden in an icy place away from everyone that could break it and family will take you out!"

Mike interjected.

Before I could say anything else, Mike was walking out of the room, while throwing up a peace sign.

With China's hands rubbing me down like a magic potion, it didn't take much massaging and I was out for the count.

The comfort of the big house and the many women around, doing anything asked of them, made me feel right at home.

The morning caught me slipping in and out of a dream-state. The hot stream of the shower hit my face.

The sun crept through the window of the mini mansion and it washed upon my face with the traces of a new beginning.

I couldn't shake the day-mares I was having about my brother having the body of a man, but the face of a demon.

In the day-mare he cut my dick off and it grew back repeatedly, and he held it up for all to see.

The only saving grace seemed to appear in the fact, I was well endowed, and it grew every time he cut it, but also became more painful with size.

I sat up in the bed and immediately thought of Tina.

My head pounded me a couple times and reminded me of the bottle of Hennessey I drank during my massage.

After my shower, I looked to the right of me and there was China lying next to me in a deep sleep. Her bathing suit was still in place with that pretty, kinky hair still trying to bust its way free from each side of the cotton, two-piece bathing-suit that graced her body.

The fact that she still had it on, revealed to me that sex wasn't part of our evening, which meant I didn't break the rules. And it wasn't a concern either, because for some strange reason, pussy sandwiches kept breaking my way. I did wonder how she was able to spend the night next to me, instead of being in the streets making bread.

I later learned she was one of those chicks with a monster period and couldn't work during her cycle. I ventured into the lavish bathroom again in order to take my morning piss and found myself just staring at the beautiful décor.

I missed most if it during my shower, due to the nightmares working my mind in broad daylight. The bathroom was layered with gold and brass at each corner. There was a telephone and a T.V. in the bathroom along with an array of purple linens. I was positive my friend was Prince, or I was beginning to wonder if my brethren wasn't in love with the new, big afro wearing superstar, himself.

Mikes pad was laid out with the dreams of black men from the streets. The colors moved beyond bright and blazed at you from every room.

After using the phone and making sure Veronica had my back with Tina, I stumbled back into the bedroom. Mike was sitting on the bed fully dressed and rubbing China's hair as her voluptuous body lye sleeping.

"Look at this broad, sleeping like there's no work to be done! She's supposed to be prepping these chickens for the clucks! This here is what is called my bottom bitch.

Every pimp has a bottom and your bottom, is your one true, blue, lioness in the jungle. She helps you hunt for new game, train and turn out the new hires.

If last night wasn't her night out of the rotation, I would be tapping that ass. You see, Mackie, I give each one of my broads a day off, and it's on a rotation. When it's done right, there's work going on every day of the week, like a smooth-running production line. But understand this, pimpin' ain't easy, which means pimps don't get days off and there's always something the bottom broad should be doing.

If a pimp steps into a store, or a restaurant, or even a supermarket he's always campaigning, or lookin' for new work.

A pimp is a representation of his broads and vice versa. If his broads are two-dollar hoes, he becomes a two-dollar pimp. If he has top notch women in his stable, he becomes a top-notch pimp. Now let's go eat a soul food breakfast on me, mane. Shit, if the peckerwoods knew I was having grits and chicken in this mansion, instead of eggs Benedict; they would have a fit and be trying to hang my pretty ass!"

Mike lauded.

He stood up and slapped China on the ass and told her to get up and prepare for her day off, but check on the chickens in the rotation.

Breakfast was laid out on beautiful china and expensive silverware. It was strange eating grits, waffles and fried chicken on nice china. As we sat down to eat, Janette brought us orange juice and lingered for a moment. Mike gave her a look and demanded,

"Stop gawking at the young Mack, before I beat yo' ass, bitch! Now, just because I'm tired of talkin' to yo' ass! You on da boostin' detail today, bitch! Now get ready hoe, cuz Amber takin' y'all out early and on yo way out, put some music on the loudspeakers!"

Mike shouted.

"Hey man, can I listen to that trouble man piece by Marvin Gaye?" I asked.

It's strange how music can transcend you into a world other than that in which you live. The powers against love always said music didn't have the power to assist in our becoming what we became and was living testimony to that being a lie in the purest form.

I felt as if music was the beacon, where black men carried a good portion of their power.

Most of the dirt I had done in life started with the listening of a powerful song and once the deed was completed, a song was chosen to bring me back to normal.

Mike picked up his fork and began eating while looking at me with a smirk.

"Mane, if you don't stop hypnotizing my broads you gonna have to wear dark glasses around this mugg, like Stevie Wonder!"

He ordered.

"Come on man, what the hell are you talking about?"

I laughed.

"I don't have any hypnotizing thing going on and I haven't looked at your broads, not one time with any disrespect in mind. You're the Mack my man, not me!"

I surrendered.

"Stop with that shit, mane! You a Mack, if I ever seen a Mack and I been in the game for years. I've seen you peel bitches without even tryin'. And that poetry thang you be kickin', flips my legs to another zone! So, you keep yo' mouth shut when my broads are in the room, you magic Motherfucka!"

He laughed.

"I don't know why you keep coming at me with this pimp stuff Mike, that's not me!"

I insisted.

Mike put his drink on the table and began twisting his glass as he spoke with intent.

“Alright mane, here’s the get down! Benita is a super bad broad and she gives you everything in the world without your askin’. The Veronica girl takes care of your sister like she’s her mama and she cooks and cleans for your family all day. Not to mention she’s always ready to rub the end of your dick with her tongue at any minute.

Damn, as I think about it, I should be trying to pull the broad for my stable! And as far you’re concerned, every one of the broads in my stable, ask about yo punk ass far too much. It doesn’t make me comfortable leaving any of my hoes with you!

To top that off, we just found out that pimpin’s in your family bloodline.

Last, I gotta ask this question my young brother,

“Have you, or do you love any of the broads that’s in your day to day game, except your mama and your sister?”

I hesitated for a moment to ponder his question and felt forced to answer,

“No Mike! There’s something about me and love; we just don’t walk on the same street. Hell, most days I don’t even know if I love my own mama.”

I admitted.

“That says it all mane! You are already a pimp, without knowin’ the game! Now it’s time for you to learn the game, grasshopper!

The two biggest tricks in a Mack's bag is the ability to not love anyone **totally**, while making it appear as if you love everyone **abundantly.**

Put your lust, in the need for bread, instead of a broad. Just as a bonus, you should be mentally able to control BP's! That is, bitch problems in case you didn't know!"

Mike suggested.

He sat back in his big chair and jeered while continuing.

"Check this; I'm affording this crib just being five deep. I've got five top notch bitches and they all clockin' me major scratch. I've moved right here amongst all these rich peckerwoods and I'm makin' so much bread, I don't have to spend any time on the track, mane!"

Mike appeared to be dead set on teaching me the Mack game. It was a surprise to me, because the more he explained the essence of pimping, the more it seemed to be just natural to me.

I found it easier to respect a woman making a living off sex, rather than a woman sharing her body with hordes of men, just to feel like she was worthy, or screwing for free orgasms.

My mind began to resonate with the things that made good common sense.

The simple truth was, sex would always be one thing that would be required no matter where the world was, in its times of societal evolution. From the days of the Caesars, like Caligula and moving through time like a well-oiled wheel, sex had rolled onward and upward.

From the jungles of Africa, to the chilly cold shores of Alaska, men had always been willing to share in Eve's delight. With the slightest hint of a woman willing to spread her legs to strangers, men had always lost their minds for a chance to dive in.

It didn't matter if that woman was as big as a bus, or as ugly as a sea creature, there would always be a man willing to buy her warm spot.

Mike Love suggested, I had a cold take on women. I sat there and thought about it for a few moments, but as much as I tried to ignore it, the truth was right there hitting me in the face. It was like a hardball to the chin.

I was a bit ashamed of my thoughts, as I shared.

"I would be satisfied if they could place pussy strategically where and when I wanted it. I'd wished, when it came to women, there was a button I could push to tell them when to talk and when to be quiet. I wish I could wave my hand and tell them to occupy my space and I could use a different wave to tell them to give me my space when I asked for it."

As I prayed to a caring God every day, I knew it was wrong for me to feel so ugly, but I couldn't lie either. I didn't trust, like or admire women or their snake like habits."

Mike shook his head and admitted,

"Damn mane, your mama has created a monster! You need a hoe that's a deaf, mute! You got the potential to be colder on these hoes than me. It's no doubt that having a John, jumping up and down in some of your pussy would never be a problem for you, mane! But dig this young Mack, pussy is just like a suit from a second-hand store. After it's cleaned and pressed, it's just as good as new, despite the fit. And rarely in these United States do you get one that's not been used before.

Next to France, America is the nastiest country in da world when it comes to sex. They call it freedom and democracy, but what it really is, is a pass to no accountability.

I don't care how many dicks slide in and out a pussy, it will always return close to its original shape, like a rubber band. If a woman can deliver ten-pound babies, she can take a twelve-inch dick and shrink back. Now of course just like big assed babies there's always wear and tear over time, but since there's no love involved, all it has to be is wet and warm. Actually, most peckerwoods are so excited to be cheating on their old ladies, they almost cum before they hit the pussy.

Take note, a few of the super bad, experienced hookers can make a john bust just by touchin' her and then you can charge twice for one fuck.

You gotta understand how differently they think, versus the way we think. It's just like this Ebonics shit they figured out. We see life in a different form than them. And according to the white people that's a bad thang. But the truth is, as long as it's a secret, they want to eat the same things we eat."

Mike insisted.

"Why are you spending all this time talking about white folks, Mike?" I sounded off.

Mike smirked and responded,

"Because a smart Mack realizes that's where most of your scratch will come from! With the end of slavery, white men have had to buy extra pussy instead of going into the slave quarters and taking it.

Even in the cowboy days they were going into the saloons and getting mostly white sex. To keep it real, they have always wanted, and fantasized about having black women, because they've been the only power given to black men. The strength comes from God, but their power comes from the woman. Like Sampson and his hair, we rise and fall due to the woman. But keep in mind young Mack, we usually fall because of women as well.

We've lacked dick control from the start. You can tie most of the brotha's in jail to the breakdown of his power, the black woman. Now, it's hard for most women to accept this truth, but the truth doesn't change. The easiest way to get a hard-workin' lady love on your team is havin' shit! In this Mack-ism it takes a hoe to choose a Pimp.

Check this out young Martell! Pimpin' and whoring is life as I know it. Not every set of legs is made for selling pussy, but every real live woman is built for flat backin'. And when you think of it, most house broads sell themselves short. They've been givin' that thang up for a meal and a movie and an occasional trinket.

If they fuck well, they'll earn, ***I love you and I don't want anybody else to have you status***!

These same broads could be doing the same amount of screwin' on the blade as they do at home and make enough bread to be buying houses and Benzes of their own! Also, most women share at least one man at least mentally. But there's something about not knowing it, means less drama. Imagine, you can have a wife and while you at work she could be fucking everything movin', and as long as she doesn't change her game toward you, you'll never be the wiser.

You'll love that woman 'till the day you die.

The mind is a bitch. For example, it's just like seeing a broad in a bathing suit, dig. It's cool on the beach all day. Truth is, if they say it's the same broad on the beach in her panties and bra, men lose their minds and flip in a completely different way.

In theory there's not much difference between the two, except in our own thoughts.

Remember them broads who need the love of men to feel worthy and to build that bullshit self-esteem, they are easy prey. They usually start off stripping, until they're pulled by a real pimp or saved by a square.

You'll always run across hard heads and you'll almost always have to keep a foot off in they asses, cuz that's the only way they feel loved. It makes them believe you care and love them. Just keep a lot of make-up available for them types of legs, cuz they light a fire in yo' ass and you begin to love the physical!

Even in the jungle, the female lion goes out and does all the working and hunting.

As long as the lion protects her and keeps the sex good, he keeps his den of females and services all in his den.

It will always come down to how good you make a broad feel. Any woman can be talked out her panties with the right combo.

If you don't remember nothing' else, remember these things.

Women are like combination locks! You gotta hit them with the right combination and everything opens up for you.

I can tell you already know how to break a woman down, but when it comes to this pimp-izm every woman is individual in what she likes sexually, and always search for the unique combination to satisfy a hoe.

You gotta give her something she doesn't usually get. It doesn't matter whether it's sexually, or mentally.

Remember, pimpin' doesn't work without getting in, owning and processing a woman's mind!

If you study and can give your bottom girl somethin' special, she'll be true.

Achieving that will help you keep your stable in line. There ain't nuthin' a broad love more than to nut, except her kids and money.

Eve was the first woman to set pimping in play many years ago and as long as there's pussy, they'll be somebody to buy it.

The serpent talked her stupid ass into doing bad shit with promises of gifts and pleasures. And then Adam played the John by following her into doing the dumb shit despite the ass kickin' he had comin' from the big guy.

That's how strong that cut is, mane!

It has the best of us willing to go against God, and it's always been like that. Pussy had Adam following instead of leading. Dig this, even Jesus best friend was a whore, before he straightened her out. Mary Magdalene was a whore and that's not to be denied. What's that say about the game? I'll tell you what it says. It says that pimpin's been around forever and ain't no stoppin' it." Mike concluded.

Soon there was a blast at the doorbell which stopped us in our tracks. At the sound of the ringing doorbell Mike stopped eating and the lesson temporarily ended as he pointed out it was time for him to get his money on.

He suggested I walk with him to the front of the house. Once we reached the front of the mini mansion. There was quite a bit of noise coming from the front room. I scanned the room and noticed the front area was full of women. All of them I had seen before, except two.

The regulars were Mike's stable girls. My interest was in the other two. One was dressed like and had the mannerisms of a man. The way she stood and the way she moved, could have fooled the average Joe. She kept a close-cut hairdo and stood while rubbing her face as if she had a beard.

I read all this after giving her one glance, but the lady that stood next to her took my breath away.

Her skin was a wondrous golden tone of flawlessness. She looked as if she was dipped in honey and then was washed lightly by the sun. The small freckles on her nose gave her an uncanny look of innocence. The two ponytails that hung down well below her shoulders were braided with care. Her eyelashes curled upwards toward the heavens and her lips appeared like they were carved from an original African painting, large, bold and perfectly shaped. Her smile revealed the dental plans of kings and queens as her teeth stood out white and lay with every one of them perfectly in place.

Her eyes were as pretty green as a crisp leaf, holding strong against the wind in the spring air. They looked as if they coined the phrase, bedroom eyes.

I had to search carefully in order to uncover the one thing I could find unappealing on this heavenly angel and I found nothing.

Her shoulders were rounded and leaned into her torso. She appeared to be sculptured by a great artist. Her waist stood tiny like a small necessary evil, due to the fact that her hips were just wide enough to bless her pants. However, they were not so big to overcompensate for the perfectly rounded ass, that protruded with the unspoken words that begged to be caressed.

She had the type of body that would make all of her clothes seem as if they were tailor made. I found myself captivated by her appearance and I watched her closely. Her grace took me to a new high.

Mike noticed my immediate infatuation, because I stared at this woman in speechless splendor. He spoke to me at least three times, but I could only hear a blur tickling at my ear.

I didn't remember seeing anyone else in the room. I had totally forgotten I wasn't shined or showered yet. I only lived in the moment.

In what felt like an out of body experience, I raced passed everyone in the room, including the mannish chick standing next to the angel.

Once I reached her, I put my hand out to hold her as gently as I could, being mindful of breaking her. I whispered in her ear without thinking what I was saying. The words just slipped from brain.

I quietly promised,

"At this moment and in this place, thanks to you, I'm reborn! I promise not to ever do anything to hurt you! My heart is yours now and even in paradise, when all is new. You and I will be power! We have the ability to walk as one!"

I promised, as if in a dream state.

I stood in a daze staring in the awesome glow of her green eyes.

There was a tap on my shoulder, but for the first few moments I couldn't really feel it or didn't want to.

She looked at me and smiled, while hypnotizing me with her eyes. The tapping on my shoulder was becoming even more persistent by the minute, until it was irritable and interrupting what felt like the purest moment of affection I had ever felt in my life.

I turned sharply toward the irritation,

"What! What is it you want?"

I snapped.

"Hey bro, you think you can let go of my woman's hand, big homeboy! I don't know you!"

The mannish chick pleaded with contempt.

It was at that moment, I returned to the scene I was causing, and it was also at that moment, I realized I didn't care. After returning my gaze to the lady with my heart, I suggested.

"You must excuse me dear heart! It was a natural thing for me to do, Queen Desdemona.

Your hand has been waiting for mine and so this is the natural order of what's to come, if you can see it! Deflect all you like, but I know you feel me, straight to my soul!"

I admitted in a low hushed tone.

Lisa smiled in awe of my natural flow and then again at the thought of being called a Queen. I knew immediately that her butch girlfriend kept control by keeping Lisa's self-esteem in check.

I softly placed her hand down and turned completely to face my opposition. It wasn't a surprise to see the mannish chick change her stance and posture as if there was going to fight between us.

"You had better be careful butch, I'll fight a girl!"

I laughed.

"Naw, I'm just playing with you. But I must admit if you were a man, I would have already bitch slapped and taken my love. But since you're a bitch, I'll take my time! Just keep in mind, that's my love, right there and one day she'll come home!"

I boasted, while looking back at the blushing beauty.

"Nigga, is you crazy? That's my broad 'till death, do or die; mind your own stable! You, low down, pretty boy, Motherfucka!"

The butch spurned.

"I hate pretty niggas like you!"

She continued.

"You dare to call me Nigga again and I'm gonna remind you why you wanna be me, bitch! I'll bend you over and stick hard dick in that rarely used pussy of yours and remind you of your place, li'l' gurl! Unlike you, I don't have to cotton my ass seven days out the month. Bitch, I was made a man! I don't have to pretend. You needy, bleedy assed bitch!"

I slammed, with a sly grin.

Mike stepped in between us and became the peacekeeper.

"Alright you cats be cool! You don't even know each other to get down like that and get off to a real bad start!

Damned Mack, I ain't never seen you drop your pimp hand like that! You all smiling and shit like a smooth killer!"

He admitted in surprise.

He then looked at the short, wanna be me man and admitted,

"Tank, this is my **friend,** Mackie da Mack!"

He faced me and suggested,

"Mackie, this is one of my long-time acquaintances, Tank! Now notice I don't use that friend word often, let's keep it cool in my pad." Mike ordered.

He returned his gaze to Tank once again and inquired.

"Tank, I don't know why you trippin'. I've seen a thousand cats try and get at Lisa, without even a peep from you! Why balls up all of a sudden?"

Mike inquired.

"It's just your boy walked up on my thang like she his or sumthin'. And there's sumthin' about his cool ass I don't like! Then on top of that he got a problem knowin' he a Nigga! Man, Mike, to keep it real this the first time I ever seen stupid over there, giggling and all stuck in a man's face and shit!"

Tank admitted.

"Well, I can tell you, Mackie ain't gonna stand for nobody calling him no Nigga! Hell, Tank, I don't even do it and he's one of my best friends. He happens to be one of those intellectual players and demands that type of respect and shit."

Mike admitted.

I found myself smiling at back Lisa, stuck on her loveliness. After the air calmed and Mike gave Tank a drink, the only thing she asked me was,

"Why you got a problem being a Nigga?"

I took a nice sip of my drink and informed her,

"Well that word is the epitome of our ignorance as Moors, as Africans, as God's and the chosen. I can never stop thinking about the many Royal loved ones that died wishing they were called everything but that, while swinging from trees. It's one of the words that's been universal for the ugliness our people, when the word greatness should be attached to us. The ugliness of that word has transcended through generations, as an example of low esteem. The same men that call each other Niggas, don't believe in self, enough to call each other king.

In Africa, the white people call us Kaffir's, which means the same thing. Around the world we're called this, and we've decided to use it as a term of endearment, when it's the word that's synonymous without emotional and physical incarceration, known as slavery.

It actually means people of low desires, without substance, or ambition and my dear girl, that doesn't equate to me. Last but not least, it's makes us home-less, unless you can tell me where nigga land is?"

I insisted.

"Where in the fuck did you come from, professor? That's a fuckin' History lesson you just broke down. The truth is the way we say it is different than the way white folks say it."

She said, as if she were bragging on her smarts.
"That's a farce, because the slang word originated back South! The Southern crackas say it just like you say it."
I relayed.
I turned my gaze to Lisa Lipps and looked deep into her pretty green eyes and spoke in a dazed fashion again.
"As far as Desdemona, she was the love of Othello, the black Moor! He was highlighted in a famous play by Shakespeare. Their love was so deep that he would have died ten times just for her to live. The love also made him willing to kill for her, and eventually kill her for love. If you want to know more, I'll be glad to share. You and baby can sit down for a lesson!"
I suggested earnestly.
Tank jumped up again and snapped,
"Naw we good professor! I want my bitch to stay dumb, and far away from your ass!" She snapped.
Tank began to laugh, while rubbing Lisa's face to remove her from my gaze from me.
I looked at Tank and replied,
"Me and you good too, Miss Tank! No hard feelings. Just recognize what's meant to be!"
At that moment I looked deep into Lisa's eyes and said,
"Me and you, we better than good. Remember what I said, no pain to my Desdemona! We have a destiny that says we belong together, in this lifetime! And I'm gonna find you baby, so you can

know true love!"

Tank turned toward Mike while speaking to me and complained,

"I ain't no Miss! It's Mr. Tank, buddy!"

She turned to Mike and asked,

"Mike can you just show me the threads man and get this Casanova Mothafucka away from my work?"

I grabbed my private area slightly and teased, "From the doggy-style position, you'll always be Miss to me, and I bet you got a fat juicy pussy hidden under there huh, **baby**!"

Mike wrapped his arm around Tanks shoulder and chuckled,

"Shit, I got him this time, Tank, cuz you here on my dime, but you know da game! You gotta control your own thang! For the first time ever, it looks like Lipps slippin' a li'l' mane! The young Mack is somethin' else!"

Mike suggested.

He let go of Tank and grabbed my arm, while laughing and pulling me away.

Upon entering his favorite room, Mike took the cognac flask and turned it up. After taking a big swig, he looked at me and wiped the drizzle from his mouth and handed the flask to me.

"What in da hell is up with that?"

He asked me.

I took a nice hard swig and emotionally responded.

"I don't give a damn, Mike! Without question, that **is** my woman right there! That is going to be my bottom woman, if I have to sell ice water in hell! I have got to have those green eyes on my team by any means necessary!"

I smiled.

My words were more like a demand.

"I don't know what to tell you young Mack, but both them bitches is dykes! I know Lisa is about the finest broad on the streets and every pimp I know den tried to pull her, but it's hard as hell to peel a gay bitch, mane! Before you say it, I know, it's hard to figure a broad that fine being in the game and controlled by a wanna be man. But her and Tank been through a lot a shit together. They were both in foster care and had a foster daddy that took Tank as his lover.

Sick fuck turned out to be gay and wanted Tank because she reminded him of a dude he was in love with.

He passed on Lisa, which means he was all kinds of crazy!

The two girls, went from huggin' and comfortin' each other, to full fledge fuckin'! And from what I know, neither of 'em been with a dude, since he went to jail.

I tried to get 'em to do that threesome for some real dough, but they flat out refused.

To make things worse, Tank only let's Lisa trick with white broads! She allows no sticks in the tunnel, mane! But I gotta admit, I ain't never seen Lisa allow a man to touch her before! Your magic ass held her hand and her attention like no nig, I mean no brotha has ever done, before.

And oh yeah, for the record, I can dig your trip on that Nigga thang! I'ma stop sayin' it myself."

Mike surrendered.

I took the last sip of my drink and made it known.

"Like I said, I don't give a fuck, Mike Love! That's going to be my woman, no matter what I have to do, and I got an idea that's gonna blow her socks off!

I'm going to call my boy at the Red and White fleet on the Wharf, and I'm going to have a boat ride! So be ready!

It's gonna be the monster jam in the Bay!"

I relayed with determination.

"If you can pull that one off my brotha, you will be off to a flying start! That some boss shit you talkin' bout! Not to mention, you'll automatically be a pimp hero, from L.A to the Bay and back, because everybody's been tryin' to get that fox on their team!

A party like that will make you the envy of the STROLL!

Damn Mackey, you know I'm in. I remember one-time Lipps got picked up for a curfew violation when she was underage and every pimp in the area stood in line trying to post the bitches bail."

Mike informed me.

"I don't care Mike. I plan on figuring a way to have her with me and that's that!"

I interjected.

"I can't believe the way all that went down, and I wish you luck tryin' to pull a dyke. I sure would love to see that fine thang with a

real pimp and getting' the dick down she deserves!"
Mike insisted.
"Is Tank the partying type?"
I asked.
I had a true thirst for all of the information available in reference to these two women.
"Yeah and the man-bitch is a tease too! She likes showing Lisa off at the pimp events.
As a matter of fact, there's a Players ball in Oakland next month and I guarantee she'll be there with Lisa Lipps looking, as fine as a vintage wine, mane."
Mike smiled.
"I don't know if I can wait that long, Mike! I need to have that green-eyed angel with me right now! And I'm telling you I saw it in her eyes, she wants to be with me.
I need to find out where they live in order to get my show on the road."
I suggested, while rubbing my chin.
Mike took on a serious tone and shared,
"Look mane, you know I would violate Tanks trust by giving out that information! You better be glad I'm not opposed to lying and saying it wasn't me.
Okay switching gears, because you and Tank ruining my thigh! I got some news! I know what club yo brotha is at every Saturday night. Since he sales that yayo, he gives his girls Saturday's off, in

order to show the other players, he's makin' all the scratch.
You let me know when you ready to see him and we'll fall in. I can't wait to see old Teddy Shines face when he meets you."
Mike jeered.

Janette walked me to the door and if I didn't know better, it felt as if she was really working on getting my attention.

I promised Mike I wouldn't mess with Tank on my way out, but I also informed him that I was nowhere close to letting my feelings go for Lisa Lipps.

I knew I wanted to care for and grow with Lisa after our first meet, and that never happened before. However, Mike suggested I wanted to conquer Lisa, because whether I accepted it or not, pimping was in my blood.

Mike also wanted me to accept, that through the confines of my life, I was damaged like most black men, thanks to mama's bad assed ways.

Her bitterness toward me, placed me in a position, not to respect, or like women much.

As I walked out, I was thinking about Lisa and hoping he was wrong but accepting more than likely he was right.

The drive home was a blur of the many things that were happening in my life and I couldn't keep them straight.

The women in my life had turned it upside down.

First there was Tina and her need to know our no-good daddy and the reality that I was the only person that could bring that closure.

Then there was Veronica and her deep feelings for me. I knew our relationship would be complex, because I never saw it coming. Was her love misguided? I was riddled with so many new things in my path. My head was beginning to spin like a toy.

Thanks to a chance meeting, I met Lisa Lipps and felt emotions I'd never felt before. There would be no way I could let her escape. I was feeling as if I had to put forth a life changing effort to have her.

Last but certainly not least, was Simone, my mama. The coldest chick I had ever met in my short life. I wondered how could an educated and lovely young woman get so twisted and ugly in life? Why was it that our father, as well as our grandparents didn't want anything to do with Tina and me? Why was mama killing every possibility of a good life? Why was she hoping my life would be as dead as her love? Why was she hiding our other family from us? The older I was getting, I realized there were more questions than answers, but there were some things that were certain.

I had a crew and with my cunning and their fearlessness, we were as dangerous as any posse in the streets.

The most amazing part of the equation was I was somehow their appointed leader. And as ugly as life was, I would still pray to God to lead us in our good and our bad ways. I was enjoying my life now, but I knew on any given Sunday death waited around the corner.

I considered every piece of information that crossed my path, an education. Some would be good, and some would be bad, like the lie that Chris Columbus discovered America.

I just knew I had to be a sponge and I had to face my future, without fear. This Bay area was home to some of the meanest streets in the United States and all the young men I ran with, didn't expect to live long. I would fight to cheat death as long as I could and fight for life at every step. I was aware that a man could only climb by stacking the building blocks of life. I would have to accept the education of a Mack!

IT STARTS

Book 1 of 3

Made in the USA
Coppell, TX
10 June 2026

80004659R10166